Consider the Lilies

Consider the Lilies

Carol Fenlon

First Published 2008
by Impress Books Ltd
Innovation Centre, Rennes Drive,
University of Exeter Campus, Exeter EX4 4RN

Typeset in 10/12 Sabon by Swales and Willis Ltd, Exeter, Devon

Printed and bound in England by imprint-academic.com

British Library Cataloguing in Publication Data
A catalogue record for this book is available from the British Library

ISBN: 978 0 95562 39 1 2

For Amanda Richardson,
who made me do it.

Acknowledgements

First and foremost my thanks are due to Robert Sheppard and Ailsa Cox. Their advice and guidance have been invaluable as has been their support and their faith in me.

Secondly, thanks go to Arthur Scarisbrick, who has always believed in me and been there for me through the thick and thin of writing this book.

Thanks also to Angela Keaton for her support and constructive criticism, to members of Edge Hill University's 4th room writers group and Narrative Research Group, Ormskirk Writers and Literary Society and Skelmersdale Writers, all of whom have been instrumental in critiquing and correcting early drafts.

Finally, many thanks to Richard and Julie Willis, Colin Morgan and all at Impress Books, together with everyone at Exeter University who has been involved in organizing the Impress Prize For New Writers and in the publication of this book.

CHAPTER ONE

"We don't want any bad habits here mate – know what I mean?" Ray's eyes glitter at me under his cap. He looks like a bad habit himself rather than a saviour, but I can't refuse his offer of a roof over my head on a wet night.

"Yeah," I say. It takes all my breath to keep up with him on the uneven paving and it's raining – that drizzle that gets into every crevice.

"Down here." He turns into a side street and I wonder what I'm walking into. But what's the point? It's two in the morning and even now the back streets of Liverpool aren't quiet. The dispossessed are ever roaming, but down here it's as still as it gets. Nevertheless, I'm nervous. There's that don't-walk-alone kind of menace you get in an empty street.

"Here." He points down an alley. I wonder why me? What made him pick me up off the street tonight, when I'm at such a low point, pain throbbing through my hip, breaching my defences, letting the memories push through? Maybe I've read him wrong but I've got nothing to lose if he turns nasty. No point in doing me except for the pure psychopathic pleasure of it and he doesn't look that type.

We turn into a back yard with no gate and up a pathway lined with bags of rubbish. I think of our house; of Corinne and Angela. Corinne used to nag me about the garden. I refused to have a gardener but never had time to look after it myself. I wonder who lives there now?

This house has boarded windows. Ray gives a series of knocks on the back door, which still looks fairly sound, despite the scabby paint. I'm still back at that other house, my home, standing under the flowering cherry by the pond, until the door opens.

"What's your name?" Ray says, distracting my attention so I don't look at the person behind the door, only the shadow as the door closes after me.

"They call me the Hermit." The hall smells of cigarettes, candlewax and damp and there's a dark room that looks like a kitchen. He's leading me up bare stairs and I can see into doorless rooms below, full of shadows thrown up by guttering candles. It's a fire trap waiting to happen except you can smell the whole place is so rotten damp it would never ignite. There are dim shapes: murmurings and mutterings like a restless crowd. We come to a landing, go up another set of stairs. The room he brings me to is dark and empty.

"You'll have to share."

Even without light I can see there's nothing here except an empty fireplace and something that might be a mattress or bedding against one wall.

"Okay by me." I slip the pack off my back onto the floor. What a relief. There's a door in one corner of the room, a built-in wardrobe or something.

He's watching me. "Got a bad leg?"

"Yeah." Right now it aches like fuck.

I go over to the cupboard and open the door. A great hiss comes out at me and I slam the door and jump back quicker than I would have thought possible. "Jesus, what is it?" I almost lose my balance and my hip screams as it twists. Only the wall stops me from falling. All I can remember is a pair of eyes rolling, black and white like spotted eggs and a lot of very sharp-looking teeth.

Ray's laughing at me. "It's okay. It's only Cupboard Girl."

'Calm down,' I tell myself and get the primus stove out of my pack and set myself to the familiar routine of making a brew.

"Organised aren't you?" His voice sounds mocking.

"You didn't say I had to share with a fucking she-wolf." My fingers shake as I light the stove.

"She's okay. She's just scared. She'll be all right when she gets to know you."

I settle myself on the floor. There's a circle of light from the stove. It's dark and peaceful after the watchfulness needed on the streets, but there is fear in the room, mine and hers, and that stops me relaxing. Stirring the water in the pan is soothing. I don't have to stay here, I could be on my way right now, but it's cold and wet outside, I'm tired and my leg –

"What's your story?" He rolls a fag. I look at the tobacco tin and he looks at my pan of water. I get out the milks and sugar sachets I picked up in McDonalds earlier in the day and find two squashed paper cups in my pack that are reasonably clean. He offers me the tin. I don't smoke much but I take it and roll up.

"I dunno," I say. "Haven't got one." I'm too tired for parlour talk.

"Everyone's got one." He squints at me as he lights up. "What happened to your leg?"

"War." I accept a light and drop a tea bag in the pan. It's one I used earlier but he won't know that.

"Which one?"

"It doesn't matter." I can't be bothered elaborating the lie. I just don't want to tell him the truth.

"It's permanent then?"

"Yeah." I pour the tea.

He keeps asking things but I don't answer. We smoke our fags and drink our tea then the silence gets awkward and he goes away. I settle myself in my sleeping bag but let the stove burn for a few minutes. The blue flame takes my mind off the shadows and the thing in the cupboard. I keep staring at the door, straining my ears but not a sound comes out. Is it – she – asleep or like me, sitting motionless, listening? I turn the stove off, listen to the clicking noises as the metal cools. Other noises float up from below but can't dispel the silence in the room. I can't sleep. Her eyes are in my mind. I try to think of something else and then the nightmare begins. I can see Angela. Her face is white; her hair is matted with blood. I can see Corinne. Her face is grey; her eyes are blank. Her fingers claw hate on my shoulders. I'd give anything for a Glenfiddich, but that's a door that I've shut. Corinne is shouting. I can't make out the words because someone is screaming but I know she's saying that it's all my fault and then someone comes and gives me an injection and I slip . . .

man sleep   oldgreybeardman
sleep bed warm bed
beardoldgreyman sleep warm

sleepnoise   nonoise
sleepnoise   nonoise
sleepnoise   nonoise
sleepnoise   nonoise nonoise
nonoise nonoise   sleepnoise
nonoise sleepnoise nonoise
sleepnoise nonoise
sleepnoise nonoise
nomorenoise greyoldbeardman
vicky wakeup vicky sleep vicky
go sleep nomore stopit

I'm awake suddenly and know better than to move, even though I'm still half asleep and I just lie here, hardly breathing in the strange darkness. For a moment I don't know where I am, then I remember.

oldgreybeardman not hurt not hit not kill vicky oldgreybeardman wakeup vicky nomore   stopit oldgreybeardman sad sleep sad

I can't see anything. My stuff is safe, I've got it in my sleeping bag with me but something's wrong. Gradually I begin to see a little in the dark. Someone's standing over me, watching. I can feel my muscles rising and falling with every breath as I struggle to hold myself still.

oldgreybeardman   nonoise
nonoise nonoise
oldbeardgreyman no sleep eye move
no sleep no body move.

I slit my eyes open just a fraction and it's a few moments before I realise it's the girl from the cupboard.

see vicky vicky scared vicky no body move
oldgreybeardman scared scared vicky

Is she going to attack me? Maybe she's got a knife or something but she's just standing there and I start to feel bad about the way I'm thinking about her. She's another human being isn't she?

4

no hurt vicky

greyoldbeardman talk   vicky
not   know

        talk
talk

vicky know

vicky know oldgreybeardman
not like vicky not like ray   not
like doctorsoames   not like rita
not like   oldgreybeardman like
bird in street vicky see bird in
street car run over bird not walk

The fear in the room is melting away and I start to relax. Being on the street makes you like this – ready for anything. You may be free of the niceties that stopped you being you, but you've got to be ready to drop into hell at any moment.

Time now for some parlour talk.

"Hi. Can't you sleep?"

I try to whisper but it sounds like a cannon going off. There's an immediate charge in the room but she doesn't move. Should I risk sitting up?

"They call me the Hermit. How about you?"

Nothing.

This is stupid. How long has she been standing there? Has she been in the cupboard all night or did she sneak out into that nest of a bed after I'd gone to sleep?

I want to get up and take a piss but I daren't move yet. I don't know what to do if she's not going to say anything. Maybe she can't talk. Maybe she can't hear. Ray never said.

Why does she just keep standing there? Does she want me to do something?

I can't see in the dark what she's like. I guess she's not a young woman, she's got the thickset outline that comes with middle age, though it's difficult to tell, could just be clothes.

Her eyes gleam white in the

5

bird not walk leg leg
greyoldbeardman jump vicky
scared greyoldbeardman scared

run vicky run

okay in cupboard dark no oldgreybeardman come   no man
come   vicky hold door no man
come

okay vicky okay

dark, not as bad as before but I still can't help shuddering and suddenly she squats down and puts her hands right on my false leg.

I freeze, although in my mind I've hit the ceiling.

How could she know?

I open my eyes fully and look at her. I can't stop myself sitting up and at once she's up and off like a deer, the cupboard door squealing shut and I'm left here thinking about those quick dim images: her nostrils quivering like a wary dog sniffing out answers; gentleness in her eyes as she examined me; and the touch of her hands asking questions of the metal and leather of my leg. There's something familiar about her but I just can't get hold of it.

I've got to piss but don't know where and everyone seems to have disappeared, so I go down to the back door and piss in the yard. It's cold and quiet. The stars are fading in the greyness as dawn comes. I look up and remember Ray asking about my leg as we came into the room so that explains how she knew about it, doesn't it?

* * *

Light squeezes round the boards on the windows when I wake and the mattress in the corner is empty. Faint street noises come into the room. I listen for clues, trying to get my bearings. It can't be far from Bold Street, where I met Ray last night, but in the dark and the

6

struggle to keep up with him I lost my sense of direction when we turned off somewhere after the ruined church.

In the room scraps of grimy wallpaper speak of past home comforts. Once, this was someone's cosy bedroom. At home, our bedroom was decorated in quiet shades of green. It's like a scene in a story I once read. It's tempting to picture happy times: Corinne and I cuddled together, Angela bouncing on the bed, but those times didn't last. I close the book. The cupboard door is shut and I can't hear anything inside.

I shoulder my pack and set out in search of Ray. There's just enough light to see by. On the landing one floor down I find a door with TOILET scrawled on it in black felt pen. Inside, it smells but it's reasonably clean and there is water in it. I take my pants down and sit gingerly. My hip hurts and I wonder how many painkillers I have in my bag and if I've enough money to get more. The toilet pan is sturdy and takes my weight without rocking. It's an old fashioned cistern with a long chain. When I pull it there's a healthy flush and I get a small shower on my head. There's even a toilet roll. I'm almost happy as I go down the final set of stairs.

No sign of Ray but there's a woman moving round in the back of the house where we came in last night. It's a kitchen or once was one. There's a cooker that looks unused and none of the paraphernalia you'd expect in a working kitchen, but there's a sink with taps and water running out.

The woman fills a plastic cup. She turns and looks at me, weighing me up as she drinks from the cup.

"Hi, I'm Rita. Who are you?"

"They call me the Hermit. Ray brought me last night."

"Ray's our Good Samaritan." She smiles, drains the cup and fills it again. I can see right away she's no smackhead. She's thin but she looks strong and capable. She's wearing a long skirt, a brown cardigan and woolly socks. She's got a bandanna tied round her head and auburn hair pokes out round the edges.

"You new round here? I don't know your face." She's studying me again, making me feel uncomfortable. I take my pack off and start setting up my stove.

"Can I get some water?" I assume there's no electricity, judging by the state of the kitchen and the candles last night. She holds her hand out for the bottle, fills it and gives it back to me. She's waiting so I have to answer.

"I've been around for a while."

"You're not a scouser." She says it pleasantly but I sense a hidden accusation.

"No." That's as far as I'm willing to go right now and she looks at me and decides to respect that.

"I'm from Croxteth." I don't know where that is but it doesn't matter. "I left my husband." She drains the cup again and looks at me. It's a sign that's as far as she wants to go and that's okay with me.

"How many people are here?" I stir the water and give her the two cups from last night to rinse out. It's easier to ask questions when you're doing something practical.

"These are manky." She puts them in a bag of rubbish, opens a cupboard and takes out a roll of unused plastic cups.

"About twelve. It varies." She laughs and the pleasure in it surprises me. "People come and go."

"So who's in charge?" I give her one of the cups of tea.

"Got sugar?" She keeps her hand open as I dole out the sachets, closing her hand when I get to four. "Thanks. I don't know. No one really. We just all muck in."

"Yeah?" My voice is full of sarcasm. I've been in squats before. She looks hurt.

"Course we have problems, but it works. You'll see."

"I don't plan to be here long enough to see. How long have you been here?"

"Three weeks."

I laugh and she looks nervous.

"I was in a refuge before, but my husband found me." She looks down and picks at her skirt. "What time is it, do you know?"

I shrug. "Feels about nine o'clock. That girl – woman upstairs: Cupboard Girl. What's that all about?"

She smiles. "Vicky? Is that where Ray put you? The house must be full. We usually try to leave her alone."

So she's got a name. Vicky. Sounds normal, ordinary, a schoolgirl's name or a page three girl. Victoria – posh, regal, a plum, an It girl, not that thing in the cupboard. Then I remember her gentle touch on my leg. It's difficult to marry the two images. Do they leave her alone because she's dangerous?

"What's her story?"

"Who knows?" She shrugs. "She doesn't say much."

"She can talk then?"

"Oh yes, in her own way."

"What does she do?"

"Do?" She looks at me puzzled.

"Well, she can't stay in the cupboard all the time. Food? Drink? Money?"

Someone else comes into the kitchen. He's tall, skinny and looks miserable as sin.

"Hi Peter," Rita says brightly.

"Going to rain all fucking day." He looks at the boarded window, takes a cup from the roll and rinses it out before filling it with water. He eyes our cups before drinking from his. He looks like he's been having nightmares all night. I'm glad we've almost finished our tea, I've got no intention of brewing up for the whole house. I start packing up my bag. Rita follows me into the hall.

"Sally Army caff'll be open." She shuts the door on Peter. "Fancy some breakfast? I'll treat you."

I want to say no but I'm curious about Cupboard Girl. "I've got my own money. I'll get my sleeping bag."

"You can leave it upstairs, it'll be okay," she says, but I'm already climbing the stairs.

"I don't think I'll be coming back," I say from the landing.

* * *

In the Sally Army caff, Rita fills me in on the house rules and the residents over tea and bacon sandwiches. The house is in the top half of Falkner Street, which is pretty well what I'd figured.

"Never use the front door, only the back."

"Goes without saying."

"And you need to use the special knock. I'll show you when we get back."

"What if no one's in?"

"There's always someone in." She's laughing at me as she takes a bite of her sandwich. "If it does happen that no one's in, there's a key hidden in the yard. I'll show you. Let me tell you about the others."

I'm not really interested in them, only in Cupboard Girl, but I let her rattle on while I'm eating.

"There's Peter. You saw him before. He's a bit of a drag, always looking on the bad side. I think he used to be in a mental hospital although he doesn't talk much."

"Clinically depressed," I say. "Who isn't nowadays?"

9

"And there's Mabel. She's a tough old boot. She told me she's seventy-two and she's been on the streets for five years. Mind you she's always bladdered, but the drink makes things bearable, doesn't it? I like a drink myself." Her voice tails off and she looks at me.

In the light I can see the signs; a slight tremor, a liverish colour. I realise she's younger than she looks, perhaps only about twenty-nine. I see myself in the kitchen, watching breakfast TV. There's a tumbler of Glenfiddich on the worktop. Corinne has already rushed off to her job at Caddick and Co., otherwise the whisky wouldn't be there. I'd promised her I wouldn't drink before the evening.

"I don't drink as much as I used to." Her hand goes up and plays with the fringe of hair sticking out from the bandanna. "Not now that I've got away from Steve."

She's looking at me but she's in some other place for a moment. Then she snaps back, smiles, lifts her mug again.

"There's Kindi. She won't tell us where she's from but she's got a Brummy accent. She's only a kid. She ran away from home because her dad wanted to send her to Bangladesh to marry some feller she'd never seen. There's two guys on the first floor, Russians or Czechs or something. They don't speak hardly any English. I think they're illegal immigrants."

" And Ray?" I drink my tea and look interested.

"Ray's wife left him. Took the kids and ran off with a Scot. She lives in Glasgow and Ray never gets to see the kids. He just went to pieces. Lost his job and his house. He thinks the world of them kids. He doesn't talk about it but one night me and him had a few drinks and got talking. He doesn't care nothing about himself, but he looks after everyone else here. It's like it gives him something to hang on to. He's like a bloody social worker, except he doesn't try to tell you what to do."

"I'll get some fresh tea." I get up and gather the mugs. She'll want to know about me next.

"And Cupboard Girl?" I say when I come back. "What about her?"

"We don't know much about her." She takes the tea, glances round the room. "She can talk but she doesn't most of the time. She'll answer you if you talk to her, sometimes, once she gets to know you, that is. When she does talk, most of it doesn't make sense."

"What do you mean?"

"She jumbles her words up. Sometimes you can figure it out in the end, or you think you do, but it's hard work. You can't have a laugh and a joke with her. She doesn't seem to understand. She speaks funny too, sort of all one tone. We think she's retarded, got out of a mental institution or home or something."

"Care in the community?"

"Yeah," she laughs, "that's us. We all look after her."

"Why?"

"I dunno. I really don't know why we do it. She's the only one doesn't do any work, but we still look after her. Ray found her one night in a back street with three men. He heard her screaming. He went down the alley and the men ran off. She was in a right state."

I'm struggling with the thought of being down an alley with those rolling eyes and vicious teeth but at the same time anger stirs. How can people mistreat someone like that?

"It was her own fault in a way. We felt sorry for her and that's why we took her in but we soon found out that she likes men. Young men. These ones just went too far with her. You should be safe." She looks at me and grins.

"So Ray brought her back here. What does she live on?"

"We all feed her. That's all she seems to need really. We take her shopping sometimes. She loves the shops. She's like a kid with toys. She shoplifts like mad, but sometimes we have to do that too. We just have to stop her because she'd get caught. She's got no idea. Oh, but there's a queer thing. Sometimes people just come up and give her things. Sometimes it's money, and if it was just that you could understand it because they feel sorry for her, but sometimes it's pieces of jewellery they're wearing or a toy they've just bought for their kid. She just looks at them and they come over and give her things. It's weird."

"And the cupboard? Why does she live in the cupboard?"

"She doesn't. Not all the time. It's where she feels safe I suppose, when something threatens her. She goes there when she's scared. It must be something to do with her life before, but who knows what?"

"Doesn't she ever talk about what happened to her before?"

"No. I've never heard her."

* * *

vicky wake up   oldgreybeardman gone   vicky hungry   rain outside – sad air sad vicky go to kitchen   peter in kitchen   peter say what you want vicky wicky peter say want cornflakes vicky peter get bowl get cornflakes get milk peter say fuck off vicky get your own fucking cornflakes peter eat cornflakes cornflakes on face milk on face spill milk on table peter sad bad inside black inside make vicky sad inside black inside sadbadblack peter say what you fucking crying for you crazy cunt black comes out of peter black all round peter vicky scared peter say what you fucking staring at go get in your fucking cupboard peter mouth open cornflakes inside black come out of peter mouth come to vicky vicky scared peter say fucking crazy bitch kindi come in kindi say leave her alone peter peter say fucking crazy cunt kindi say she's hungry aren't you vicky peter say she's fucking nuts kindi get two bananas out of cupboard kindi give vicky banana kindi eat banana vicky look at peter look at banana black round peter peter bowl empty peter stand up go to door open door peter say fucking rain vicky put banana in pocket vicky eat banana in cupboard no black peter in cupboard kindi say it's okay vicky vicky see rita come in gate oldgreybeardman come in gate oldbeardgreymannoleg hurt vicky scared oldmangreybeard scared peter rita come in rita say it's okay vicky peter say fucking nutty cow rita say stopit peter vicky say stopitstopitstopitstopit rita say stopit vicky okay vicky vicky say nomorenomorenomore rita say stopit vicky oldbeardgreyman come in put bag on floor kindi say it's okay vicky peter say back again staying are you rita say what's it to you peter say go and fuck yourselves peter go out of kitchen up stairs peter take black away up stairs vicky say sadblackpeter badsadpeter rita say it's okay vicky kindi say sit down vicky eat your banana vicky sit down oldgreybeardman sit down hurt oldgreybeardman put leg out straight noleg hurt red round leg oldmangreybeard not black rita not black kindi not black black go upstairs with peter rita say don't be scared vicky this is the hermit he is coming to stay for a bit oldgreybeardman say jack greyoldbeardman hold out hand vicky look at hand kindi say hi jack kindi hold oldgreybeardman hand vicky say hermitjack kindi laugh rita laugh that's right oldgreybeardman say hermitjack hermitjack laugh vicky laugh no black in kitchen rain outside vicky eat banana hermitjack take things out of bag hermitjack make tea hermitjack give vicky tea vicky like tea vicky like hermitjack hermitjack not black

* * *

In the kitchen when we come back, Rita and me, there's some kind of row going on; the air in the room is zinging with it. There're three of them in there. The Indian girl, thin as a knife, in jeans and tee shirt, must be Kindi. That long, streaky miserable guy, Peter, is still there, standing by the back door. Kindi stands between him and another woman.

The other woman has tears on her face but she's not crying now. Her eyes are squeezed shut and she's shouting, "Stop it! Stop it! Stop it!"

My insides are churning. Something is wrong here, something is happening to me. I don't know what it is and I'm scared.

Kindi leans towards her protectively. "Stop it, Vicky!"

So this is Cupboard Girl. Rita and Kindi are fussing round her, calming her down. Peter looks at me slyly.

"Back again? Staying are you?" I can't answer him, I'm too busy looking at Cupboard Girl. She's not a girl, she's a woman and in the daylight nothing to be scared of. So why am I getting alarm signals? My body chemistry's practically out of control. She looks just like any forty-year-old bag lady you can see any day on the street; thin mousy hair cut with a knife and fork; shapeless skirt and sweater, but an odd touch, a bright lime green and blue scarf wound round her neck with careless style.

She senses my gaze and opens her eyes. My breath stops in my chest. I see Angela's eyes staring at me, grey and full of tears. A thousand images of Angela crying flash before me. Joy rushes through me for a second, then terror strikes. This can't be. Angela is dead. I visit her in the morgue every night. I see her blue-white face; the dried blood; her grey eyes, dead like stones. My leg gives way and I reach out for the chair in front of me.

Peter stomps out of the kitchen. Kindi says, "Sit down, Vicky," and the moment is gone.

I sit down opposite Vicky. I sit carefully yet my hip still creaks with pain. I get my things out and make tea and feel her watching every move. The air is more relaxed now Peter has gone and I sense that Vicky doesn't feel afraid of me, but I'm still in turmoil. I won't let myself look at her eyes. I keep telling myself I'm mistaken. Slowly I become calmer.

Rita introduces me. "Vicky this is the Hermit."

Before I know it, I say, "Jack," then immediately bite my lip. I've always made a point of never telling anyone my real name. What's got into me?

Vicky says, "Hermitjack," and everybody laughs. I stir the cups of tea. Ray comes into the kitchen. He too looks more normal in daylight, less haunted, despite the stubble on his chin. He rubs his hands together when I pass him a plastic cup half filled with tea.

"I'm going down to Lime Street Station for a wash and brush up. Anyone coming?"

"Shall we go?" Kindi asks Rita. "Then we can go straight to the agency."

Rita shrugs and smiles, gets up. Vicky looks from one to another.

"You stay here," Rita says to Vicky. "You'll be all right." She smiles encouragingly.

"Decided whether to move on or not?" Ray looks at me, raises an eyebrow.

I look at Vicky. She's staring at me and I can't read her expression. Who is she? Where has she come from? What's wrong with her? And why has she got the eyes of my fourteen-year-old daughter?

"Angela," Vicky mutters, and suddenly everything stops for me, inside and out.

"Are you okay?" Ray's at my side. The others are staring. "You don't look too good."

"You'd better stay here for a while." Rita puts her hand on mine.

"Yeah, I think I will, if it's okay." I turn off the stove.

* * *

quiet

      all gone

hermitjack sadsick
  scared

see angela
make vicky sad
  hermitjack   not hurt
no

It's quiet in the kitchen once the others have gone although there are muffled noises upstairs reminding me that there are still people in the house.

I'm still stunned, don't know what to say, can't think even.

I just keep looking at her.

I know I never mentioned Angela. I never talk about her to anyone. It's only myself I torture with her memory.

So how does she know?

She sits there eating her banana and I want to shake her, shake it out of her.

14

no stopit hermitjack

stopitstopitstopit

no redblack
hermitjack
not bad

hermitjack cross
    run vicky

no
    wait

okay, vicky

hermitjack redleg hurt

vicky eat banana
    sweet sticky vicky like

    hermitjack talk

talk vicky
    nomoreangela

nomorebanana

The silence goes on. It gets harder to break. She jumps when I clear my throat.

"Vicky – you said 'Angela'."

She looks straight at me and again those grey eyes hit me. I hold my muscles tight so that I won't cry out.

"What do you mean, 'not bad'?"

She jumps. I realise I am shouting, scaring her. She drops the banana on the table and I can see she's poised to run. There's a delicacy about her, a faun-like quality that belies her shapeless figure.

"Okay, Vicky, take it easy. It's okay."

My hip twinges sharply and the pain radiates right down into the memory of where my leg used to be, where she touched me last night.

Christ, what kind of creature is she? She knows about Angela, she knows about my leg.

The painkillers are in my bag. I swill them down with the last of the tea. I'll need to get more somewhere today. "How long have you been here Vicky?"

I pluck up the courage to look in her eyes. She's not Angela and whatever she knows I see no understanding there.

I don't think she understands what I'm saying. She looks at me, then says, "Vicky like banana."

itchy
itchy
  want tickle

vicky itch

sore notleg

      poor leg

nomore angela
nomore leg

      car
silvercar

itchy
    tickle now

"Yeah, bananas are good." I smile. After a moment she smiles too but it's like something she's realised you're supposed to do. I try again.

"Where were you before? Before you came here?"

She stares at me. Her face is unreadable. She squirms in her chair.

"I came yesterday." It seems like a lifetime ago. "With Ray. You came – when? Last month?"

There must be some way of getting through to her. I rack my brains trying to think of what to say. My hip twinges again, sending another bolt of pain down my non-existent leg.

Suddenly she reaches forward and strokes my leg. There's nothing sexual about it but there is curiosity in her fingers. Her hand's moving down to the false part and I swear I can feel her touching it as if it were still flesh and not just metal. A memory shoots up in me so strongly that I feel it in my flesh, my no longer existing flesh; me and Jed playing badminton, my legs strong and athletic, leaping for the shuttlecock.

"Poor Hermit Jack," she says and her eyes look full of tears.

She takes her hand away.

"Vicky itch," she says.

She shifts again. Her hand is up her skirt. She's playing with nice tickle

yes, good

hermitjack angrysad . . . vicky go
find laszlonik

herself under the table, right in front of me. Blood rushes into my face and I look away, at the boarded window, not seeing anything. My leg still feels her touch. The same hand.

I'm bewildered. I want to get up and leave the room but I'm in a daze, I sense that she knows something, feels something about me. She can't tell me but it's in her touch. I feel this without being able to explain it to myself.

So I just sit there watching her wanking. Even though I'm disgusted I just can't pull away from her.

"Don't do that, Vicky," I say weakly and it's she who gets up and leaves me.

By the time I heave myself to my feet and get my bag together, I can hear her feet on the stairs and by the time I get to the bottom step, she's disappeared and I just hear the slam of a door somewhere.

She must be headed for the cupboard and I've half a mind to leave her to it at the thought of climbing all those stairs but I want to know more. What does she know about me?

I nearly fall over a huddled figure sitting on the top step on the first floor landing near the toilet.

"Has Vicky gone up?" My breath scrapes in my chest, slowing my words.

"Don't fucking bother. She's in the Russkies' room."

It's Peter. He's wearing a hoodie that's pulled right over his head and he's slumped with his head on his knees.

"Russkies?" I'm breathing easier now and the painkillers are starting to kick in.

"She's screwing them. She's always in there."

"What? Both of them?" I can't marry that innocent fragile look with this masturbating nympho, and blurring into both images is

Angela. I'm looking at all the doors. Which one is it? I want to kill them. She's an innocent.

"Told you, she's fucking crackers. She can't get enough of it."

I want to thump him as well but I remember Rita saying Vicky likes young men.

"What about you? Does she come on to you? And Ray?" I can hear anguish in my voice and suddenly I think, why should I care? I've only just met her and she means nothing to me – nothing. I've only seen her twice, yet it's as if she's got some kind of pull on me.

"I wouldn't touch her with a bargepole. She's probably riddled with all kinds." There is slight movement from under the hood. "Anyway, it'd be like shagging a baby, wouldn't it? And she's old enough to be my mother."

I turn and lower myself carefully down to sit beside Peter. He shrinks away from me towards the banister.

"Laszlo and Nik aren't so fussy. They must be fucking desperate."

I sit and wonder about Laszlo and Nik. My mind fills with pictures of what is going on behind that door. I don't know the right thing to do. Should I break down the door and play the rescuing knight or would that frighten her away from me altogether? Peter's gloom begins to envelop me. I can feel it weighing me down like a wet cloud.

"Anyway I wouldn't care if she looked like Britney Spears. Sex, women, they just cause trouble. What's the fucking point?"

Now I really look at Peter. The misery coming out of him is almost palpable. I want to ask if he's getting medication but think better of it.

"Someone give you a bad time?"

"What do you fucking care?" He pushes himself further away from me, as if he wants to crawl right into the banister and become part of the rotten wood.

It doesn't look too steady and I reach out a hand to stop him going through it but he pushes me away.

"You know fuck all, granddad." The hood starts to slip and he pulls it down again, wraps his arms round his knees and begins to rock back and forth. "Just fuck off. Leave me alone."

The door creaks open and Vicky comes out. I pull myself to my feet.

"Christ that was quick," I say.

There is a muffled grunt from under the hood. Vicky looks at Peter, steps carefully round him to join me on the stairs.

"Hermit Jack Vicky go shopping," she says looking up at me and plucking my arm. In her hand she has a five pound note.

*　*　*

outside

light
no sadpeterblack . . .
skynowall smell rain smell clean rain cold
   vicky mouth open rain cold in mouth　vicky in rain
    rain on vicky rain in vicky vicky smell flowers in rain

hermitjack cross　vicky scared

hermitjack scared

hermitjack put hood on vicky stop rain on vicky　hermitjack not cross not hurt vicky

big road car noise red car blue car black car white van　people noise foot noise talk noise ladypinkcoat smell nice　ladyredumbrella push vicky　vicky see noroofchurch

black car black car black car

It's still raining but not as heavily as before. It's good to get out of the house, away from the gloomy half light and decrepit atmosphere; away from Peter and his depression. The pain in my leg is fading as we step into the damp air. Outside in the alley she stops and turns. Her eyes are closed; her face is turned up to the rain. Round and round she goes, letting the rain fall on her face.

"Come on," I say, but she takes no notice. I get my wool cap out of my pocket and put it on.

"Come on, you'll get wet." Impatience leaks through my voice. She stops and looks at me. The shock blanks my brain all over again. Her eyes are grey and clear. There is a sense of alarm in them as she studies my face.

"Come on." I lift the hood of the old anorak she's wearing up over her hair. I start to walk along and she follows.

We go down Falkner Street and Rice Street and into Pilgrim Street. It's almost lunchtime and the pubs and cafes are opening up by the time we get to Bold Street. I can't think of much to say. I'm trying to get myself together. I look at the street life going on

manbrowncoat smell bad

shops

    shops

vicky like shops

bookshop toyshop clotheshop shoeshop

fruitshop meatshop cakeshop supermarket

foodsmell
vicky hungry vicky see caff

hungrythirsty
               want coke

hermitjack say no point big road
vicky hungry see big shops little
shops ladybabypram baby cry
make vicky want cry

around us. Today it seems surreal like one of those films where everything seems normal but you can tell something weird is going to happen any minute.

She turns, stares at people as they pass, stops here and there with her nose in the air like a dog. In the light I see she's cleaner than I expected. Her mousy hair is shiny and her clothes are shabby but pretty clean. Kindi and Rita must take her for a shower.

She's got nothing with her except presumably the five pound note which she must have tucked away somewhere.

I bet she keeps her belongings upstairs in that cupboard. I wouldn't leave anything in there myself, but then maybe she hasn't anything worth stealing.

Suddenly she says, "Hungry," and points at a bistro on the other side of the street. Smells of garlic and good coffee waft across. I look at the window. It's too pricey for the likes of us.

"Not here." I point towards Church Street. McDonalds is more in our line.

She looks at me but doesn't say anything. We walk on. Church Street is full of shoppers and office workers on early lunch breaks. The street is getting re-surfaced so we're all crowded down one side, but everybody's used to the road-works by now. It's all part of the

no crybaby   nocry

poorbaby
        nicebluerabbit

baby cry no
no

vicky see balloons   vicky like
balloons blue balloons   silver
balloons
red balloons green balloons

balloons have pictures

softrabbit

        bluebunnyfluffy

mcdonalds smell cheeseburgerfries

cheeseburgerfriescoke   vicky
give mcdonaldsman get money
back ...

City of Culture improvements and maybe it will look good when it's finished but I don't think I'll be around to find out.

Suddenly this woman comes over with a baby in a pram and gives Vicky a toy rabbit. Whatever went on I missed it while I was looking at the cranes behind the street façade, and while I'm still wondering about it Vicky pulls me towards a stall selling souvenir rubbish down a side street.

"The rabbit, Vicky. What happened? Why did she give it to you?"

She ignores me, her whole body's straining towards some balloons but I turn away and she follows. I watch her cuddling the rabbit and there's something almost alien about her till she glances at me with Angela's eyes and I forget everything. She's looking and sniffing at everything but I keep walking automatically. My mind's a blank until she tugs my arm and I look up and see we're outside McDonalds.

She's straight up to the counter, luckily there's no queue. She orders cheeseburger, fries and coke with no problem at all, paying for it with the five pound note which she extracts from somewhere inside her clothes. She takes the change without counting it and puts it in

hermitjack get tea   no cheeseburgerfries   cheeseburgerfries
smell good   vicky like

hungry
cheeseburgerfries   taste   good
drink coke like coke   coke
bubble make vicky sneeze

hermitjack drink tea

hermitjack sad   hermitjack dark
not black like peter
hermitjack dark   brown   grey
man shout mcdonald man shout
scared. men shout   red round
counter make vicky red   scared
redblackpolice run in   look for
vicky take vicky back hide vicky
hide   hermitjack help vicky
shout shout shout   all red all
black   close eyes

redblackpolice pull vicky hand
nomorenomorenomore no
nomore medoban   nomore
medoban   nomore   medobannomore   medobannomore
medobannomoremedoban   no
moremedobanno   medobannomore
nomorenomorenomorenomoreno
moreno

her anorak pocket. She's getting
by but does she understand
money – exchange? I doubt it.

I buy a cup of tea. I'm not
really hungry yet and I don't
have much money left. Soon I'll
have to find a few hours' casual
work but not until I'm desperate.

We sit at a table some distance
from the doors and the counter.
She nibbles her food, looking all
around at the people: the colours
and pictures on the walls.

She's such a mystery. Where's
she come from? What's she
doing here?

She looks at me timidly. God
she reminds me of Angela but
Angela would only be twenty
now if she were still alive.

I can hear raised voices.
There's some kind of row going
on at the counter and the next
minute two policemen barge
through the doors. Before I
know it, Vicky's under the table
clinging to my good leg.

"What's the matter?" I
splutter through a mouthful of
hot tea. I can feel her shaking
down there. I reach down a
hand to pull her up but she digs
her nails into it and I let go
quick.

She's muttering over and
over, "No no medoban." At
least that's what it sounds
like.

Two girls at the next table
are staring and giggling, other-

morenomorenomorenomore
medoban
nomedobanno
nomorenomorenomore
noise   nomorenoise   nomore
nomore
no more noise

baby see vicky baby not red not
black baby like vicky baby not
shout   like baby
no redblackpolice come no man
shout
hermitjack hide vicky   hermitjack say
redblackpolice gone
get on chair
look   no police come   no redblack police come take vicky.

no redblack police take vicky
baby eat fries   baby cry

medoban
                              nomore

no moreno moremnomore

wise no one seems to have
noticed. They're all too busy
watching the fun at the counter.
After a few moments the two
coppers frogmarch someone out
and peace returns after some
excited whisperings among the
staff.

The two girls get up and leave,
giving me curious stares. Their
place is taken by a young couple
with a toddler. The little boy
crawls under the table and says
hello to Vicky.

"It's   okay,"   I   whisper.
"They're gone." I don't know if
she'll understand me. I can see
her eyes staring and for a
moment I remember last night
when I opened the cupboard,
how much she had scared me.
She didn't look at all like Angela
then. She comes up and sits back
on her seat, all the time looking
round as if ready to leap up and
run away.

"Did you find it?" I say loudly
for the benefit of the couple at
the next table, but they just give
Vicky a glance, then carry on
trying to feed their child.

"They weren't looking for
you. Why would they come for
you?"

"Medoban," she says. She's
shaking so much I can hardly
make out the words.

"Medoban?"

"No more, no more, no
more . . ."

stopitstopitstopitstopitstopit-
stopitstopitstop
stopitstophermitjack
hermitjack no hurt vicky
hold vicky hand   hermitjack
hand warm

okay vicky okay
eat cheeseburgerfries   fries cold
drink coke   coke
bubbles good
hermitjack drink tea   hermitjack
no
talk   hermitjack sad

cheeseburger allgone

one fry two fry threefry
all gone
   coke all gone
vicky want go shop

hermitjack vicky go shop   smells
in shop
flowersmell fruitsmell seasmell
lemonsmell
lipstick pink red purple
brown   lipstick smell good
red blue pink purple put on nails
little bottles   vicky like little
bottles

"Stop it Vicky," I say, remembering Rita earlier.

"Stop it stop it stop it. . . ."

She's got her eyes shut so I stop her hand that's shaking on the table, put the cup of Coke in it and hold on to it till she opens her eyes and calms down.

"Take it easy. No one's coming for you. Calm down and eat your food."

She eats but her eyes still dart about like a frightened animal. I drink my tea and try not to think about Angela. Medoban? What does that mean? It seems to be the first clue to her past.

She must have been in care somewhere, or someone must have looked after her.

From what I've seen of her so far, I can't see how she could have survived on her own for any length of time. She seems to know about the police and it looks like her previous experiences of them haven't been to her liking.

When she's finished eating we go out into the street and I take her into Boots so I can stock up on co-codamol.

She sniffs at and picks up everything and I have a hard time stopping her from putting things in her pockets. I daren't take my eyes off her for a minute. I get her to the pharmacy counter without her actually pocketing anything. She stuffs the blue

hermitjack buy pills in box
vicky
like little boxes, redbluegreen
cleansmell medicinesmell

ladywhitecoat see vicky

hermitjack give vicky littlebot-
tlebag
like littlebottlebagsmell
littlebottles   redbluegreenpink
ladywhitecoat smile vicky

hermitjackvicky go in big road
vicky open littlebottles like
tops on littlebottles pinkbrown-
blue

pink bottle smell flowers

pink bottle smell bath medoban
no like medoban
no like pink bottle smell

no like pink bottle

police

run vicky run nogomedoban

run

rabbit in her coat pocket and runs her fingers over the boxes in the displays in front of the counter while I pay for my tablets. The assistant looks at me, looks at her. Her expression softens. She rummages under the counter.

"Here's a few free samples for your friend."

The bag is full of little bottles; shampoos, shower gels, stuff like that. Vicky takes it with a brilliant smile. The assistant smiles back.

"Thank you," I say.

Vicky makes happy grunting sounds while she roots in the bag. It keeps her occupied while I lead her to the top of Lord Street, away from any more big shops. My leg is complaining again but there's nowhere to rest. Apart from the main street the whole area is a vast building site. It's like the middle's being ripped out of the city. Cranes scrape the sky and the air is full of dust.

I think about sitting on a bench at the Pierhead, having a nice rest and taking in the sea breeze.

The rain is easing off and there are glints of blue sky out over the Mersey. Gulls shriek from the tops of tall buildings and I can smell the river. Suddenly two policemen come out of Harrington Street and almost bump into us. Vicky squeaks, drops her bag of bottles and she's off before I have time to think.

The police watch her running, then look suspiciously at me. I daren't chase after her. I walk on slowly, trying to look nonchalant and after a moment or two they carry on and turn down Lord Street towards Church Street.

Vicky's disappeared. I walk all round Derby Square and up and down James Street, looking down all the alleys and in all the shops and bars but there's no sign of her. I call her name and people look at me. I don't care. I just want to find her. I do this for ages but with no luck. In the end I've no choice but to give up. My hip's telling me I have to rest, right now. I limp to the Pierhead and sit down by the ferry terminal and wonder what to do.

I don't want to go back to the house without her. Kindi and Rita expected me to look after her. 'It's not your responsibility,' someone says in my head, but I know it *is* my responsibility – just as it was my responsibility to look after Angela that day. I feel like crying but I can't. My heart and my eyes are dry and have been ever since that day.

It's the quiet time of the afternoon before parents come on the streets with school-kids; before people start rushing home from work. There are still quite a few foreign tourists and pensioner day-trippers milling about. I have to scrutinise the groups of passers-by to make sure she's not among them.

A young Japanese girl suddenly stops and puts a pound coin on the bench beside me. "Cup tea," she says with a shy smile and flits away. Christ, I must look rough.

I don't have to go back to the house. I hadn't intended to stay more than one night, only till the rain cleared. I'd been thinking about leaving Liverpool anyway. I've been here a few weeks now and I don't like to stay anywhere for too long.

I'm kidding myself. I can't leave this unfinished, can't just walk away. She's got Angela's eyes and she knows things about me without having been told anything. How did she know Angela's name? I feel like she can read my mind, but that's crazy, she can't even speak properly. And then there's the way she touched my leg. I think about the shy gaucheness of her; the masturbation; the sex with the Russians. None of the pieces seem to fit together.

And now I've lost her. Anything could happen to her. I have visions of rape, abduction, arrest for shoplifting. I might never see her again, never find out what she knows. Hopelessness translates to stiffness as I creak upright and plod back up James Street.

I've a vague hope that she'll be there when I get back to the house but she isn't. Ray is sitting at the kitchen table alongside an old woman with wild grey hair. There's a bottle of wine that's three-quarters empty in front of her.

"Mabel, this is the Hermit," Ray says as I come in through the open back door.

"Oo d'yer say, love?" She peers at me but her eyes are glazed.

I know that place she's in. It's a comfortable hideout, but I don't go there any more.

"Kermit did yer say? Isn't he a frog?"

"Hermit!" Ray shouts down her ear.

"That's a funny name." She looks at me suspiciously for a moment then shrugs and laughs. "Pleased to meet yer, I'm Mrs Mabel Hardaker, formerly of Boaler Street. Ah those were the days when my Jimmy was alive." She swigs from the bottle.

"I've lost Vicky." I watch Ray for signs of anger, disgust. I remember how Corinne's lip curled that day, how her eyes burned into me, after the first cold shock. She couldn't even speak to me, her hatred was so fierce. I remember this, and little else, through the fog of shock and morphine I was wrapped in at the time. I remember feeling detached as the emergency team rushed round me, as if I were watching a film about somebody else. I don't remember any pain, but Corinne's expression is etched on my memory.

"She'll be back." Ray smiles. "Don't worry, she always finds her way back. She's like a homing pigeon."

"There were these policemen."

"Yeah, we know. She runs a mile. Honestly, don't worry. She does it all the time."

"Oo's he lost, love?" Mabel's head swings from me to Ray.

"Vicky. Cupboard Girl." Ray tries to stay her hand on the bottle but she pulls it away and clasps the bottle to her chest.

"Oh, her." She chuckles and looks me up and down. "Don't you worry about her, she'll be havin' it away off down some jigger." She laughs again and raises the bottle to her lips. A trickle of wine escapes and dribbles off her chin to join the other stains on the front of her jumper.

"Rita and Kindi asked me to keep an eye on her."

"Well, what can you do?" Ray shrugs. "She could be anywhere. Where did you lose her?"

"Top of Lord Street. Anything could happen to her."

"She'll come back. She always does."

"But how does she know the way?"

"She's a blooming homing pigeon." Mabel laughs and swigs from her bottle. "She's got ESP or something."

"What's it to you?" Ray's staring at me.

"I just feel responsible."

"Why? Why should you?"

I shrug. How can I explain? I don't even know myself why I feel responsible. It's not for her sake, it's a selfish curiosity. I want to know how she knows what's in my mind, if that's what she does know. Is it some kind of ESP, my guilty secret laid bare? If so, thank God she *can't* speak. Or is it possible she knows something else, something I don't know myself?

Mabel sings, "*Come round any old time,*
Make yourself at home."

"Shut up Mabel," Ray says. "She's always turned up before. If she's not back by five, we'll go and look for her."

"*Put your feet on the mantelshelf,*
Open the cupboard and help yourself."

She shakes the bottle. "Got anything to drink?"

"No." I go out of the kitchen. I don't like the way Ray is looking at me. He thinks I fancy Vicky but nothing could be further from the truth. I go up the stairs and into the toilet. No one else is around. I think about Vicky earlier, coming out of the Russians' room. There's tenderness now when I picture her. I've overcome the fright she gave me when I first saw her. It's not sex. It's not even because she reminds me of Angela. It's something in me that responds to the way she moves, the gaucheness. There's an innocence about her, as if she's less knowing even than a child, despite her sexualised behaviour. Something in me calls to her, or is it that she is in my mind, calling to me? And she sees Angela, of that I'm sure. Mabel's singing floats up the stairs;

"*Rich or poor, come knock at the door*
And make yourself at h-o-o-m-e."

I go up to the next floor and into 'our' room. Maybe she's sneaked in without anyone seeing her. Maybe she's hiding in the cupboard right now, holding her breath in the silence, but I know that's not so. I can sense the emptiness in there.

I open the cupboard door. It's a nest of brightly coloured knick knacks; scarves, plastic toys, perfume bottles, clothes and shoes all jumbled together on the floor. There's a mixed smell of perfumes and mustiness. There are a couple of children's picture books, a few fast food and chocolate wrappers. My gaze stops on an old hardback notebook that looks incongruous amongst all the rest of the stuff.

I pick it up with difficulty. The hardboard covers are worn away at the corners but there's nothing on them to identify it. I turn it over in my hands and open it then something lands on my back and almost knocks the breath out of me. I stagger forward catching hold of the doorpost to save myself from falling.

hermitjack in cupboard hermitjack take vicky book
stopitstopitstopitstopitstopit
hermitjack

give vicky bookgivebookvicky-
givevickybookgive
stopitstopitstopgivebookvicky
vickybook

hermitjack hurt notleg

vicky hurt hermitjack
not take vicky book   not take
book
vicky book

hermitjack laugh
vicky cross   no laugh

vicky hold book
hermitjack look at book

"Fucking hell!" I know it's her before I even turn round because she's screaming, "Stop it, stop it, stop it" and who else does that?

I have to hold on to the doorpost with one hand while I try to dislodge her with the other. After a moment I succeed and she snatches the book out of my hand and stops screeching.

I can hear her panting before I turn around and see her. As well as the blue scarf she's now wearing a pink fluffy hat and sweat is running down the side of her face.

She looks so funny and I'm so pleased to see her unharmed that I can't help laughing till tears come in my eyes while she just stares at me.

She's still panting and her lips quiver. She holds the book tight to her chest and says, "Vicky book." Her eyes flash angrily. I see Angela; at seven, on holiday in Cornwall, throwing a tantrum over an ice cream; at fourteen demanding to be

hermitjack no take vicky book

hermitjack sad   no take vicky book

allowed to stay out till after eleven at night.

I sag against the doorpost.

"Vicky book," she says again. "No Hermit Jack."

I wonder what's in the book. Why is she getting so worked up about it? She can't have written in it, can she? I shouldn't think she'd be able to write, or even read for that matter. Maybe I'm wrong.

She clutches it tighter as if she thinks I'm trying to take it from her but no, let her keep her secrets. I've got a book like that too, but mine is in my head.

"Yeah, okay, vicky book," I say. "Let's go find something to eat."

CHAPTER TWO

It's two days later, late morning. I'm alone in the house, I think, unless Peter's skulking about somewhere. I'm in my room, tucked up in my sleeping bag. My hip's so bad today, I need to rest.

Yesterday I did four hours' casual work, washing up on the lunchtime session at the Golden Peacock restaurant in Chinatown. This morning I woke up in agony. After all the pain I went through with the amputation and getting used to the prosthesis, you'd think a touch of arthritis in the hip would be a doddle, but it's no joke. Thank God for co-codamol and hot tea.

I'm beginning to feel warm and cosy and my mind drifts to yesterday, to the good feeling of having enough cash for a few days; me, who used to throw more than that away on a pub lunch with Jed. I wonder how Jed is now, whether he has a new partner in the practice we used to share and if Gladys, our menopausal practice manager has retired yet. The patients stream past, some nameless, faceless; others well remembered from years of chronic illness, both real and imaginary.

There's a rosy nostalgia in these memories as I sink towards sleep then I remember the whisky bottle in my desk drawer and the way Jed started covering up for me, although it was ages before he tackled me directly about it.

It wasn't a problem then, at least I didn't think so.

"You need to face up to things. You're drinking too much."

"I can handle it. It's not affecting my work. Don't sit in judgement on me, you like a drink yourself."

"You missed an important meeting last Tuesday, you've been late for surgery twice this week, and that mouthwash doesn't fool anybody. People are starting to talk."

"Talk? People always talk, make mountains out of molehills." I couldn't let him see how his words had shaken me. I hadn't realised anyone knew. And it was only the odd nip, or so it seemed to me then.

"What is it, Buster? The stress of the job? Maybe I can help. Or is it something at home? Is it Corinne?"

Only Jed could get away with quizzing me like that. We'd been friends so long he knew he could talk straight to me and I knew he only had my welfare at heart. That didn't stop the acid rising in my stomach. I choked on anger and embarrassment. Corinne! There it was. He'd hit me in a tender spot. The acid erupted into my throat as I turned on him and told him to mind his own business before I went in search of a drink.

What did make me drink like that? Now I can see how bad it was, but at the time I didn't notice it happening. I'd always liked a drink, nothing wrong with that. I didn't drink cheap stuff, good quality whisky and most doctors need a nip of something after the pressures of a day's work for the NHS. Changes at work meant bigger workloads, more responsibilities. I was continually tired, but Corinne always wanted more.

She'd got a good job. As a busy lawyer, she had plenty of intellectual stimulation, her own life, friends and colleagues, besides the nice house, beautiful baby girl and reasonably successful husband, but it wasn't enough. I idolised her but I couldn't meet her standards. When I couldn't perform, first at climbing the social ladder and then, as the drink took hold, not even in bed, that's when the coldness, the contempt, the crushing comments began.

The medical community in a city like Worcester is fairly close knit. I gradually became aware of whispers, sidelong glances from my colleagues, despite Jed's efforts to protect me. Drinking more meant I didn't have to care until the day I got stopped for drink driving.

I'm wide awake now, distress and adrenalin coursing through my body because it's there in front of me, that place surrounded by thorns and briars, like Sleeping Beauty's castle. Angela is inside and I don't want to look, won't look.

This no man's land is for my own protection. Even if I did want to look, nothing comes. I know this because in desperate moments I've tried, over and over, to remember, but only bits and pieces come like dreams. I've closed it off so well but after all these precautions, now it seems I'm given the slip.

Just when I think Angela's sleeping, if not peacefully then at least quietly, I find her echo haunting me in Vicky; in the turn of her head, the flash of her eyes and, most disturbing of all, in this wordless knowledge she seems to have.

I ought to get out of here, go to a new city, away from this girl/woman who's stirring up old thoughts and feelings, but I can't. I don't know what pulls me to her and it disturbs me. The cosy warm feeling has gone and the sleeping bag feels hot and uncomfortable. My head feels like an upset stomach.

It's strange how she went for me when I looked in the cupboard, the way she clung to that funny old notebook. I'm tempted to get it now and read it while she's out with Kindi and Rita, but I think they have come back. I can hear noises downstairs so I get up and put my leg on. The newly washed sock is soft on my stump. It's the one thing I have to be really careful about and it's a nightmare trying to wash and dry them. I inspect the socket too and oil the foot.

At least because of my profession, I had a good surgeon and a good prosthetist. It means I can walk a good distance without too much discomfort, or at least I could until the arthritis kicked in.

Vicky is in the kitchen with Rita and Kindi, sitting round the table eating chips out of a big paper parcel, which is opened in the middle. They look so normal, the distress inside me starts to subside.

"Help yourself," Rita smiles. Her red hair is up in a ponytail today and it looks shiny and clean in the sunlight coming through the open back door.

"We're going to the laundrette this afternoon," Kindi says. "If you've got any washing we'll take it." She looks fresh in a clean white tee shirt and I'm suddenly conscious of my grubby shirt and cords.

"Thanks." I sit down on the only empty chair, tear off a bit of the paper and put a few chips on it. Vicky also looks squeaky clean and her hair looks damp at the ends so I suppose they've all been to the station for a shower.

33

"Can Vicky stay with you this afternoon? We've got two hours' cleaning at St John's market."

"Fine with me. Okay with you Vicky?"

She doesn't answer, doesn't even look up. She picks up chips, measuring one against another, then stuffing them in her mouth. Rita grabs her sleeve.

"Vicky, you stay with Jack. Me and Kindi go to work."

Vicky stops chewing, looks from Rita to Kindi to me.

"Kindi go to work," she says.

"No Vicky, I go too. Rita go to work. Kindi go to work. "She points to herself and Kindi. "Vicky." She taps Vicky's chest. "Vicky stay with Jack." She points to me. Vicky watches in silence. She eats another chip, looks round again, then smiles.

"Vicky stay Hermit Jack. Rita Kindi go work. Okay."

"I'll get my stove. Make us some tea." I have to hold on to the table to get out of the chair. I need painkillers again.

First thing I do upstairs is get two co-codamols out of my bag and wash them down with a drink of water. My spare clothes are even dirtier than the ones I have on.

Downstairs, the chips are all gone. Kindi and Rita are stuffing black bin bags with clothes for washing. I hand over my black cords and blue shirt but not my Y fronts or socks. I can wash those out myself with the bit of soap I've got in my bag.

"How much?" I say as I get my stove out and set it up on the table.

"Is that all you've got?" Kindi looks at the little bundle. "Oh, call it quits. You've given us plenty of free tea the last couple of days. Don't bother with tea for us." She stops me pouring more water in the pan. "We're going now. We'll be back about six. We usually get leftover sandwiches and fruit so don't buy any food. Okay?"

"Okay," Vicky repeats as they go out of the door.

	I watch her while I stir the water on the stove and wait to see if
hermitjack make tea	she'll be the first to speak.
	She gets up and washes her hands at the sink but doesn't say anything. She wipes her hands
fingers sticky	on her skirt.
wash hands	
wetbubble	The water boils. I ponder

bubble
cupspooncup

roundandroundspoon
    roundbubbles

sugarsweet
black

    peter
peter come peter black   black
   yespeterblack

spoon   black come out of peter
all over vicky   squash vickysad-
petersosad
        make peter better
peter shout

vicky wet
    vicky scared

        vicky run

petershout make vickyrun

peter redblackangrysad
shout   red words
    black words

while I make the tea. She watches every move, says nothing. It's unnerving that she speaks so little. I'm realising now that in the four days I've been here I don't think I've heard her ask a question or start a conversation, except for screaming, "Stop it" and "No more". Even making a simple reply to a question seems to be difficult.

I get some sugar packets out and give two to Vicky. Suddenly Peter walks in with a paper cup in his hand. He fills it at the sink, drinks it down, fills it again.

Vicky gets up and goes to the sink. She picks up a plastic spoon. "Peter sad," she says and reaches out to touch his arm.

"Get away from me you fucking loon." Peter twists violently away, spilling water over himself and Vicky. Vicky jumps back and stands there holding the spoon.

"There's no need for that," I stir my tea, keeping my voice calm, although I want to flatten him.

"Mind your own business, you old bastard." He seems to squeeze the words out as if some great force from outside is constricting him.

"Just don't talk to her like that." I speak quietly but I can feel my temper rising.

"Fucking shut up, can't you? I only come in here for a fucking drink and this bitch starts on me, and now you."

hermitjack notscared
make vicky notscared

black   vicky sick
drink tea

badroom   thickblack
hermitjack vicky go out of house
leave redsadblackpeter in badroom

sun yellowshine
vicky hot

vicky see ladygreendress
nice greendress

hermitjack walk slow   vicky see
manwithdog   dog sniff wall
sniff floor
ladyhighheels tap tap flowers in
box on wall   red flowers
blueflowers yellowflowers
whiteflowers
girlyellowtop yellowsun
yellowhair
girl laugh kiss boy boyredshirt
laszloredshirt   vicky kiss laszlonik   boygirl go bookshop
vicky want go shop

He's got his back to us and his voice comes out of the hood but I can hear the anger, see it in the way he's gripping the edges of the sink, both arms rigid.

No one speaks for a few moments. I can hear Peter's breathing rasping in the silence. Peter's presence is heavy. It's as if he knows it. He just stands there.

I empty my cup. I've had enough. The stove is cool enough to pack away.

"Come on Vicky," I say. She follows me without a word.

It feels about two o'clock. It's warm and sunny and the streets are choked with women still in summer dresses, shorts and tight tops, breasts and navels showing; men in tee shirts or looking uncomfortable in suits. What's happened to the British autumn?

I feel more relaxed walking like this with Vicky. It's companionable, even though she doesn't speak. The tension created by the scene with Peter eases away just like the pain in my hip has done.

I don't know where to take her. If I was on my own I'd go to the library and read, but I can't see her sitting still while I do that. I think about the museum or art gallery but decide against it. In the end I take her to St John's Gardens.

She tries to pull me into various

vicky want
icecreamchocolate

hermitjack give vicky chocolate
icecream   like hermitjack
icecream coldsweetsticky

hermitjack sad . . . hermitjack no
get ice cream
        eat   icecream   yellowsun
behind tree

ice cream good

hermitjack talk ladybabypram
go past
        hermitjack sad

shops on the way down but I don't let her. I just keep walking and thankfully she follows me.

There's an ice cream van outside St John's Market and I stop to buy her one. She points at the picture of the ice cream cone with a flake in it and gives me a smile when the man hands her the cone.

Something twists inside me when I see how her eyes light up. How little it takes to please her.

Going into the garden makes me feel better. It's peaceful here now that the office workers have finished their lunches and gone back to work.

I sit down on a bench and wait for Vicky to sit beside me. She's busy eating her ice cream and I watch her in silence for a few moments.

"You like ice cream, don't you?" She doesn't answer.

"Did you get lots of ice cream when you were a little girl?"

It's as if she hasn't heard me. She carries on eating.

"Vicky. Haven't you got any family?"

She looks at me but there's no response.

"Mum, dad, brother, sister"

Nothing.

She licks the last of the ice cream from her fingers and glances at a woman with a pushchair on the other side of the garden.

hermitjack talk sad see bin red-
paper bluepaper angela sweet-
paper
crisppaper icecreampaper
wasp in bin no like wasp
wasp go bzzz
yellowblack silvercar yellow-
blackbzzz

hermitjack darksad
grey come out of hermitjack
grey come to vicky angela   talk
grey
no
        grey nono dark
hermitjack hold vickyhand
no

hermitjack hurt vicky
        silvercar

vicky hand hurt

nonolikesilvercar
        see silvercar
seeangelahermitjack nono
stopithermitjackletgovickyhand
nonostopit
        bird   birdongrass
        bigbird   bigredeyebird

"I have – had – a wife, and a daughter."

Nothing. She's looking at a nearby rubbish bin. A few wasps hover round it and she watches them without fear.

"Do you hear me? Do you know what I'm saying?"

"Bzzz," she says.

"You remind me of my daughter. Her name was Angela."

"Angela," she says, and I look up but see no understanding in her eyes. Maybe she's just repeating what I said.

"My wife's name is Corinne." Vicky doesn't seem to hear me. She's looking at the roses in their beds, the flower borders along the paths and the wasps buzzing round the bin.

Suddenly it starts to come out. "I wasn't drunk. They said I wasn't drunk. Corinne was working late. Corinne was always working late. Angela came home from school. I'd had a drink, but I wasn't drunk. That's what they told me, so how?" It stops. I can't go any further.

"Ow!" says Vicky. I find myself back on the bench in the gardens. I realise I'm holding her hand and squeezing her fingers. I don't know where I've been for the last thirty seconds.

"Sorry." I let go of Vicky's hand. I can see she's ready to run. Her eyes are full of horror.

silvercar

nonononononononononono
redblood
hermitjackangela

nomorestopitstopitstop

black   black

blackbadhurt

bad   badblood

nomoreangela

nomore   sadhermitjack

poorhermitjack

poor hermitjack
hermitjack scared scared vicky

redblack paper smell sweet
redblack hermitjack

redblackangela

redblackpeter

vicky see
stopitstopitstopit   peterblack

She's looking at two pigeons pecking about on the grass.

"What? What is it?" I jump up and look round but can't see anything.

"Silver car," she says and I feel as if a chunk of ice has suddenly formed in my stomach.

"What? What did you say?" She's looking at the pigeons but when she turns to me it's as if she doesn't see me.

"Stop it, stop it," she wails and I realise I'm shaking her. I let go and slump back on the bench. You can't see the road from here. There's no silver car, only the one in the past.

She must see it, she must. Sweat breaks out on my forehead. If she sees it, she knows, she must know what happened.

"What do you see? What? Tell me. Vicky, you have to tell me."

She bends down and picks up a faded chocolate wrapper from under the bench and begins to fold it this way and that.

"Not hermitjack," she says. What does she mean? Suddenly she stiffens. There's something else.

"What is it Vicky? Tell me, please, tell me. Vicky? Vicky?"

It's as if she's listening to something. Her eyes are closed and there's a strange absence about her that makes the hairs stand up on the back of my neck.

blackstopitsadblackpeter-
stopvickygo
nonostopitstopitstop

hermitjack back   vickyhermit-
jack back

peterblackpeternono

stopitstopitstopitstop

run vicky

            run blackblack

run

            back

            hermitjackrun

house   shut   open   door
hermitjack open door   vicky
push   door no open
opendoornowopen

She grabs my sleeve and pulls
me and starts running out of the
garden. I lose my balance and
nearly fall.

"Hey!" I shout. "Stop. Vicky,
stop! What's the matter?"

"Stop it, stop it, stop it," she
shouts and her eyes are wild with
fear. People are staring at us.

"Stop it!" I pull her back to a
walk. "Calm down."

She slows to a fast walk but
she's still pulling me along and
twisting in my grip. She's muttering under her breath. I so
badly need to know what she
sees, but she's obviously so
frightened I need to calm her
down before I can get any sense
out of her.

She's got tight hold of my
sleeve and she's walking so fast
that I haven't any breath to
speak, all my effort is going into
keeping up with her.

She mustn't run off and get
lost again. I limp along as fast as
I can. My hip's screaming com-
plaints but I'm so unnerved by
the wild look in her eyes and the
crazy muttering, that I hardly
notice it.

People stare as she barges past
them, pulling me along with her.
By the time we get to Falkner
Street we're practically running
again.

The back door is locked.

The key isn't in its hiding
place behind the ivy. Vicky

stopitstopitstopit

hermitjack open dooropen-
doornow
vicky push door.doornoopenn-
odooropen
pushvicky push   push
opendoor hermitjack opendoor

    hermitjack open window
open   door hermitjack   open
door hermitjack open door
quick hermitjack
hermitjack open door
black in house
black in vicky   stopitstopit

        peter
peter
peterpeterpeternomoreno
morenomore
see peterfeet   peterface

black go out of peter red gone
out of peter
nomorepeter

hermitjack hold peterfeet hermitjack cryshout
vicky   hold   nomorepeter
nomorefoot

throws herself against the door.
It's not giving.

I'm caught up in her panic,
not even wondering why she's so
anxious to get back in the house.
There's a loose plank on the window by the door and it comes off
easily enough. The glass behind
the board is broken. Somebody
has done this before. I put my
hand through carefully and feel
about for the door handle. The
key is in the lock on the inside
and I struggle to turn it while
Vicky bleats and fusses behind
me.

The kitchen is empty. Vicky
pushes past me and into the hall
and stops short.

At first the dangling feet don't
mean anything. I look up. Peter
hangs from the landing, swaying
slowly in the breeze from the
open back door.

The rope is an old sheet torn
into strips and tied together. It's
tied to the banister. I rush forward and try to take the weight
off Peter's neck by supporting
his legs.

"Get the rope – upstairs –
untie it!" Vicky just stands and
stares at me. She puts a hand on
Peter's left foot. His trainers sit
neatly side by side on the bottom
step.

She looks at me as if to say it's
pointless. I'm pretty sure she's
right judging by the angle of his
neck but I can't give up so soon.

41

nomorepeter shoes on stairs
shoes nomore go peterfeet

laszlo nik laszlonik shout hermitjack shout peternomore not
speak

nomorepeter fall down fall on
hermitjack cry notleg sore

poor hermitjack poor peter

hermitjack kiss peter push peter
chest
push breath in out of peter
hermitjack stop no breath come
in out of nomorepeter

hermitjack shout

vicky scared no want see police
police take vicky medoban
vicky scared
vicky scared police

"Upstairs," I incline my head,
"untie the rope. Vicky – please!"
She doesn't move.

Horror must be in my voice
because a door on the landing
opens and Laszlo or Nik comes
out. He chatters something to
the other one and they both rush
out and untie the rope.

Peter's weight lands on me
and we both fall down. My hip
twists and I scream but ignore it.
I feel for signs of life but there's
nothing.

He's still warm but I can tell
he's been dead too long for there
to be much hope of resuscitation. Still, I make the effort for as
long as I can. The pain in my
knee is terrible when I kneel. The
Russians watch and chatter
while Vicky seems frozen.

"Get an ambulance!" I hiss
between breaths. Laszlo or Nik
takes a mobile phone from his
pocket but the other one stops
him and says something in
Russian.

"What are you waiting for?" I
can't get my breath.
"Ambulance."

"No ambulance," says the
other one. "Police come. He is
dead anyway."

I check again for vital signs.
Nothing. I sit back.

"So fucking what?"

"Dead," says Laszlo or Nik.
"No need for ambulance."

Ray comes in from the back,

42

ray

hermitjack kiss nomorepeter

ray phone   laszlo pull ray

vicky scared

ray cry
sad greysad
ray sad nomorepeter

laszlonik run   up stairs

hermitjack sad   ray sad vicky
sad
touch nomorepeterface hair feel
peternomore peternomoresad

peternomoreblack
redblack paper for nomorepeter

laszlonik go out not talk

hermitjack sad nomorepeter like
angela

singing to himself. He sees Peter.
His face sags and he drops the
plastic bag he's carrying. There's
a sound of breaking glass.

"Get an ambulance," I hiss
and go back to CPR.

"He is dead," Laszlo or Nik
says again. "No fetch police."

Ray is talking into his mobile.
Laszlo or Nik pulls at his sleeve.

"Piss off!" Ray shouts breaking off his conversation. "Clear
off out of the way if you're bothered about the police." I see he is
crying.

He puts the phone back in his
pocket and covers his mouth
with his hand, watching me. I
give up. I'm exhausted. Peter lies
there relaxed.

I get to my feet and lean
against the banister. I'm
defeated.

Vicky moves, kneels down by
Peter and touches his face, his
hair. She closes his eyes then she
takes the folded sweet wrapper
out of her pocket and arranges it
on Peter's chest. I half expect him
to open his eyes and shout, "Get
off me you fucking moron!"

Laszlo and Nik come running
downstairs with overflowing
backpacks. They rush past without even looking at us.

Vicky smoothes Peter's hair and
straightens his clothes. "Angela,"
she says and looks at me.

I freeze.

"Who's Angela?" says Ray.

I barely hear the ambulance siren. The paramedics are knocking at the front door and Ray has to shout through the letterbox and tell them to go round the back because the front door is nailed shut.

"We came in and found him hanging off the banister. I'm pretty sure he's dead. I've been giving him CPR for about fifteen minutes and there's no sign of life."

Now they've taken over, I realise how exhausted I am. I need to sit down. I turn round but only Ray is there. Vicky has disappeared. Has she gone out the back or up the stairs? My guess is she's headed for the cupboard.

My leg grumbles all the way upstairs. I listen on the landing. Not a sound. Seems that no one else is in.

In our room, the cupboard door stands ajar.

"It's okay, Vicky, it's only me." I open the door. She's not there. The silence is watchful as if someone, Peter maybe, is waiting to see what I do next.

Vicky's belongings are a pathetic heap. The blue fluffy rabbit lies on top. I see the notebook half hidden in the jumble of items. Soon the police will arrive. I might be invited to assist with their enquiries. It's time to go. Maybe I'll find Vicky outside in the street.

The notebook goes in my pocket. My bag is downstairs by Peter's body. I tread carefully on the side edges of the stairs to avoid the creaks. The paramedics are still working on Peter, and Ray stands there watching. I get my bag and start to sneak past when one of the paramedics looks up.

"Hey! You! You stay here. You're a witness."

I pretend I haven't heard and keep on walking. I want to tell Ray to get the hell out but I daren't look back.

In the yard I breathe out and get a lungful of fresh air. The bright ambulance looks incongruous among the skinny weeds and peeling gates of the alley. I keep to the back streets to avoid the police cars that I expect will be speeding towards the front of the house. Maybe Vicky is round this corner, skulking in that doorway. I search all the alleyways, look in back gardens until I'm exhausted. The streets are empty.

* * *

houseblack   streetblack   vickysick
      ambulancepolice come   runvickyhide vicky

44

no no no housebad streetbad nopeter binshide smellbad man come hide quick look nolook vicky scared man go hermitjack vicky want hermitjack tell hermitjack vickygo no vicky scared ambulancepolice come nogomedoban hide here gate garden tree bin silvercar tell hermitjack wait no stay no run black-badhousegarden black nomore stay peter gone yes wait wait hermitjack comeback tree nothurt angela

noise come noise mouse rat vicky scared mouse rat no no stop it stop it oh no rat cat blackkitty hello kitty

* * *

All seems quiet on the way down to Lime Street, too quiet. I can't believe I've escaped so easily. I don't know what to do next, where to look for Vicky. I want to keep searching but I'm done in. I have to rest. Right now my head is rattling. I head for the library. The building swallows me up. The graceful architecture in the Picton Room soothes me instantly. It's like entering a sanctuary. I give myself up to the huge circular room. The muted colours of the leather bound books on the shelves are easy on my eyes.

It's tea time and the library is almost empty. I can hear my own breathing. I sit with the *Daily Post* in front of me and look up at the vast glass dome way above my head. I think of Peter hanging off the landing. Tomorrow the newspaper will carry a few lines on his death. I wonder if anyone will know who he was. I admire the way the spiral staircases wend their graceful way up the tiers of books and I see Peter's swinging feet, his empty face as I tried to push the life back into him. I knew he was depressed but I didn't expect him to top himself. He seemed too angry for that.

The pictures unreel. Peter's dead face; Vicky touching him. Was she feeling for herself that he really was dead?

I never saw Angela in the mortuary, never felt for myself the certainty of her death, that cold unresponsiveness. For a long time I didn't believe she was dead. Angela loved me. She was warm and she warmed me; only her touch could warm me in that cold box my life had become. I was always afraid that she would grow away from me, take Corinne's side as she got older. I never thought she might die.

All the time I lay in hospital I kept thinking, if only they'd let me see her, touch her, she would be alive. There was nothing and no one to make her death true for me. I was at home, having my first scotch of the day. Angela was going for her riding lesson, and then I was in the hospital. It was like a disjointed nightmare with people appearing and disappearing and someone telling me that they couldn't save my leg.

As if that mattered. That time in between, where did it go? Why can't I get it back? Christ knows I've tried.

I come back to the library. My fingers are gripping something hard. It's Vicky's notebook. Vicky looked at Peter, said, 'Angela.' And in the gardens, 'silver car.'

The Jaguar I was so proud of. How could she see it? What did she see? The sleek beauty I brought from the showroom, or the death dealing monster, the mangled wreck it was when I'd finished.

I have to stop this. The notebook falls open. Its pages whisper in the silence.

In the afternoon we went along the hedges picking blackberries. Michael pulled me down in the grass and kissed me. My blood fired up like the sun and his hands were all over me. Everything in me shouted for him and I forgot all I had been taught. I kissed and touched, I let my hands wander just as he did. I listened only to what I felt and it rushed and roared and ran away with me. There were pain but there were pleasure too so I couldn't stop even though I were scared. It were like when I were little and I used to jump off the top of the brow and roll all the way down to the bottom field. Afterwards, we lay in the grass and I saw rabbits hopping across the field and I wondered if it were like this for them too.

But later in my room, Dad's words came back to me, beware the filthiness of fornication and be sure to deny your mother's blood. I looked at the purple juice fingermarks, the nettle stings on my body, evidence of our lust. I picked the thorns from my white flesh and felt the desire of the harlot that I've inherited from my mother. There were blood in my knickers. I thought of sacrifice and a warm wet soreness in the middle of me reminded me that I were . . .

"The library closes in five minutes."

I look up at the assistant. The light has changed. Is it six o'clock already? All the other readers have gone. My hip creaks. The assistant shifts her feet. She's anxious to lock up and go home. I put the notebook back in my pocket. All I can see is those lovers in the brambles. Who has written this? Not Vicky, surely? She can barely speak.

Outside the traffic is thinning. The colours are leaving the grass and the flowers in the garden, the same garden I sat in with Vicky just a few hours ago. I stand on the pavement watching the rush hour traffic and try to think where she might have gone.

Maybe Kindi and Rita would know but St John's market is closed now. There are lights in the windows of the Playhouse and neon signs flash against the dimming sky.

I'm still dog tired and I need a cup of tea. I want to read the rest of the notebook.

The Sally Army café is still open. It's a different waitress. She looks tired but summons a smile.

"There you go luv, fresh brewed just for you."

"Thanks."

The table furthest from the door is a good choice where I won't be disturbed.

The hot tea kicks in. I open the book at the beginning. The pages are thin and yellowed. At first there are figures written in thick soft pencil. Some kind of accounts for things sold in dozens. Eggs maybe? The sums are in old pounds, shillings and pence, so it must be pre-1972. Looking closer, all the sales are dated in 1964. After this comes the writing, in a thinner pencil and a different hand. The pages are crowded with it, but it's the pothook style of a child, not the kind of writing you'd associate with fluency. The first entry is dated 15th July 1964.

Ted Bracewell brung me back after the funeral. Asked me how I'm going to manage now without Dad. He said, you're on your own now girl. I told him, the Lord will protect me. This afternoon the vicar come but I never asked him in. He stood on the step and asked me how I were going to manage. Hadn't I got no relations? Nosey parker, asking where Mother were. As if I know or care. He said I could count on him and Mrs Swinson for help. Told him I don't need no help. Dad had no time for St Stephen's. Whited sepulchres, he used to call them down there. I walked round the farm when he were gone. This is my farm now, my land. Not milk and honey, like Canaan but mine. I am strong and used to hard work. In the sweat of thy face shalt thou eat bread till thou return to the ground.

I turned to the Bible for advice and my eye were drawn to the family names all written in the front and back. The names go back to 1840, a record of all those who have lived here on this farm. All the pages are filled up, there is no space left for any to come after me. Like Moses and the tablets of stone, God set my hand to find this book, its empty pages waiting for my record. Some things should be written. God will direct me.

Monday 10th August 1964

Today Bill Stanley brung a letter. Now he is postman instead of Reg Wilson. Bill Stanley said Gordon starts work for the post office too in Upholland. Gordon Stanley were one of them as used to laugh at me in school. Bill were hanging round, waiting to see what were in my letter but I come inside and shut the door. This letter is from Ginnigle and Marsh Solicitors in Wigan. Says I must go to Wigan next Tuesday about Dad's estate. Does this mean the farm? I am frickened by this but excited too. I've never been to Wigan since I were a little girl with Mother. What if I have to leave the farm? I will put my trust in the Lord and take no thought for the future. Ted Bracewell come for eggs. Brung groceries and old newspapers for me to read. The devil tempted me and I turned the pages. People called mods fighting on beaches. Girls with skirts up showing their legs. How could I live like this? Even reading this paper is sinful. I felt Dad watching. I burned the paper. Dug tatties all afternoon.

Tuesday 18th August 1964

Wigan is a sinful place, like Babylon. Ginnigle or Marsh told me Mother could not be found and the estate is left to me. I cannot have the paper till I am twenty one but I can stay on the farm as there is no one to look after me. There is only the farm. There is no money left after paying the funeral and Ginnigle and Marsh. I remembered the publicans in the temple and held my peace. On the bus back I laughed to myself. Who ever looked after me? I been worked like a horse ever since I were big enough to heft a potato sack. Kids from the council estate chased after me almost to Ashurst Beacon after I got off the bus. Took Barney for a walk tonight and looked out over the fields to Shevington. It's lonely here without Dad but it's peaceful. Top potato field is almost all dug. I wonder where Mother went.

Saturday 29th August 1964

Gordon Stanley brung a letter today. He's taken over his dad's round already. Bill has a cushy job now, working in the sorting office. I took the letter and turned away but he started talking to me about the new houses that are getting built in Skem and then he tried to kiss me. I pushed him so hard he fell over and Barney chased him all down the path. I watched him get through the gate. He shouted at me, You're fucking crazy Mary Appleton, you always were. His face were bleeding. Don't come here no more I said. I come inside and washed my mouth till the uncleanness were gone. I nailed a box on the gate and wrote POST on it in white paint. The letter were from someone called Inland Revenue. It didn't make sense. I put it on the fire. Ted Bracewell come this afternoon and took six sacks of spuds and eggs as usual. Ted says we will be overrun with Scousers when this new town is finished. He says they will have to build a prison to hold all the criminals. I thought it can't be a more sinful place than Wigan but I held my tongue.

Tuesday 8th September 1964
Today is my eighteenth birthday.

Thursday 11th February 1965
Today have happened a strange thing that makes me so I don't know what to do. I were in Dad's room, looking for one of his jumpers to unravel to knit up again for myself and in back of the draw I found a sock stuffed full of paper money. When I pulled it out, there is more money than I ever saw in my hands, greasy notes, worn with work. This winter have been hard for me on my own, hauling potato sacks, cutting leeks and cabbage. I laughed, then cried, looking at all that money. I put it back in the draw but could not stop thinking about it. I can be like the lilies of the field, neither toiling nor spinning. Then I remember the parable of the two talents so I don't know what to do. I asked Dad to help me but there were no answer. Elsie Bracewell come to bring chicken feed. Ted is sick in bed. I never seen another woman since I went to Wigan last August but she were soon away as there were no one to mind the shop only Simple Ellen. Elsie took two stone of cabbage and a stone of leeks. Dad always said they had wagging tongues anyway. In the night I took Barney up to the top of the hill. I knelt down and telled the secret to the earth. Rich, I am rich I telled Barney but a rich man cannot enter into the kingdom of God. I will pray to the Lord to guide me. First egg laid today.

Wednesday 17th March 1965

Spring comes in at last. Ted Bracewell brung red diesel and checked tractor over for me. Set tatties to chit and ploughed bottom field before the rain come. It's hard work but I am my father's daughter. It's all I know. Money would only turn my head from the Lord. This is why Dad kept it out of sight – to keep us both safe. Ted says Skem is like a building site. Thank the Lord I am up here away from it all.

Friday 24th September 1965.

Behold a stranger comes and I don't know what to make of him. The sun is still strong but the days are shorter and work is easier though there are still potatoes to dig and cabbage to cut. When Ted come, I asked him to bring sugar next week for jam. The blackberries are heavy on the brambles. I watched Ted's van go up the lane and I come back in to count jam jars and check for rubber bands and no sooner had I got out half a dozen jars than Barney set up such a racket and started the chickens all a squawking. In the doorway I could see only the dark forked shape of a man that frickened me half to death till I thought it must be Ted come back for something but when I got out in the light it were a stranger but so beautiful with long fair hair like the Lord Jesus and a shirt all different colours, like Joseph's coat. He asked for a drink of water and his voice were soft and kind so I didn't feel afraid but when I brung the water, he watched me while he drank and I remembered the bad things Dad telled me about men and women and I remembered Gordon Stanley and the boys at school and I begun to feel scared again. But then he talked to me so kind and telled me about places he had been. I asked him where he were going and he said it didn't matter and would I let him stay here tonight. The sun were going and it were getting cold. The path to the lane were already dark under the trees. He had a sleeping bag rolled on his back so I said he could sleep in the old empty chicken shed. I brung Barney inside with me. I can't sleep for thinking of him out there, although all is quiet. His name is Michael and his beauty and kindness run against Dad's warning voice in my mind. I have been reading my bible for guidance and the pages I turned tell only of wandering. Israel wandering the deserts, Jesus and his disciples going from town to town. This man wanders too, while I am planted in the ground. What does this mean? Still, he will be gone tomorrow.

Saturday 25th September 1965

Last night I dreamed of serpents. Michael is still here. He has been helping me with the chickens and with the vegetable garden. The sun seems twice as hot and bright as yesterday. Michael talked to me about the sun and colours and flowers. There are no flowers here. Dad used to say you can't eat flowers. Michael has a little radio – he calls it a tranny. It plays songs about love. Sitting in the sunshine felt good. Michael made me laugh. I laughed more today than I ever laughed before. Tonight is almost cold enough for frost. Michael is sleeping on the sofa in front of the fire. Barney knows him already and doesn't bark. I telled Michael Dad would turn in his grave. Michael said your dad is dead and we are alive. It's true. I feel more alive than I ever did but it makes me restless. Tonight I have not read my bible.

Tuesday 28th September 1965.

Michael has been here four days. The weather holds good. I made him hide in the shed when Ted Bracewell come for the eggs and potatoes. Ted were full of news about the Scousers that are already arriving. Michael came here from Liverpool but he is not from there. All he says is I've been around. I were weighing the sugar Ted brought for the jam when Michael come behind me and put his arms round me and kissed my neck. It stung me so I dropped the spoon and my breath choked in my throat. You're so beautiful he said but I knew this were not true. My hair is long, uncut, untidy and my clothes are old cut-downs from Dad's things or pieced together from things I grew out of years ago. When I go out children run after me and call me names. Michael got his pack and took out a little mirror and showed me myself. There are no mirrors in this house and all I see of myself is the blurred reflection sometimes in the windows when it is dark. Dad told me I must not look at this for fear of vanity but when Michael showed me I could not help myself. I looked and saw my eyes bright and happy, my lips red, my cheeks flushed. It were true. I am beautiful. It felt good to be beautiful, not wicked like my dad said. In the afternoon we went along the hedges picking blackberries. Michael pulled me down in the grass and kissed me. My blood fired up like the sun and his hands were all over me.

I sit back and lift my cup but it's empty. The café has filled up a bit without me noticing.

"More tea, luv?"

51

"Thanks."

I wait for the fresh cup and think about the dates in the diary – if that's what it is. 1964. I was six years old. I don't doubt it's that old. The covers are worn and the pages have that brittle texture like weary skin and the smell of old paper.

"Going to be a chilly night." She puts down my tea and smiles. She's got me marked for a down and out.

"Yes." I give her the money. My finger's already marking the next entry. She shrugs and moves away.

But later in my room, Dad's words came back to me, beware the filthiness of fornication and be sure to deny your mother's blood. I looked at the purple juice fingermarks, the nettle stings on my body, evidence of our lust. I picked the thorns from my white flesh and felt the desire of the harlot that I've inherited from my mother. There were blood in my knickers. I thought of sacrifice and a warm wet soreness in the middle of me reminded me that I were no longer a separate whole. Michael had changed me. The old Mary were gone forever. How could something so beautiful be evil? I know now that Dad were wrong.

Sunday 3rd October 1965
Everything is stocked up for winter and the sun loses its strength. Life is easy with Michael to help and love makes every job a joy. The farm feels happy. There is no corner of the barns, sheds and house where we have not made love – even in my father's bed. I wish Dad could have been happy like this. With him I knew only coldness and anger. I thought it were because Mother ran away and I were evil like her, but now I think maybe that is why she ran away, that he drove her away with his coldness. I would run anywhere to share this with Michael. Would I even leave my home?

Monday 11th October 1965.
He is gone and I can't believe it. The house still seems to ring with his laughter. I were feeding the hens this morning when he come out with his pack on his back and said it were time for him to move on. I just stared. I'd not given a thought to a day or time when he wouldn't be there. In my mind we'd go on forever digging tatties and making love. I begged him to stay but he were closed like a stone. I said I'll go with you, even though I were afraid to leave the farm which is all I know.

At last I saw that he didn't want me. He said I shouldn't try to tie him down, that both of us were free and that's how we should stay. He kissed me and promised to come back. Can this be true? I will wait here for him. I have nowhere else to go.

Thursday 14th October
His kiss still stings my lips. Everywhere I look, he's not there. Barney will not come to me. He is moping in the barn.

Thursday 28th October
Winter is coming and he has not come back. I think now I will never see him again.

Tuesday 2nd November
I have spent all day on my knees, begging forgiveness of both my heavenly Father and my earthly one. How did I fall into such madness? It must be true, I have my mother's nature, to be tempted and give in so easily. This torment I now suffer is just punishment for my sins.

Sunday 7th November
The Bible comforts me. God can forgive all sins if the sinner repents.

Monday 22nd November
The Devil were in Michael and now is in me. My monthlies didn't show and now this sickness leaves no doubt. What I have suffered so far is nothing to what is to come. What shall I do? There is no one I can tell.

Thursday 10th February 1966
I have prayed and prayed to God to take this evidence of sin away from me but my belly swells daily. Today I felt it move, a horrible flutter. It will not go away. Maybe I will have to go away from here.

Friday 25th February
Michael has taken most of Dad's money. I thought I might go some- where else to hide my shame until it is born. I went to the draw to count the money but the sock is much thinner than before. I don't know how much he took. I suppose I should be glad he didn't take it all.

Tuesday March 29th
My belly is huge. The evidence of my sin kicks at me day and night as

if it knows how I hate it. It is eager to be free of me. I put on a big coat when Ted Bracewell comes. Last week he said how peaky I look and asked if I were all right. He has taken the last of the potatoes. I been too sick to plant any yet this year. There are plenty of eggs already and I've got my vegetable patch. I pray it will be born dead but I can feel its strength and its anger.

Tuesday April 19th
Last night I dreamed it were born on the kitchen floor. Instead of feet it had little cloven hooves. What am I to do when it really does come? I still can't believe it is really going to happen. God forgive me I have thoughts of drowning it in the kitchen sink. Who would know? But that would be piling sin on sin. Please God, take this cup from me. I will not transgress again.

Sunday June 26th
My belly can get no bigger. I am sure to burst. I left the eggs out in a basket for Ted and called through the window with my list of what I want. I pretended to be busy washing. I have cut up some of Dad's shirts and got out a box to put it in. I spread some of Ted's old newspapers on the bed. What else is there to do? I am frickened now of how to bear it alone but it must be so. I pray we both will not live.

Tuesday June 28th 1966
It came yesterday in the early morning and a horrible squiggling thing it is. I knew it were evil by the way it tore itself out of me. I looked at it and its face were as red as the Devil. Dad were right; sin begets sin.

It screamed while I looked after all the mess and stickiness. I burned the newspapers and everything in the kitchen range. It were still screaming when I come back. Its eyes were fierce and angry and it twisted itself about. It hardly looked human.

I cried all the way through. I were scared of the blood and slime and I were sick and so tired but I knew it were my punishment and even though I were scared being on my own, I were glad Dad weren't here.

I must have fell asleep and when I woke up the afternoon were full of shadows and the room stank of rotting blood and it were still screaming and now its face were purple and it had pissed all over the bedclothes.

Its hair were stuck down black and I got up even though I felt sick and dizzy and took it to the sink and washed it with the dishrag and it stopped for a minute then started up again worse than ever.

I wrapped it up in a towel and put it on my breast and its head bumped about like a blind thing and I squeezed my nipple into its mouth and its gums clamped hard on me and an awful want run through me like when I were with Michael so I knew it were wicked, a memory of my sin and I threw it down on the bed and it screamed and screamed.

There were a terrible pain in my gut and blood run down my legs even though I put a rag there before I got up. I sat down and cried and it screamed and screamed so I couldn't stand it no more and I took it out to the old chicken shed and put it down in the straw. In the other shed the chickens were fussing. Like in a dream I went in and filled the feed hoppers and the water dishes, all the time thinking, maybe God will take it away but in my heart I know that won't happen, because sin is hard to shift. I felt so weak, I struggled to get back to the house then I crawled into the bed and slept.

Wednesday 29th June

This morning when I woke up I thought at first it were a dream. I've had such dreams before, but there were the smell, the stains, the blood, the pain and the slack in my belly. I made some tea and got some bread and jam. I were so hungry it blotted out the fear of what would be in the shed.

At last I made myself go and I could hear it crying before I got out the back door so I knew it were still alive, but it were a pitiful sort of cry, tired like and soon as I heard it, milk run out of my breasts and all down the front of my nightie. I let the chickens out and threw some feed down in the yard. The sun were shining like it were an ordinary day but all the time I could hear it whimpering. At last I went in and looked in the towel. It stopped crying when I touched the towel and its eyes wandered about like it were searching for me. The towel were soaked with piss and sticky black shit. I didn't want it to see me.

It wanted my breasts but I couldn't stand to feel that shame again. There were an old sack in the corner and I thought about just covering it up and pressing down on it but I couldn't do that either. That would be leading myself into worse sin.

I went back to the house and went through the kitchen cupboards till I found the old beer bottles Dad used to use for feeding motherless lambs. They still had the rubber teats on the ends. I started trying to squeeze milk out of my breasts into a jug but it weren't so easy and I were soon sore and crying. When I thought I had enough I put it in one of the bottles, took the dishrag and went back to the shed.

It were howling, but I hardened my heart. Dad told me evil has many forms. I pushed the teat in its mouth and it screamed and choked, then must have got a swallow of the milk and it started to suck. I could see its true nature in its greed. It were like a devilish animal.

I didn't touch it. I didn't want to look at it. The smell of it made me feel sick but already I realised what I have to do. I have to feed it and clean it. If I don't that's like murdering it, but if I do these things and it dies anyway, it won't be my fault.

When the milk were gone, I cleaned it with the dishrag as quick as I could, not touching it any more than I had to. It stopped crying but its breath caught in little sobs and when I put the clean sack down, its eyes were rolling asleep. It looked innocent and helpless but I knew different. How could it be? It were a girl. My mam ran off with another man. She were a dirty whore. And look at me.

I must pray for absolution. Perhaps yet it will be taken away. This would be a sign of forgiveness.

I lift my eyes away from the book, away from the nightmare. The café is bright against the darkness outside. The waitress's blonde hair and red lips seem surreal after what I've just read. So does the friendly chatter going on at the other tables.

My rational mind says this must be a work of fiction, but I know it isn't. I've already jumped to the conclusion that the baby is Vicky. The horror of it scalds my brain but I don't doubt it. I have to find her right now, even though I want to read the rest, as if I'm drawn to the madness of it.

My hip's stiff from sitting. As I struggle up Mount Pleasant, I try to comfort myself with phoney explanations. Vicky's found the book somewhere, it's nothing to do with her. It's some amateur writer's idea for a horror flick, but I'm already cataloguing her speech problems, her shyness, her odd behaviour and the cupboard, oh God, the cupboard.

Everywhere is quiet as I turn into the lower half of Falkner Street. The darkening buildings loom against the still bright sky with a melancholy watchfulness. Suddenly I remember Peter.

"*Ma-ake yourse-e-elf at 'o-o-ome.*" The singing is thin and reedy but echoes down the street and fades away into muttering. Mabel appears round the corner of Catharine Street. She is weighed down on either side by a ballast of bulky carrier bags. My heart sinks.

"Mabel? Where are you going?"

"Oo is it? What do you want?"

"Mabel, it's me, Jack. I was at the house. Remember?"

"The 'ouse?" She laughs, showing a few broken teeth. "It's all locked up, dear."

"Where are the others? Ray? Rita?"

She puts her bags down and rubs her back. "Sure I don't know dear. They're all gone. I packed me bags before the police come. One of them students in the 'ouse next door give me a cup of tea so I waited a bit in case the law pushed off again once they'd took him away. No such luck, though. They locked the place up good and proper."

"Have you seen Vicky?"

"Vicky? Oo's Vicky?"

"Vicky. You know, she was in the house. Cupboard Girl."

"Oh, her."

"I thought she might come back to the house. I need to find her."

"Fancy her, do you dear? Well, there's no accounting for taste. Anyhow, you won't be seeing her again. Haven't got a drink on you, have you, dear?"

"What do you mean? You've seen her then?"

"Police took her away. She was hiding in the yard and they caught her."

"In the yard?" She must have come back. Maybe she was looking for me. "What did you do?"

"What could I do?"

"You could have brought her into that house next door."

"Not my place is it dear? Anyway, they'd already caught hold of her when I saw her. It was only all the screeching she was doing that made us look and it was too late then."

"Where did they take her?" I want to shake the information out of her.

"How should I know dear? All I know is, it took four of them to get her into the car." She bends down and picks up her bags. "Look, I can't stand talking to you all night. Got to find meself a new little nest."

"Which police station would they take her to?" I don't want to get involved with the law but I have to find her.

"Can't help you there dear. There used to be a cop shop on Church Street but it ain't there no more. Anyway I must get off." She pushes past me with a whiff of unwashed body and cheap brandy. "Toodle-oo old bean. Don't forget, *Co-ome round any old ti-i-me, make yourself at 'o-o-me.*"

As I cross Catharine Street I can see a patrol car parked outside the house. I stay on the other side of the street till I've passed it, then go up the side street to the back, but when I look down the alley I can see crime scene tape across the gate and a uniformed officer on guard outside.

A slim girl with long dark hair comes out of the gate of the student house next door to ours. I move under the streetlight. I don't want to startle her as she comes past.

"Excuse me. I'm from next door – the squat." She looks doubtfully at me. "I'm looking for a woman who was there, Vicky. Do you know Vicky?"

"Someone killed himself." She looks up at me.

"I know, but I need to find Vicky. Do you know her?"

"Is she the old one that sings? She was in our house before."

"No." We walk past the patrol car. It's empty but lights shine round the edges of the boarded windows in the house. "Vicky's about forty. She can't talk properly."

"The police took a woman away. They brought her out of the yard. But she could talk. She kept screaming, 'Stop it. Stop it.' She put up a good fight." She smiles at me.

"Sorry I can't help. I haven't seen any of the others."

"It's okay. Do you know where they might have taken her?"

"Try St Anne Street police station. It's the only one I know."

"Thanks." My heart is in my boots. She'll be halfway to some institution by now.

"Have you got somewhere to go tonight?"

"I'll be okay. Thanks for your help."

* * *

It's not my problem, she's not my problem. I should just let it go, melt into the shadows, but I can't. I feel sorry for her, I know how scared she is of the police, but that's not the real reason is it? There's the diary business but even that's not it. It's the growing certainty that she sees things I don't. Maybe she can fill in my missing links. I struggle with my own difficulties in going to the police but in the end I make my way to St Anne Street. It's a long walk and my leg complains but I keep going. When I get there it's much as I expected.

"I'm enquiring about someone – a woman. She was brought in a couple of hours ago from a house in Falkner Street. I heard someone killed himself there. Her name's Vicky."

"Full name?"

"Vicky – I'm not sure. I think it might be Appleton."

"Your name?"

"Phil Williams." Best not to give real names to anyone official. For a second I think of telling him I'm a doctor. I could say I'm Vicky's GP or her psychiatrist. Maybe they'd let me in to see her. Then I look down at my stained trousers and worn out trainers. I look up and see contempt in his eyes.

"Address?" He puts the pen down on the paper. Just another street bum. "Are you related to this person?"

"No. We're just friends. She hasn't got anyone, I don't think." It was a bad idea to come here. Everything I say sounds ridiculous. There's no way they're going to tell me anything.

"Were you at this house in Falkner Street too?" The pen is poised now.

"No. No, I was supposed to meet Vicky in McDonalds and she didn't show so I went up to Falkner Street and someone told me she was here." Does this sound feasible? I don't think so.

"Take a seat and wait."

I sit down on one of a row of linked seats. No one else is here. Another uniform comes and takes the paper from the duty officer.

My stomach grumbles. I haven't eaten all day. The clock on the wall says seven forty. I'm getting really bad vibes about being here. It reminds me of the past.

That night I was arrested for drink driving, I wasn't really drunk, not as drunk as I wanted to be. They didn't understand.

"I've only had a couple." The light hurt my eyes, bright light bouncing off the white painted walls. I wanted to escape but the voices were unrelenting, calm and polite but the contempt was there. You'd think I'd committed a murder.

They put me in a cell. "Till you sober up," they said and then the worst thing happened. Corinne, dressed in her evening gown, came to get me. Jed had come with her, he looked handsome in his bow tie and dinner jacket, a change from the baggy sweats he usually knocked round in outside work. I'd forgotten about the formal dinner we were supposed to attend.

The Jag purred under her hands as she drove us home. She didn't speak and Jed just squirmed in his seat while I told them both how I'd had enough of dinners and boring speeches, of pretending to be committed to my work when my days were filled with mindless paperwork, patients wanting sick notes and disability benefits, and cost cutting exercises that had me jumping through hoops.

"I'm sick of being a pet poodle." No one answered me. Jed stared out of the car window and Corinne screwed her mouth up into a tight little purse like she hated me, and I couldn't wait to get home for another drink. For a moment I worried about being found out, being in the papers for all my colleagues and patients to see. I knew Corinne would chill me to the bone but the whisky took care of my worries. I never gave a thought to what could have happened, what I might have done to someone else. That came later.

"Mr Williams?"

Christ! Have I been asleep?

"Mr Williams, I'm DC Porter. I'd like to ask you a few questions."

"I don't want to answer any questions. I haven't done anything wrong. I just want to see Vicky."

"No one has said you've done anything wrong. But we can't let you see anyone held here. It's not police procedure. You're not even a relative. You said so."

"I'm not going to be interviewed. I don't know anything."

"Did you know the deceased?"

"No. I don't know anything. I met Vicky and we are friends. I'm worried about her. That's all."

"Look, we're not interested in you. We need to trace the family of the deceased, Peter Snelgrove and —"

"Vicky?" I think of the notebook. "I can't help you."

"How long have you known her? Does she have any friends, relatives that you know of? Did she say where she came from?"

"I haven't known her very long." He looks quizzically at me. What am I doing here? How can I explain about Angela? "I just felt sorry for her."

"Were you at the house where Peter Snelgrove died?"

"I'm not answering any more questions. Are you going to arrest me?"

"No." He seems tired. "You're free to go Mr Williams. I can tell you your friend has been passed to the care of Social Services. Maybe you should try there."

* * *

coldroom   policelady say begood

        cupboardroom   bed   vicky scared   nosto-
pitstopitstopitnononon   police say stopitvicky   stopit lady go
away vicky sick   vicky scared   nomorenomore nonoise
no one come room grey vicky grey

                        ladygreendress come say gohome-
marjorie   mrsmitchell worry   nomarjorie no marjorie no
mrsmitchell vickyvickyvickyvickyvicky   hermitjack want hermitjack helpvicky   run
run run hardwalls doorstop; no run ladygreendress say stopitmar-
jorie   stopitstopitstopitstopitstopit   stopitstopit   policelady come redpolicelady redround grab vicky hurt vicky more police
more redpolice shout stopitstopit no no fall down fall on floor redpolice fall hurt vicky police say doctorspencer sort you out   grey-
suitman come doctorspencer   say make you feel better
nonono notneedle stopitstopit nomore   nomore   no   more
no
        mo

CHAPTER THREE

I sit in McDonalds for as long as I can with a single cup of tea and a cheeseburger. Money's low and I'll need to find more from somewhere tomorrow. Time's running out now, it's dark. I haven't found Vicky and I need somewhere to sleep.

It's noisy here with crowds of young people but as soon as I open the whispering pages of the notebook, I'm in another world.

Thursday 21st July

It lives on. I should of known it would. It's my punishment and there's no end to it. It's been three weeks now and I'm wore out what with the chickens to see to and the endless milk and bottles and cleaning of it.

I try not to look at it when I go in. It looks so helpless and I have to remind myself that it's easy to love sin, like I loved Michael with his golden hair and the Devil's silver tongue.

I got to be careful even though no one comes here only Ted Bracewell to take the eggs and bring the groceries. I make sure to have the eggs ready. Soon as I hear the van I go down to meet him so he won't hear it cry. He looks at me suspicious but he don't know nothing. Last week he asked if I weren't hot wearing Dad's overcoat in middle of June. I've wore it right the way through so's he wouldn't notice and I can't take it off yet. I'm still swelled up like a rotten fruit. I just took the groceries and talked about next week's egg order, to remind him to mind his own business. His thoughts are on other things anyway, all he talks about is new Skem and the goings on there.

Last night I went out to the back field when it had finally stopped crying. The night were still with a full moon up. The grass is grown to my waist now without Dad here to cut it. I looked at the cart and the tractor all rusting and disappearing into the grass and thought how they were never going to move again. All I need is the spade and fork to keep the vegetable patch.

Across the plain the new motorway were sparkling and I thought how I've been here on this hill for all my life and always will be. I thought about the new people living down in Skem and wondered how it feels to leave your home for a strange place. At least I have my land. How happy I would be if Michael came back but I don't think he ever will.

When Dad died, I thought for a while that I might go away, maybe to Wigan or even to Liverpool. Maybe I'd have got work in one of the factories, lived in a little room and gone to pubs like the girls in the papers Ted Bracewell gives me. Maybe I'd have married and lived in one of them little houses all stuck together, but maybe I wouldn't like not to be able to walk out and stand alone on the hill, looking down the dark valley at night with only the moon watching. At least here secrets can be kept. Who knows what things this land has seen? But change comes — the motorway, this new town. This makes me fearful. People have had their land, their homes taken away. Pray God this won't happen here.

Thursday 8th September 1966
Today I am twenty.

Saturday 24th September
It is twelve months since Michael came. I watch at the window but the path is empty. There is silence except for it crying. Even Barney is quiet.

It doesn't cry so much now. Maybe it knows it can't soften my heart. It watches me when I go in but I turn my eyes away.

Tuesday 11th October
Today is a year since Michael went away. Not like my sin that is

63

always with me. Yesterday I seen it catching its toes. Today it tried to lift the bottle from the sacks I prop it on.

Wednesday 12th October
Ted come for eggs. I seen him

"Scuse me mate, anyone sitting here?" It takes me a second or two to pull myself back. I stare at the hulking boy in front of me. He chews gum and looks me up and down.

"No." I wave at the chair. "Help yourself." I turn my body away so he won't talk to me but he's already talking into his mobile, his tray of food congealing before him.

I seen him looking at the weeds sprouting through the cobbles in the yard and at the top field, all fallow and overgrown. You should get out of here Mary he said It's too much for you. I think I see the Devil in him. I must be wary.

Thursday 3rd November
When I took its milk it were trying to roll over. Soon it will begin to move about. I must pray for guidance.

Wednesday 14th December
Now it sits up. It eats bits of egg. I have made it more clothes cut from Dad's things. A harsh winter may yet carry it off. If this happens it is God's will but my life will change again.

Wednesday 21st December
Ted Bracewell brung a Christmas card. From Ted and Elsie it said. Ted asked me to come for Christmas dinner but I told him Christmas is for prayer and meditation, not for vanity and greed. I burned the card on the range when he'd gone.

Wednesday 8th March 1967
First eggs laid this week. It has seemed a long winter but now Spring breaks out. It has survived. Now it eats eggs, potatoes, bread wet with water. Ted come and said I should be planting. He said I should get someone to help. I don't need nothing I told him but he says it's a waste. Consider the lilies I told him. This is my land, my business, not yours. Ted Bracewell is like the serpent in the Garden of Eden but I need the groceries he brings for the eggs.

64

Thursday March 23rd

Found Barney dead on the rug in front of the range this morning. I cried all day. He were a good and faithful servant and has been here almost as long as I can remember. I think Dad fetched him not long after Mother went.

I buried him on the top field under the rowan tree. Poor old dog, he is in a better place now and I am alone.

Saturday 6th May

I've spent all day in the chicken shed. Now it has started crawling about and this morning it were pulling itself up on the door post and trying to walk.

I put in the bit of carpet that Barney used to sleep on and hung up a chicken hopper with water in. It will get no more milk now it has teeth. I shall be glad to dry my breasts. It is mostly quiet except for grunts when I feed it. I don't speak to it but sometimes I forget and shout if it gets in my way when I sweep out the shed. I have nailed a strong bar outside the door. I must make sure it can't get out.

Friday 25th August

A letter come from Ginnigle and Marsh to say I must go to Wigan again to sign the paper for the farm. I had forgotten my birthday were near.

Monday September 11th

Yesterday I were twenty one. I catched the bus to Wigan. I took a pound note out of Dad's money to buy myself a birthday present. I were worried about leaving the farm all day but I fed it before I left and made sure the shed were safely barred. I left the chooks outside. Who would come here anyway? No one except Ted and he only comes on a Wednesday.

I got the paper from Ginnigle and Marsh and whichever one of them it were wished me happy birthday. They wanted me to leave the paper in their safe but I said no. I know these people have evil natures and the paper belongs on the farm. Ginnigle and Marsh sent a letter to something called the Land Registry for me. I signed it but I didn't understand what it said.

I bought a cup of tea afterwards and watched the sinful sights in Wigan. The boys with their long hair and flowery shirts reminded me of Michael so I longed to be back on the farm away from all this visiting of pubs and kissing on the streets. Ted Bracewell telled me that New Skem is a den of iniquity with wife swapping and such going on. Yet I think of my own sin and can't condemn others.

I couldn't think what to buy for my birthday and it seemed a vanity for there is nothing that I need. In the end I bought a new notebook for this one is nearly full. I worried all the way home about the farm and the shed but when I got back everything was just as usual.

Sunday 24th September
I have cut and dried as much grass as I can and saved it all summer. The eggs won't pay for enough straw for the chickens. I thought I might put straw down for it in the other shed but it has Barney's rug and it is easy enough to keep the bare floor scrubbed. It walks sometimes now but it's not much trouble except when it wants food.

Tuesday October 17th
A paper come from the Land Registry. I put it in the draw under Dad's sock where I put the paper for the farm.

Monday 19th February 1968
A stranger come today. I were frickened half to death when he knocked on the front door. I were in the shed seeing to it and I never seen him coming. There is no Barney now to warn me.

He said he were from the Inland Revenue which I don't understand and he said I should be paying tax on what I earn. I telled him I don't earn nothing but he wanted to look all around. I showed him the house and the fields all left fallow. I showed him Dad's machinery all rusting away. And how do you live then? he said and I telled him how Ted brings me flour and butter and such for the eggs and I pointed to the chooks in the yard and then I seen I'd left the other shed door unlatched and my heart flew up in my mouth in case he went and looked in there.

The Lord will provide I said and I asked him in the house for a cup of tea while he filled in his big forms. All the time I kept looking at the shed door and praying that it wouldn't make a noise.

He made me sign the form and then he went away. I followed him down the path to make sure he were gone and then I run all the way back up to shut the shed door but it had got out and were creeping about in the yard. What a dreadful deformed thing it were when I saw it in the day light with its eyes screwed up against God's good sunshine. It looked just how I imagined the devils to look that Dad used to tell me about when I were little. I got the yardbrush and shouted at it till it went grunting back in the shed. It is strange how some bad things show their evil natures on the outside by their ugliness and others are all beauty and sweet words on the outside yet filled with filth like Michael and that tax collector that come today. It must be the Lord's way of making you watchful. And what of me? My sin is neither hidden inside nor shown outside, but is split off from me, yet grows and grows. Even though it is kept apart in the shed, I am bound to it, it is my eternal punishment. Can there ever be an atonement?

Wednesday 28th March.
Ted Bracewell brung me a new cockerel someone had give him. I wrung old Roosty's neck though I had the devil of a job to catch him. He has had his day and precious few new chicks the last year. Ted says he can sell more eggs to the New Skem people. They are used to a lot of shops in Liverpool and there aren't enough here for them. Ted says he can take his van

There it ends. The notebook is full. I flick at the last page angrily. I want more than the wringing of a cockerel's neck. What happened, for Christ's sake?

People around me are laughing, chattering, arguing. Ronald McDonald and the bright colours are a million miles away from the bleak farm life led by Mary.

Yet who knows what secrets are hidden behind this normal scene?

She was twenty-one in 1967. Today is 24th September. That makes her just turned fifty-nine. What the hell happened to her? One part of me is still trying to say the whole thing is fiction but the horror is too real. I retreat to my own childhood.

In 1967 we lived in a quiet suburb of Worcester. I was ten years old, too young for the swinging sixties, but I can remember the ethos of hope, peace and fun. This kid in front of me is stuffing down his Big Mac and looking suspiciously round at everyone else, like a dog with a bone. Were we like *that* in those days or did we really all love each other in the way we're told so many times in books and on TV? I can remember my brother Matt, like the Michael in the notebook, with long hair and multicoloured tee shirts. I remember our parents' scandalised faces when my sister Penny appeared in bell-bottom jeans with huge fringes.

I can't recall anything about a child found in a shed. The sixties are just a blur of people and events I've learned to think of as ground-breaking – Marilyn Monroe, JFK, the first space walks, England winning the World Cup. What's history to me? Just a patchwork woven with my own views of school and family relationships, mem-ories of *The Avengers*, *Ready Steady Go*, football, science fiction films, the space race – the everyday world of a ten-year-old at that time. None of it seems real now, I can't bring back a single vivid memory.

The boy opposite me scrapes his chair back and leaves. He doesn't give me a look. His eyes are glued to his phone. I look at the littered tray he's left on the table and wonder if he had a happy childhood.

The only stories I recall of children locked away from human con-tact are rehashed accounts, dramatised in histories, novels and plays, and one or two cases in medical journals. I can't remember much about them.

"Closing up now mate." The boy wiping the table looks about fourteen. I heave myself to my feet and get my arms in the straps of my pack. It feels twice as heavy as usual and my hip complains. I feel exhausted and depressed. I've nowhere to go and still haven't decided what to do next.

* * *

I don't get much sleep. The night is spent mostly tramping about and moving from one doorway to another. Each time I settle I get dis-turbed and I can't sleep anyway for the images of Mary sweeping at her monster child with the yardbrush. What kind of child would this creature be, if it was rescued, after so long without love or comfort, deprived of stimulation and the opportunity to hear and learn speech? Could such a child become the shy innocent I see in Vicky? I think of her baring her teeth in the cupboard, playing with herself under the table, having it off with the Russians. I think of the warmth and love Angela was bathed in during the good days, when Corinne and I were happy and Angela was a carefree infant. I remember how she grew to give that love back, especially to her daddy. No matter what Corinne or anyone else thinks, I always loved Angela more than anything. I still do.

Morning sees me back at the library as soon as it opens. The only national daily paper on archive is *The Times*. I check all the dates around the end of the diary and for a while after the last entry but find nothing. I beg a sheet of paper from the library assistant and go through the diary again making a list of possible clues:

1. The farm is somewhere near Wigan.
2. Also mentioned – Upholland, Shevington and Skem. Skem is a new town?
   Maybe Skelmersdale?
3. Mary's name is Appleton. Is her father's the same?
4. Other names mentioned: Ted and Elsie Bracewell, Bill and Gordon Stanley, Reg Wilson, Simple Ellen.
5. St Stephen's is a church somewhere near the farm. The vicar's name is Swinson.
6. There is a place near the farm called Ashurst Beacon.

The list seems promising. The local newspaper archive is on another floor. I don't expect to find a birth announcement, given the circumstances in the diary, but there just might be a record of Mary's father's death.

I check the *Liverpool Daily Post* from a week before the first diary entry. The reports of the day seem odd, from today's viewpoint. Columns are given over to lengthy coverage of divorce decrees. A report of an unlawful abortion performed by a local doctor jostles pictures of Southport's English Rose contest. Ringo's twenty-fourth birthday gets more space than ethical questions about Rhodesia. Still, I suppose if you change the names, the conflicts and moral dilemmas are the same as ever.

The death notices produce no results. Most of them seem to be from Wales and Cheshire. *The Echo* is no better. Every edition is full of the exploits of the Beatles and their satellite Merseyside pop stars. Hardly surprising. Saturday 11th July's edition culminates with the headline, "Night of a Thousand Screams," commemorating the Beatles' arrival in town for the northern premiere of *Hard Day's Night*. There are many more death notices in the *Echo* than in the *Post* but they are all from Liverpool families with a sprinkling of Welsh. I give up and return the microfilm lens to the library assistant.

"Not found what you were looking for?" She smiles. My dejection must show.

"I'm trying to trace someone from around Wigan, but I don't even know where these places are."

She looks at my list. "All those places are near Wigan, I think." She finds me a map of West Lancashire. Her finger traces the elongated diamond formed by Skelmersdale, Upholland, Wigan and Shevington. Excitement stirs in me. The M6 motorway cuts through the middle of the diamond – the new motorway Mary watched from the fields of her farm.

Is the key to Vicky's identity somewhere in this space or am I chasing a fantasy? Maybe I'd be better going to Social Services and trying to find out where they've taken her but it's like the trip to the police station last night; I don't want to go and doubt if they will tell me anything.

The excitement evaporates and I'm suddenly exhausted. I head for the refreshment area to rest for a while with a cup of tea and think what to do next. The little diamond on the map doesn't look that difficult to reach. The best place to start is probably Wigan. I remember going there a long time ago to a medical conference. All I recall is a grim railway station and some Victorian red brick buildings shouting of industrial wealth. For a moment I see myself in my neat suit, carrying my briefcase. I'm standing outside the station and waving down a taxi. In those days I didn't worry how to get from one place to another.

I go back to the helpful assistant in the local history department.

"You can get to Wigan by bus or train, but where exactly are you trying to reach?"

"It's somewhere round Ashurst Beacon, I think."

"That's near Skelmersdale. I think there's a bus goes from the back of St Johns Market, or you can get a train to Ormskirk and then I'm sure there'll be a local bus to Skelmersdale."

I'll need to raise some money to get there so I can't go right away. And the Social Services are niggling at me. This hunt for Vicky's history is helping me to find who she is but not where she is. Social Services hold that key.

* * *

"Can I see the duty officer please?"

I wait a long time. An unhappy looking young woman with a baby goes in before me.

"Won't you sit down?" The duty social worker smiles but I know that appraising look. It's one I used to wear myself. I explain about Vicky. Should I pretend to be a relative? No, it won't wash once she starts asking questions.

"So why are you so concerned?" She doesn't even write anything down.

"I'm worried about her. She's my friend." I don't tell her we've only just met.

"Don't you think she's safer off the street?"

"Yes, but I'd like to keep in touch with her."

"You know I can't divulge information." If she's thinking I'm some kind of old pervert she does a good job of hiding it. "I can't even confirm that this person is a client of our service."

"Yes, but —"

She rustles papers. "I can take your details. If this person is in our care, someone will let you know if she wants to have contact with you and if it's deemed appropriate." She examines me, draws conclusions. "Is there somewhere I can leave messages? Do you have a phone?"

"It doesn't matter."

I get to my feet.

* * *

It takes me three days to scrape the fare together. One of the fruit and veg stalls on the market gives me some work carting boxes but it's only a couple of hours morning and evening and they pay me buttons. It's heavy work anyway, my leg's screaming after two hours. I couldn't do more if it was offered.

Monday morning and at last I'm travelling. The cheapest way to get to Skelmersdale is by bus and I try to stay awake as it crawls through the traffic in Walton Vale and eventually out to another overspill district called Kirkby. After that it's curious flat countryside, dotted with white farmhouses and covered with huge fields full of sprouts and cabbages.

Skelmersdale is a mass of tall trees that takes my breath away. I'd expected the wide roads, the sixties link-housing and concrete bridges, even the roundabouts, but this graceful autumn glory edging the roads and housing estates is something else.

The bus terminates at a glass shopping mall full of the usual chain stores and cake shops. I get tea and toast in one of the cafés and find out from the waitress that there is a library next to the shopping centre. There are people walking around but it's quiet compared with Liverpool.

I wash and brush up in the toilets in the centre, and take my leg off in one of the cubicles to change the sock. I've no spare clothes now and no real prospect of getting any more. I use lots of the liquid soap in the effort to disguise any developing smells.

The library is between a swimming pool and a police station that I pass as quickly as possible. The library building is surprisingly large. Inside it is light and cheerful. The assistant is really helpful.

"I'm looking for newspapers, going back to 1964."

"We've got local ones – Skelmersdale and Ormskirk, but no national ones before 1990."

She sets up the microfilm machine for me while I take off my pack and my coat.

"Can I look at the Skelmersdale papers for July 1964?"

"Oh, they don't go that far back. There's only the *Ormskirk Advertiser* but all the Skelmersdale news is reported in that."

I skim through the editions for June. This paper contains little national news. Its pages are taken up with sports days, carnivals and flower shows. The financial pages discuss cattle shows and agricultural sales. The only flaw in this cosy rural existence is expressed in the repeated fears of residents about the new town that is taking shape in their midst.

The paper is published once a week. I start serious reading at the 9th July edition. There are only three funerals reported and nine deaths but one of the deceased lived in Ashurst, so I feel I am on the right track. Excitement makes me rush through the pages even though I know I'm clutching at straws. Mary hardly seems the kind of person to have put family notices in the newspaper. The 9th July is probably too early anyway. I flick through accounts of Ormskirk's annual horse show and the exploits of the cricket team, to get to the next edition.

Here there are five funerals reported. If Mary's father is going to be in, it will surely be here – but it's not. I get out the diary and check the date. No, it won't be in this one. Maybe the 23rd July – it's not there either. I'm deflated. I roll the film forward, scrutinising the pages right through August but I don't find a thing.

I slump back in the chair. Maybe I should just accept this as proof that the diary is fiction. I start to rewind the film, then something catches my eye.

The notice is small, tucked away at the end of a column devoted to prayers to the Blessed Virgin and reports of lost kittens.

JEAN APPLETON. If anyone knows of the whereabouts of Jean Appleton, nee Wilshaw, wife of William Appleton, formerly of Brow Lane Farm, Scarclough, last heard of in Wigan, please contact Ginnigle and Marsh, solicitors of Market Street, Wigan.

Ginnigle and Marsh! I check the diary. It's there! This must be Mary's missing mother. The diary is real. Scarclough! At last, the name of the village where the farm is located.

I'm feverish now. Can't wait to get this reel out and find more. It takes forever. I scan all the reels from '65 to '67 until my eyes are sore but find nothing – no babies rescued from sheds, no mention of any of the other names in the diary.

I quiz the assistant about Scarclough.

"It's up by Ashurst Beacon." This means nothing to me, except that Mary mentions it in the diary.

"I'm trying to trace some relatives, name of Appleton. They live – lived on a farm around there."

"Appleton's a very common Lancashire name." She looks at me kindly. "I'll show you the maps. Sometimes the farms are marked."

She takes me to the Ordnance Survey maps. The names don't mean much; Newburgh, Parbold, but St Stephen's leaps out at me.

"The road runs from Parbold to Upholland and you can turn off here," she points a finger, "and come out in Skelmersdale."

"Brow Lane." I lean over the map and it's there, near a public house.

"If you haven't a car," she looks at me doubtfully, "you're best getting the bus to Upholland and walking from there. It's quite a long way." She traces the road with her finger.

"Thanks." I get my bag and coat. There's a café across the way and the smell of chips tempts me in. While I'm eating I think how the people in the diary have taken on a reality for me that I didn't feel before. Still, knowing where she came from doesn't help me to find out where she is now. Time is going by and she could be anywhere. I keep thinking that if I knew where she had been brought up in the first place, it would be easier to find her. Maybe they will take her back to the same place. Maybe she has a family somewhere.

There must be clues, in something she said. After all, I was with her for most of last week. Why was she so afraid of the police? I remember her hiding under the table in McDonalds. "Medoban," she kept saying. It's a medical sounding name. I roll the syllables about in my mouth. It sounds like a drug but it can't be. "No go medoban," she said. It must be a place.

Back at the library I search the Yellow Pages but can't find anything under residential homes or hospitals that sound anything like it. It was a long shot anyway. It's unlikely to be local. People get sent all over the country for specialised treatment.

I feel like setting off for Scarclough right away but it's already mid-afternoon and it sounds like it's still an isolated place. I need to think about where I'm going to stay tonight.

Outside, the air is cooling and clouds are gathering over the hills beyond the buildings. There's a bench on a path at the side of the library, near some trees; a place to sit and plan what to do next. Once it was a playground or leisure area but brambles have grown over the seats and railings and there's rubbish everywhere. Behind the railings the remains of a stream disappear into a concrete tunnel after flowing through upturned shopping trolleys and old tyres.

People are walking along a path to my right that leads towards the shopping centre but they don't come down here. I can see why. There are needles and beer cans lying around and the atmosphere is slightly menacing. I was thinking maybe I could sleep down here under the trees, but perhaps it's not such a good idea.

"All right there mate?" Three smackheads appear from nowhere. One has a black eye. "Looking for something?" He grins, showing rotten teeth.

"Just taking a rest." I suppose I'm sitting in the middle of the local dealer shop.

"No, you're all right, stay there." He sits down beside me as I move to get up.

One of the other two sits on the other side but the third remains standing, flicking glances towards the shops then back at me. He stamps his feet and rubs his hands.

"Not from round here, are you?"

"Just visiting." I'm glad of the people walking around up on the path. At least they're unlikely to have a go at me while it's so busy.

"I'm Robbie. This is Den and Stuie. What's your name mate?"

"Tommy."

"Want a fag, Tommy?" He starts to roll up.

"I don't smoke." I try again to get up but his hand's on my arm. I try to avoid looking at him, at any of them. Their eyes are so deep and dark I might drown in there. One look and you can see the peaks and troughs that shape their lives. Stuie's making me twitchy. He paces up and down, short nervous steps, obviously looking for somebody.

God help their families. At least I've been spared that. Imagine if Angela – but I think maybe I'd even accept that, just to have her here and alive.

"I've got no money." I feel I need to make the point even though they can tell that just by looking at me.

"Got somewhere to stay? What you doing here anyway?"

"I'm looking for a woman." Stuie stops pacing and snickers. "A woman called Vicky." They all look blank. "She lives in Scarclough."

"That's fucking miles away." Robbie giggles. "Too posh for you mate, or for the likes of us. You can stay in our flat for a day or two if you like. There's no place to doss round here."

"Thanks, but I'll be okay." I can imagine what kind of place they live in. Even I can't sleep with my eyes open all night.

"There's the hostel." Stuie stops for a moment, then resumes pacing. "Come on Mouse, you fucker. Where is he? He's always fucking late."

"Yeah, I forgot about them. They might take you in. We'll take you up there in a minute."

A hostel sounds good, just for one night. A proper bed, maybe some hot food, even a bath. It's been a long time since I slept in a bed and this is a new place. I don't know good spots to sleep, like I did in Liverpool. The shopping mall will be closed up at night and down here – well I don't think so.

A lanky boy rides up on a bike.

"Where've you been, Mouse, you twat." Den suddenly bursts into life.

"Come on, hurry up." Stuie is almost dancing.

Mouse jerks his head at me.

Robbie grins. "It's okay. He's just a dosser. We're taking him up to the hostel."

They turn their backs in a huddle and I watch a young girl pass along the top path with a baby in a pushchair. She keeps her head averted.

"Okay, come on." Robbie touches my arm. Mouse is already riding away, towards the shops. "I'll take you. Stuie and Den, they got business to attend to."

I creak to my feet and follow him past the police station. "Isn't it a bit dodgy, outside the cop shop?"

"Never see a fucking copper here." He spits on the ground.

Where he's taking me I've no idea. I just limp along and we go through a complicated system of footpaths and underpasses all hedged with bushes full of red berries. Now and again we cross wide roads with huge sweeps of grass verges and monster roundabouts. Everywhere tall trees are ripening red and brown, preparing for winter, making a contrast to the grey concrete box houses.

The thought of winter makes me shiver. I spent most of last winter in Manchester. Ended up in Hope hospital three days before Christmas. It was almost worth the beating I'd got off some yobby Mancs to sleep in a clean bed for once and be spoken to like a human being. Not that they had much time for me and they still put me out the next morning with just the address of a hostel that was already full. That was one of the few times I almost phoned Jed.

As we walk, Robbie rattles on about the flat he shares with his girl Sharon and her two kids, Justine and Ben, as well as with a floating population of other people with nowhere to stay. I learn how Social Services are always poking their noses in and trying to take the kids away. I hear the stories of people who drift in and out of the flat for a few days and nights here and there and I find out about his mum's arthritis, this last information brought on by him observing my limp, which is getting worse as the day draws to a close.

"How far is it to Scarclough?" Robbie stops in midflow, grins and points ahead. The hill rises above the town. The ground beneath our feet is just beginning to slope upwards as we move towards the incline. A thick nest of flat-roofed grey houses cluster on the lower slopes.

"See that?" He points at a stubby needle sticking up on the top of the hill.

"That's Ashurst Beacon. They used to light fires on it to warn people."

"What about?"

"I don't know. Invasion I suppose. That's what they told us at school."

"And Scarclough?

"Scarclough's there too. Right by it."

My fingers curl round the notebook in my pocket. "You ever go up there?"

"Nah." He looks at me as if I'm crazy. "Nothing up there. And it's miles. Me ma used to take us there for picnics when we were kids. You can see for miles around. We used to think it was great, but that was when we were kids. Not now."

"Here it is." We cross a road into a pedestrianised estate of identical pebbledashed houses with blue front doors. "That one there." He points to the third house on the row. "Just ring the bell. I better get off."

"Thanks, mate." Despite the way he looks and the way he probably lives, he's done me a good turn for no reason at all.

A voice comes out of the intercom when I ring the bell and after I've explained about having nowhere to go, the door opens.

"Up here." There's a woman at the top of the stairs. She's dressed casually in leggings and a sweater but there's nothing casual in the way she looks me over. She's assessed me before I open my mouth and evidently finds me wanting.

"Are you resident in this area?" is the first question she asks as soon as she's got me sitting in her office.

I explain about coming up from Liverpool but I don't say anything about Vicky and going to Scarclough. "I was hoping to stay with my cousin but he doesn't seem to live here any more. It's years since I've seen him."

"Where did your cousin live?" She frowns.

I struggle to remember the names of the streets Robbie brought me through but my mind's a blank. At last something comes.

"Ashurst."

The frown deepens. "This hostel is for people who are made unintentionally homeless and who were living in the area and are therefore eligible for rehousing by the district council."

She looks at her watch. "The council offices will be closing now. Look, I'll give you a bed for the night but that's all, unless tomorrow you can convince the council that you were actually living with this cousin and you can no longer stay there."

I try to hide my delight. One night will suit me fine. I mutter thanks.

"Come on." She takes me across a small landing to a bedroom. The place seems quite small, just an ordinary house, with four or five bedrooms.

"You'll have to share with Terry. He's been here for a while."

Terry's bed is made with military precision and his possessions: hairbrush, razor, small radio, framed photograph of two children, are lined up in a neat row on his bedside table.

"I'll get you some bedding later. Come down to the kitchen first."

The kitchen is large and warm with a communal pine table. People come and go, there are kids running around. A young man with an anxious look says, "Elaine, I n-n-n-need to t-t-t-t-talk about something."

"Bit later Geoff. Busy right now."

"Got any food?" I shake my head.

"Here." She unlocks a cupboard, gives me two tins of soup and one of Irish stew. "Help yourself to tea and coffee." She nods at the canisters on the worktop. "You can use the washing machine. I'll give you some soap powder. Don't suppose you've got spare clothes?"

She frogmarches me back up the stairs, unlocks another cupboard and starts pulling things out.

"What size are you?" She doesn't wait for a reply but holds things up against me. I get a baggy pair of sweat pants, a tee shirt and a grey V-neck sweater, black socks and underpants.

"Here's your bedding." She thrusts a duvet and pillows at me.

"Bathroom's here." She opens a door. "I'll leave you to it."

When she's marched away I go back to the bedroom and dump everything on the bed. There's a greyish towel and a small bar of soap among the other things. I can't believe my luck.

The bath is the best thing that's happened to me in a long time and I stay there for as long as I can until someone starts banging on the door and a male voice tells me to hurry the fuck up.

Back in the bedroom I take the time to give my prosthesis a thorough clean and hang my freshly washed stump socks on the radiator to dry.

My new clothes feel soft and comfortable, except that the underpants are too tight so I leave them off, and the pants are too big but I fix this with a piece of string I have in my pack.

Maybe I could borrow Terry's razor and shave my beard off, but I don't expect he'd take kindly to that and once you start shaving you have to keep on, so I just give it a bit of a trim with the scissors on my penknife. I always had a beard in the old days, but it was short and neat then. An excellent barber was one of the luxuries I allowed myself. I used to think I looked very distinguished. Still, looking in the mirror now, my skin's a bit rough and my eyes a bit red but I don't look too bad.

By the time I've had a cup of tea and eaten my Irish stew, I'm falling asleep. I don't want to sit in the lounge with the other residents watching *Neighbours* and *Big Brother*. This woman with a ponytail has already been asking awkward questions while I've been sitting at the kitchen table but I have to hang around for a bit while my clothes are in the washing machine. Elaine has gone off duty after handing over to a young man called Greg who looks like a social worker.

A man comes in with a toothbrush moustache, a blazer with brass buttons and very shiny shoes. I know right away that this is Terry. He follows me when I go to the room with my armful of clean clothes.

While I make up the bed I'm forced to listen to the story about his wife who was a slattern that couldn't keep the house or the kids clean and who had eventually turned him out of his own home.

"She got the police. To me! In my own house! Said I'd beaten her up. It was a tap. No more than a little smack. God knows I was provoked, I can tell you."

He's working himself up, arranging and re-arranging his little row of belongings. "Now she's sitting pretty in the house – the house I'm paying for," he jabs his finger at me, "and I end up in here, like some nomark."

I don't care. I just want to get in the delicious bed and go to sleep.

"I suppose the same thing happened to you?" He sits on his own bed and waits for me to commiserate.

"No." I get under the duvet and turn my back.

"Oh well, suit yourself." The bed creaks as he gets up. "Bloody dosser," he mutters as he leaves the room.

Now, even though I was falling asleep before, I can't sleep now. It's too comfortable, feels strange compared with what I'm used to and Terry's made me think about Corinne, started up the memories again.

Is Corinne sitting pretty? Is she still in the big house out on the edge of town? How empty that house must seem now without Angela knocking a tennis ball against the garage wall or sunbathing at the bottom of the garden. Has Corinne kept Angie's yellow and white bedroom the same, with her 'Take That' posters and her guitar?

I realise I'm holding myself tight round the middle, trying to hold the pain in, stop it exploding out into the room, out into the rest of the world. If only I could be like Terry so that I could never be wrong, would never have to suffer this guilt.

Something wakes me in the middle of the night. I sit up covered in sweat. I don't know where I am. Is it Vicky, standing beside me in the mouldering bedroom in Falkner Street?

My eyes grow accustomed to the dark while I fumble for my pack, looking for my lighter. I remember where I am, realise it's not Falkner Street and Vicky's not here. I find a switch and light floods the room, shows me Terry's humped shape, his bedding tidy even in his sleep and his shiny shoes sitting neatly beside the bed.

Tuesday morning I leave early, before Elaine, the sergeant major, comes on duty. The woman with the ponytail, whose name is Janice, feeds me tea and toast alongside her kids. I get my stuff together right after they've gone off to school looking like a row of penguins in their uniforms. Greg gives me a card with the hostel phone number on and the address of another hostel on the other side of Wigan.

"Sorry we can't do more for you." He looks at me earnestly over his wire-rimmed spectacles. "If you get any joy with the council, come back this afternoon and we'll try to help you."

In the street I meet Terry coming back with a newspaper under his arm and a carton of milk in his hand. In the daylight he is even more pink and shiny.

"You're out early." I can't pass without saying something.

"Some of us have to go to work." He looks down his nose at me and doesn't stop.

It promises to be another fine day. The sun shines through the trees as I follow Greg's directions across the estates to get to the bus station. It's quite a walk but I feel rested.

When I ask for a bus to Scarclough at the bus station, the driver I approach laughs.

"No bus goes there, pal. You'll have to get the Wigan bus, get off at Upholland, the Golden Lion, and walk up the brow."

I check my money. I've still quite a bit left. Enough to last a couple of days, after that I don't know. This area doesn't look the kind of place to find casual work except maybe for farming and I don't feel fit enough for that. There's no point in worrying about it now.

The bus wends its way through more housing estates, wide roads and trees. My spirits are high. If I can find out who Vicky is – give her a name and a history – I've got more chance of finding out where she's gone. But to do this I'll have to contact old friends from a life I've tried to escape.

Thoughts of the past throw gloom over my good mood. Memories crowd in of the different persons I've been; respected and admired, vilified and disgraced, humble and abject. At least now I'm distanced, closed off. Most of the time, only my guilty thoughts can hurt me. I'm none of these people or maybe I'm all of them rolled up into an unrecognisable mixture, like a ball of Plasticene made up of different coloured sticks that ends up just a murky brown lump.

"Golden Lion." The driver jerks the bus to a stop and I get out into the real world. It's a crossroads on a hill. The pub is on my left and across the road there's a chip shop and a convenience store. I ask a passing woman the way to Scarclough and she points up the road to my left.

"It's a good walk. Two or three miles." She smiles at me. My heart sinks and my hip twinges in anticipation of the pain I know is coming.

The road climbs sharply and I'm soon feeling the strain. I make myself take it slowly even though excitement's mounting at the thought of finding Vicky's birthplace.

There's council housing bordering the left side of the road; one of those solidly built post-war estates. The notebook mentioned something. The children! The children from the council estate chased Mary on her way back from Wigan. It's another little confirmation that gives me a buzz and lends fresh energy as I reflect that I'm retracing Mary Appleton's footsteps.

After a long haul the hill flattens out but there's no sign of habitation once I get past the estate, just untended fields that slope sharply on either side. There are fantastic views though. On my left there's a great plain and the silver line on the horizon could be the sea. Skelmersdale is clustered below. On my right the buildings of a big industrial town clutter the land as far as the eye can see. This must be Wigan.

I pass the odd house but no farms. I'm getting tired and when I come to a pull in picnic area, I stop to rest. There are a couple of cars parked up and there are people walking dogs in the bushes and on the grass.

I check the photocopied map I got from the library. Brow Lane is on the right and still a good way from where I am now. I've already walked at least a mile and the lane is as far again, if not further.

It's a long slog and the landscape gets bleaker. The hilltop is wind ravaged with crumbling dry stone walls, long yellow whips of grass and wild gorse bushes. As if in sympathy the earlier sunshine has disappeared, the sky turns grey and darker clouds gather in the distance.

The lane comes upon me suddenly when I have drifted into a plodding motion of one foot in front of the other, ignoring the backdrop of pain. A flush of anticipation turns almost to dread when I look down the turning and see how overgrown trees meet overhead, making a dark tunnel barely wide enough for a single car to pass.

Even though rusty ferns colour the verges and the trees themselves are fiery with autumn golds, the leaves drifting to the ground and the bony branches poking through strengthen my sense of foreboding as I pass under the canopy.

My footsteps crunch on the metalled road and seem to echo back at me. The hairs on my neck rise, as if there are hidden watchers.

Further down, the trees are cut back, the road bends and widens, houses are dotted here and there, the atmosphere lightens. Occasional cars pass. Steep banks and thick hedges obscure the view. I want badly to rest again but I keep on for about half a mile until I see a youngish woman weeding the front garden of one of a pair of whitewashed cottages.

"There's a big dairy farm on the main road," she says in answer to my question, "but that's not down here. Go back to the top road and it's about two miles along on the right."

"No, it's here. I'm looking for some friends who used to live there. Definitely Brow Lane. Their name's Appleton."

She looks me up and down. "I don't know any Appletons." There's disdain in her voice. "Mind you, I've not lived here very long. Try Mrs Thornton next door, she's been here twenty years. She'll know if anyone will."

I'm opening the gate when she says, "There's an old place up the road. You've come past it, but no one lives there. It's been abandoned God knows how long. No one seems to know who owns it."

It's like a jolt of electricity, blocking out the pain in my hip. I close the gate, all thoughts of Mrs Thornton gone.

"Where?" My voice is hoarse.

She looks dubious. "It's up near the top of the road, where the bend is. There's a metal gate, but it's all overgrown. There's no one there."

I can feel her eyes on me as I hurry back the way I came. Adrenalin gives me energy even though it's now midday and I'm tired and hungry.

It's not surprising I missed the gate. It's set back off the road on the bend and it's overgrown with tall grass, gorse and brambles.

Luckily there's a gap in the hedge by the gate that I can just squeeze through. As soon as I set foot in the deep leafmould on the path an eerie quiet assails me. Not a bird twitters. The trees on either side soar in fantastic untamed shapes over my head.

The house is to the right, low and ancient, although little is left of it, just some tumbled walls, all overgrown with ivy. The ground beneath feels stony, like there might be a yard beneath it, but it's solid with dead leaves, layers of weeds and soil. On the left, heaps of broken bricks may once have been a barn.

There is nothing to suggest habitation, any sheds have long gone. The house roof has disappeared. Only vaguely does the brickwork retain the shape of a home, suggest that someone once lived here. Nothing to conjure up the picture of Mary making love with Michael, sitting with her diary, feeding her chickens or even her child, and yet there's a sense of watching, no, maybe just of being, a feeling of containment, something dark, unredeemed, like a ghost trace of the poor stunted creature shut up in the shed. My eyes are drawn to this heap of rotten wood, that clump of stones, and like leaves rustling, a voice in my head whispers, "Was it here, was it here, was it here?"

I have to walk away, out to the fields at the end of the path behind the ruins. The wide sweep of the hill behind the house is cleansing and heartening. The grass here is short and turfy. Cars pass along the road at the top, the road I walked along only a little while ago. Already it seems like another world, another time.

Out here in the open, life seems normal. Here Ted Bracewell ploughed the ground for Mary's potatoes, as did her father and who knows how many before him?

I turn and make my way through the undergrowth back past the old barn. Other people have trodden through here, forging pathways, but not too recently. Bleached crisp packets and rusty beer cans are mementoes of their presence.

The tangle of blackberry bushes is heavy with fruit, the briars arching down to the ground with its weight. The berries are swollen to bursting ... *My blood fired up ... his hands ... the purple finger-marks ... evidence of ... desire ... the white flesh of the harlot ...*

I half expect to see the imprint of their bodies but there is only the wilderness of couch grass and nettles.

The view when I look up stops my breath. A vista of gentle slopes in mud greens and browns, faint bluish hills forming the distance and superimposed on the natural landscape, the motorway carries its moving dots of traffic.

I need to sit down. There's a huge stone gatepost that's fallen on its side. Everything in me sinks and I can feel tears approaching. My hand in my pocket feels for the notebook. I hold on to its rigid corners. Next to me the remains of a cart are sliding into the ground, unrecognisable shards of wood, grey and paper thin, one iron wheel sticking up, still solid but pitted with rust and half-obscured by gorse bushes growing through the spokes.

Suddenly I have to get out of here. I can feel the air closing behind me as I make my way back down the path to the gate. It's damp underfoot. Despite the hot weather, little light or freshness has penetrated here.

A stinging rattle of raindrops hits me as I squeeze through the gap by the gate, borne on a sudden gust of wind that blows yellow leaves round my legs. Out on the road, that overbearing presence lifts although the tunnel of trees on my left still menaces.

I turn the other way and go back to the pair of cottages but now the garden is empty. There's a twitch of lace curtain when I knock at Mrs Thornton's cottage. After a long time the front door opens on a chain to show a slice of face, long and wrinkled with sharp brown eyes.

"I'm sorry to bother you. I'm looking for the people who used to live at the farm up there. Their name was Appleton?"

When I mention the name her face changes from suspicious to curious. She loosens the chain and opens the door wider. She's long and thin in a black skirt and jumper that are decorated with cat hairs.

"Nobody lives there." She casts a glance up the road. "Nobody's lived there – since before I came here."

"You don't remember them then?"

"Didn't say that, did I?" She peers at me. "I remember Bill Appleton all right, and mad Mary too. I were born and bred in Scarclough village. Nobody's been here for many a year asking after them." She stares past me, back in time.

"Are you some relation?"

"I think so," I lie. "I looked the family tree up on the internet."

"Internet?" She sucks her teeth. "Well, if you found so much out, you'll have found out what happened for all we've tried to keep it quiet. I'd thought it were all forgot about." She shakes her head. "Now you come along. You're not from the telly are you, digging up muck from the past?"

"No, no." I hold out a pleading hand as the gap in the doorway narrows. "I met Vicky once. I just need to get in touch."

"Vicky?" Her eyes are guarded. "I can't stand here all day and I don't want to talk about it, although there're those in the village who will. Try Jimmy Atherton, it were him as found Mary Appleton's body." The door shuts in my face.

Coming out of the tunnel of trees into the open aspect at the top of the brow is like leaving a ghost train. I look up gratefully at the sky with its smattering of blue among the grey clouds and almost get run over by a sports car that races round the bend and disappears before I even register its presence.

The road begins to slope downwards and I pass a pub on my right. It's an old stone building, it must have been there in Mary's time. I'm hungry and thirsty and I'm tempted to go in and buy a sandwich and maybe get more information from the staff but then there's the lure of the whisky bottles behind the bar and God knows I could use a stiff drink. I make myself carry on.

The road seems to go on forever but after some time I see an opening up ahead on the right and when I get up close, there's a sign saying 'Ashurst Beacon'.

Suddenly this stone finger is there in front of me, having been hidden by a steep bank at the side of the road. I sit on the stone plinth and make tea. It's such a relief to rest. I get a strange feeling here, a presence but I shrug it away. It's just because I know people have congregated here for centuries. Here, fires were lit to warn of invaders, a wordless communication system carrying those most basic signals, fear and alarm. The countryside rolls out below. It's always been here, despite the antics of civilisation. Buildings are dotted about but they're only temporary. So is this beacon, even though it's so solidly planted.

I'm still tired when I set off again but I'm too impatient to stay any longer. A couple of painkillers have subdued the gremlin in my hip.

St Stephen's Church takes me by surprise as I come round a bend. These sloping banks hide everything from view till you're right on top of them. On the left is the lane the librarian pointed out to me that leads back to Skelmersdale and next to the church is a school where small children are being called in from lunchtime play. There's no marker or sign, but this must be Scarclough.

Houses roll higgledy-piggledy down the hill and thankfully there's a small shop cum post office where I buy a sandwich and a fresh bottle of water.

"Do you know a Mr Atherton? Jimmy?" The woman at the till barely flickers.

"The gardener? End house on the terrace – over the road a bit further down. But you won't catch him in now. After getting your garden done up? He's the best round here." She looks at me with fresh interest.

"Yeah, someone told me about him." It's hardly a lie.

The house is easy to find. There's a sign in the garden. "Atherton Landscapes. Gardens by design." So, he's not your ordinary oddjob gardener. No ordinary terraced house either. These houses are set back in long gardens and Atherton's garden advertises his skills with lines of shaped bushes and the smooth lawn setting off clumps of Michaelmas daisies and chrysanthemums.

There's a truck in the driveway and a burly middle-aged man heading purposefully for the driver's door as I turn into the gravel drive.

"Yes?" He looks me up and down.

"Mr Atherton? Jimmy Atherton?"

"What can I do for you?" His face says it all. He thinks I'm a bum but he can't afford to be rude to a possible customer. I might be an eccentric millionaire. "I'm in a bit of a hurry, got to get back to work."

"Mrs Thornton told me to come and see you."

"It'll be a few weeks before I can take on any more work. I'm chasing my tail as it is."

"No. It's about the farm. The Appleton farm."

He stops with one hand on the truck door handle. His whole body is attentively still and his face changes.

"What about it? There's nobody there."

"I wanted to find out what happened to Mary." I take a deep breath. "To her child."

He leans back against the truck, folds his arms against his chest.

"Why?" I can't read his expression. "You from the press?" His blue eyes are fierce, searching. This is someone I won't be able to kid.

"I think I met her – the daughter, Vicky."

"Oooof!" The breath rushes out of him. His eyes are fixed on me. "That's not possible." He hugs his chest.

"I found this." I hold up the notebook. He takes it, frowning, turns the pages at random. His mouth drops open and he looks at me with horror.

"Where did you get this? From her?" He sags against the truck. "You think it's all over," he says slowly. "You think it's gone, forgotten but it comes back. It keeps coming back.

"I have to get back to work." He recovers himself, opens the truck door. I hold my hand out for the book. I know he wants to keep it, wants to read it in private.

"But I need to talk to you. Please, I need to find her again."

"Find her?" He seems surprised. "I didn't think she was still alive." Reluctantly he hands me the book but his eyes follow it as I stow it in my pocket.

"Come back at six o'clock. Maybe we can talk then."

*　*　*

At last the truck comes back. He sees me as he goes past and gives me a wave. It's been a long afternoon with nothing to do but sit on the bench outside the shop and think about what has happened to Vicky.

"Been here all the time?" he asks as I limp up the drive.

"No point in going away and coming back. I don't know the area."

He looks a bit guilty like he hadn't realised I'd have to hang about all this time.

"Just let me get this in the garage."

He takes me round the back of the house. The back garden is even longer than the front but just as neat. A Border collie rushes out and jumps at us when he opens the door.

"Down, Jimbo." He pushes the dog away and it disappears down the bottom of the garden.

"Tea?" He brings me in to a neat pine kitchen and puts the kettle on. "There's been other people here asking about Mary Appleton, lots of them – but no one for a long time now. I thought everyone had forgotten about it. I tell you straight, I got sick of it – TV, newspaper reporters, every so many years, digging it all up. Sometimes it were just plain nosey parkers, read about it somewhere, wanting a cheap thrill. I don't talk to anyone now." He folds his arms and stares at me.

"Mrs Thornton said you would talk to me."

"Listen mate, what's your name?"

"Bob."

"Listen Bob, the only reason I'm talking to you now is because of that book. Do you mind if I have a look at it?"

"Be my guest." I sit quietly with the mug of tea he gives me while he skims through the diary. He reads greedily, whipping over the pages. I look round the room. There's a woman's touch here, everything is shiny, clean and colour co-ordinated, but it's comfortable for all that. The dog scratches and whines at the back door.

"Let him in, will you?" He doesn't look up. The dog eyes him hopefully, then slopes off to its basket in a corner. Jimmy Atherton finishes reading, sits back, sighs.

"So where did you get this?"

I go through my story while he feeds the dog and fills its water bowl.

"On the streets? I can't believe it. I'd have thought she were dead or in some institution." He shuts the dog in another room. "Funny, I've never really thought about what became of her. I suppose the story stopped for me after they found her. I didn't even know it were a girl for ages. I thought it were a monster, you know?"

What does he mean? Then I remember that first night, the scary eyes and sharp teeth in the cupboard. He notices the way I'm looking at him.

"I were only eight year old. 'Course, later on I realised, you know, she were just a child but it didn't stop me thinking she were a monster, not deep down inside. It were that first time I saw her, you know."

He gets up and rinses his mug at the sink, stares out of the kitchen window. "I'll never forget it, never."

I think of the moment they told me Angela was dead. It was a nurse, someone impersonal. I can still see her pinched, white face. She must have drawn the short straw. It's my one clear memory of that day.

"There were stuff in the papers about her, a lot at first but I were too young to make much of it. 'Course there were loads of gossip and people coming from Skem and Wigan to find out more about it. As I got older there were bits on the news and in the papers every so often about how she were getting on in hospital and such places, but I didn't pay much attention. I were young. I had more interesting things to think about." He shrugs.

"Mrs Thornton said you found her mother's body."

"Aye, well it were before that. We used to go and play up there, you know, commandoes and space wars and stuff in the bushes. She were always a bit odd even before her dad died and she used to chase us and that. We thought it were funny. We used to dare each other. You know how kids are. It were only later I realised how crazy she really were.

"Anyway, I were up there one day on my own and I hears something thumping about in the shed and making funny noises. It give me a bit of a fright like.

"In those days I were always making things up about space monsters and stuff – all that Doctor Who on telly I suppose. I were mad on Dan Dare too. I told some of the kids at school there were a monster up at Mary's farm. I told me mam and dad too but they didn't believe me. Me dad never believed anything I said because I were forever making up stories.

"Anyway, top and bottom of it were this kid Norman, he were a bit of a bully and his family were loaded – he thought he were cock of the village – he makes us go back there after school. There were four or five of us I think.

"It were going dark when we got up there. I still have nightmares about it, about going up the path with the bushes all waving like triffids in the shadows. And when we got to the top Norman and the others were all laughing at me and saying there's nothing there, when all of a sudden there's this banging and thumping coming from the shed and we were all scared stiff, and when it started making these noises we all ran. You never heard noises like that; they weren't human nor they weren't animal neither.

"I ran with my eyes shut and when I opened them again I were outside the farm door. It's frozen in my mind. I can still see it now. This horrible face were staring at me. 'Course it were only poor Mary, but we didn't stop to look. We all ran away. We ran all the way back to the village."

He stops and looks at me like he's coming back from somewhere else.

"That's some story."

"That's only half of it." He sighs. "Fancy a butty?"

"Thanks. That'd be great." I'd eaten a pork pie from the shop while I was waiting but that was hours ago.

While he's buttering bread and getting ham and cheese out of the fridge he tells me how his wife is away visiting their daughter at university. It's her first year.

I used to plan for Angela's education. I always thought she'd follow me into the medical profession. Suddenly she's there, four years old, with a toy stethoscope and medical bag.

"Be good Daddy and you can have a sweetie," she lisps, pressing the toy syringe against my arm.

"Owww!" I cry and she shrieks with laughter.

My heart squeezes and catches my breath. Jimmy Atherton is holding out a sandwich on a plate and looking curiously at me. Did I cry out? I pull my mind back to Vicky.

"You said that was only half the story?" The fresh tea he gives me washes the dryness out of my mouth. My heartbeat goes back to normal.

"Yeah." He sits down, takes a bite of his sandwich. "When I got home that night, I tried to tell my dad there were monsters at the farm but he didn't believe me. My mam could see I were upset but she just told me off for playing up there. Next thing, Norman Forster's dad knocked on the door with Norman. Old Mr Forster were a big nob round here, richest man in the village, so my dad had to take notice of him. We all got in his car and drove up there. Big car it were, a Bentley I think. It were beautiful and any other time I'd have been over the moon to be riding in it but I were too scared to think about it and even Norman didn't have anything to say. My dad still didn't believe me, threatened to leather me if I were telling lies again but when we got there and my dad found the body in the doorway it were different.

"Mr Forster drove up to the pub and called the police and while we were waiting the noises started up in the shed. Dad said it were an animal but he didn't go near it till the police came.

"The body were Mary Appleton. She'd got electrocuted with the hoover or something. Dad kept saying that, but it still looked like a monster to me. Norman kept crying and it made me want to cry too but I managed to bite my lip, then the police came and Mr Forster came and took me and Norman back to the car. He gave me a fifty pence piece. I remember it because it were the first time I ever had one.

"While we were sitting in the car an ambulance and another

police car full of plainclothes men came, but the farm gate were rusted solid so they had to walk up with the stretcher. First they brought the body down but all you could see were a lump under a blanket, then there were a lot of shouting and banging and the policemen came down with this bundle all wrapped up in blankets and tied round with straps or belts. In the light of the torches we could see this head sticking out and it were the worst thing I ever saw, worse even than Mary Appleton's dead face. This one were alive all right, all hair and teeth and staring eyes like something out of a horror film and the noises it were making were like nothing I ever heard before. It went right through me.

"You couldn't tell what it were – human or animal, never mind whether it were a boy or a girl. It scared the shit out of all of us. Dad came running behind them and jumped in the car.

"It's a child," he shouted and his face was wild, like he couldn't control it. "Oh God, it's a child." This frightened me even more. I suddenly realised that the grownups were just as scared as us kids. I'll never forget it – never." He rubs a hand over his eyes.

"I don't know where it – she – went to. The local hospital at first, I know because my dad kept some of the newspapers. I soon forgot about it on the surface, you know the way kids are, but every so often it pops up in my mind, something triggers it off. Sometimes I've wondered if they ever found any family for her. The story goes that they can't find out who owns the property, that's why the farm's been allowed to fall to bits. So I suppose if you think about it logically that means they can't trace her, but I always supposed she were locked up somewhere. I've never thought of her as an ordinary person, only that picture that's burned into my brain, those awful teeth and that screeching. In my mind she's always been like that. I were gobsmacked when you said you met her on the street."

I'm disappointed. I'd hoped he'd be able to give me a clue, a starting point, some way of tracing her.

"Newspapers you said? You haven't still got them have you?"

"Yeah, matter of fact I have. I found them when Dad died. I'll get them."

I'm left sitting in this modern kitchen looking at the gleaming surfaces. The collie comes in and puts its head in my lap. Its eyes plead for me to stroke it. Gingerly I put my hand on the dome of its head. Between my hand and my leg, its warmth connects me to it. It's a long time since I touched another living creature.

"Here." He's back with a scrapbook, one of those cheap sugar paper ones with different coloured pages. "Get down Jimbo." The collie subsides under the table.

The covers are curled with age. "There's some later stuff in there too. Every so often some magazine or newspaper digs it all up and runs a feature on it. I got into a habit of collecting it, in case there were anything new, anything that might explain what happened. That were later on, after I grew up and got married and settled down in the late eighties, so there's a bit of a gap like."

"And was there? Anything new? Any explanations?"

He shrugs. "Nothing concrete. Experts spouting theories, making comparisons to other cases. Even then I didn't really think about it, not about understanding it. I just kept the papers for the novelty of it, it were something that related to me, my history, our village.

"But this," his hand stretches out for the diary, "this explains a lot."

There's something in his voice that makes me look up. His eyes shift away. There's something he's not telling me. Before I can speak, he lowers his eyes to the notebook again, makes a deliberate performance of reading.

I start on the scrapbook. The newspaper cuttings are yellowed. 'SCARCLOUGH WOMAN FOUND DEAD', the first headline shouts. Christ! The date is 13th November 1975 – 1975! He looks up at my gasp.

"But Vicky was born in 1966!"

"Yeah. She were around nine year old when they found her, just about the same age as me." In his eyes I can see the same horror that rocks my brain. What is there to say? I go back to the scrapbook.

SCARCLOUGH WOMAN FOUND DEAD

The body of a woman was discovered at a local farm by two Scarclough men this week. Police were summoned to Brow Lane Farm on Ashurst Beacon on Monday 11th November last at 6.30pm following the discovery of a body at the farmhouse. The body is presumed to be that of Mary Appleton who lived on at the farm after the death of her father in 1964. The police are not treating the death as suspicious. A child was removed from the farm and is currently being treated at Ormskirk Hospital.

The next clipping is also from the local paper dated Thursday, 20th November 1975.

BROW LANE FARM CHILD KEPT IN CHICKEN SHED

A child found in a chicken shed last week may have been there for years, police revealed this week. The child was removed from the shed at Brow Lane Farm last week following the discovery of a woman's body in the farmhouse. The woman has been identified by local residents as Mary Appleton who lived alone at the farm.

Mrs Appleton's body was discovered by schoolboy Norman Forster, who had gone to the farm with schoolfriends after another boy had reported seeing a monster at the farm. On returning home, Norman told his father, the well known local businessman, Robert Forster.

"My Norman's a sensible lad," Mr Forster told our reporter. "He doesn't make things up so I knew something serious had happened. I went up to Daniel Atherton's house, his son Jimmy was also involved, and we went up to Brow Lane farm with the boys where we found the body of Mary Appleton and we called the police. It was after the police arrived, we heard noises in one of the sheds and when the police broke the door down, they found a child in there. It hardly had any clothes on and its hair was all matted. You couldn't tell if it was a boy or a girl. It was dreadful. Shocking. I can't describe it."

Police have since confirmed that a female child was found on the premises in an advanced state of neglect and is currently being cared for at Ormskirk Hospital until proper arrangements can be made for her. Nursing staff have named her Vicky. It is not known if Mrs Appleton had any relatives.

Two days later it's made the *Daily Mirror*. I wonder what the TV news of the time made of it.

WILD CHILD FOUND ON REMOTE FARM – BOY HERO RESCUES CHICKEN SHED GIRL

A girl of about eight has been discovered locked in a chicken shed on a remote farm in Lancashire. Police say the child was in an advanced state of neglect and may have been in the shed for years.

The child was discovered by schoolboy Norman Forster, who led his pals to the farm, near Scarclough village, after hearing strange noises when playing in the area on a previous occasion.

On going to the farm after school on Monday 11th November, the boys discovered the body of Mary Appleton, thought to be 29 years old, who lived alone at the farm. The boys ran home and Norman alerted his father, local businessman Robert Forster.

Mr Forster called the police who then discovered the child in the chicken shed while searching the premises. Police say the child, currently being treated at Ormskirk Hospital, is probably the daughter of Mrs Appleton. They have so far been unable to trace any relatives of the dead woman. The death of Mrs Appleton is being treated as accidental.

The *Sunday Mirror,* 23rd November 1975:

MIRROR EXCLUSIVE – SECRET SHAME OF CHICKEN SHED GIRL
MY SON SAID, "THERE'S A MONSTER IN THE SHED, DAD."

In remote Lancashire the picturesque village of Scarclough has given up a shocking secret, a child hidden in a chicken shed for many years, bereft of comforts, kindness, perhaps even the sound of a human voice.

The child's torment finally came to an end with the discovery of the death of Mary Appleton, presumed to be the child's mother, by local schoolboy Norman Forster and his pals.

It is not known at present how Mrs Appleton died but the circumstances are not thought to be suspicious. Local businessman Robert Forster, Norman's father, told us in an exclusive interview that he went with the boys to the farm where he saw the body of Mrs Appleton lying in the hallway, next to a vacuum cleaner which was plugged into the electric socket.

"Brow Lane Farm is hundreds of years old and since her dad died in 1964 I don't think Mary bothered much with its upkeep," he told us. "I could see she was dead. I called the police and it was when they arrived that my Norman said, "There's a monster in the shed.""

"When the police broke the shed door down, the thing inside was making a terrible noise, not human – indescribable. When they brought it out, I was shocked. I never saw anything like it in my life. I hope I never see anything like it ever again. It looked about five years old, but nothing like any child you ever saw. I couldn't tell if it was a boy or a girl."

The body of Mrs Appleton was removed to Ormskirk Hospital for post mortem examination. The child has been taken to a secure ward at the same hospital. Medical staff say she appears to be around eight years old but looks smaller. Nurses have named her Victoria. Sister Margaret Owen told us, "The nurse looking after her is called Victoria and we all agreed the name suited the child. Also, of course we hope she will be victorious in overcoming her tragic circumstances. We call her Vicky for short and we think she responds to the name, but so far she can't repeat it. She can't speak at all."

Vicky will probably be transferred to a specialist hospital when she is physically well enough to begin her rehabilitation into society. We spoke to psychologist Peter Frame who has worked with many deprived children. He said, "This child has suffered appalling neglect. I have heard of such cases before, they are unusual but not as infrequent as we might think. Vicky will probably be unable to walk or speak and will need a long period of physical therapy before even beginning to deal with her emotional and developmental problems."

What can have happened on this farm to produce such a tragedy and how could such a thing happen in a close knit community? How could someone lock up a child for years without anyone knowing of her existence?

Brow Lane Farm is set apart from Scarclough village, a traditional rural community which itself is high on Ashurst Beacon, some three miles from the modern new town of Skelmersdale.

"Mary Appleton kept herself to herself," 74-year-old Mabel Pearce told us. "Brow Lane farm used to be a happy place when old Jim and Annie Appleton had it, but their son Billy was a different kettle of fish. He was very religious, all hellfire and damnation. He tried to keep his wife Jean the same way but she was a Wigan girl, liked a bit of life. She ran off and left him when Mary was just a little girl. Mary never left the farm. She did everything her dad said. They were always together and didn't mix with the rest of us. It's just the way things were. When her dad died, Mary stayed on alone. We never thought anything about it."

Ted Bracewell, who keeps the village shop, told us he drove up to the farm once a week with Mary's grocery order.

"I'd collect the eggs she had to sell at the same time. She hardly ever spoke to me, only to say something about her order or the eggs. I never suspected there was a child. She never ordered anything that would make you think a child lived there. I never saw any washing, never heard anything. How could she have had a child? I never saw anyone else up there. She kept herself to herself and if she wanted it like that, that was her own business. We respected that, though a lot of people thought she was a bit mad.

I couldn't believe it when I heard what happened. We were all shocked. You hear of things like this in other countries, where people don't know any better. Not here. Not here. I can't believe it."

There's more but I'm lost in the pictures of Ted Bracewell going up there week after week and never suspecting, despite the strangeness he must have been able to see in Mary. I mean, just look at the way she wrote in the diary, all that religious stuff and letting the farm go to rack and ruin.

A small item in the *Daily Mirror* on Monday, 24th November 1975 makes me smile.

CHICKEN SHED HERO'S FOOTBALL JOY
"THAT'S MY BOY," SAYS PROUD DAD

Schoolboy hero Norman Forster, who discovered Vicky the chicken shed girl at Scarclough, Lancashire last week, is to meet the Liverpool football team and be given a grand tour of the Anfield ground. Afterwards Norman will have a special afternoon tea with all his favourite football stars and their manager. Proud dad Robert Forster said, "That's my boy. He deserves it."

"There's not much about you in all this. Norman seems to have got all the kudos."

"That's life, isn't it? Norman's dad were pushy. Taught Norman to be the same. He always got anything that were going, even though he had twice as much as the rest of us and more."

"Do they still live here?"

"No they moved away around 1980. Harrogate I think. Norm's dad were a good businessman, you have to give him that. Went from butcher to manager of a string of retail outlets to owning a few meat-packing plants. I never heard from them. They never had any family here. I think they come up from Wigan originally."

He looks down at where his finger marks his place in the diary. It's a clear message. I turn the scrapbook page. The date has moved on.

The *Skelmersdale Advertiser,* Thursday, March 25th 1976

INQUEST HELD ON BROW LANE TRAGEDY

Inquiries into the death of a local woman found that faulty electrical equipment caused a tragic accident. The inquest on Mary Appleton, spinster of Brow Lane Farm, Scarclough, was held on Monday March 22nd last at Preston Coroner's Court.

Evidence was given by PC Charles Woods of Skelmersdale police station. PC Woods stated that he and PC Graham Ashworth attended Brow Lane Farm on Monday 11th November 1975 following a report by a Mr Robert Forster that there was a dead body in the farmhouse.

PC Woods stated that when they arrived they had found Mr Forster, a Mr Daniel Atherton and their sons, at the door of the farm-house. The body of a woman was lying face up on the floor in the hall-way. She was holding an electric plug in one hand which was half inserted into a socket on the wall. A vacuum cleaner lay beside her.

Suspecting electrocution and aware of possible danger to life, PC Woods stated that he asked Mr Forster, Mr Atherton and their sons to move away while he attempted to detach the plug from the socket with a wooden washing prop which he eventually managed to do. PC Ashworth had meanwhile called the police station and summoned the police doctor. Finding the body very cold, PC Woods did not attempt any resuscitation.

At this point, PC Woods stated, a lot of strange noises were heard coming from an old chicken shed in the yard. PC Woods stated that he looked through holes in the wooden planks of the shed and saw something moving about and crying inside, but he could not recognise what kind of animal it might be. Both police officers then broke down the door and discovered a small child in a neglected condition.

It hid in a corner of the shed and attempted to bite them when approached.

PC Woods then stated that the police doctor arrived with Detective Inspector Peter Venables and DC John Morgan from the Skelmersdale police. An ambulance was summoned and the child was eventually overcome and sedated, then removed to Ormskirk Hospital.

Police surgeon Dr Harold Serjeant gave evidence that he examined the body, identified as Mary Appleton, at the farmhouse and concluded that she had died at the scene and had been dead for approximately 30 hours. Death appeared to be due to electrocution.

Detective Inspector Venables of Skelmersdale police station gave evidence that the circumstances suggested accidental electrocution. The farmhouse was in poor condition and the electrical system appeared to date from the 1920s with old cables and sockets in a poor state of repair. The plug to the vacuum cleaner was not earthed and the cable was frayed in several places. There did not appear to be any suspicious circumstances and there was nothing to indicate any suicidal intention despite the tragedy of the child discovered in the shed.

The post mortem report indicated death by electrocution and stated that Mrs Appleton's body was otherwise well nourished and in good health.

Coroner Mr Alistair Forsyth gave a verdict of accidental death by electrocution and commented that the need for regular maintenance of household electric wiring and appliances could not be overstated.

He said, "This is a death that could have easily been avoided. While it is not strictly the concern of this court the only positive thing to come out of this tragic case is the rescue of the child in the shed and its return to a caring society."

We understand that the child, Vicky, is no longer at Ormskirk Hospital. She has been transferred to a specialist hospital dealing with disturbed children. Staff at Ormskirk Hospital are unable to divulge further details.

"Vicky made excellent physical progress while in our care," Sister Margaret Owens told our reporter, "but the press and public interest have made life very difficult for us all. She will now get the specialist help she needs in a quiet and peaceful environment. Our long term hope is that she may eventually be able to live in a more home-like setting."

I come back to where I'm sitting. Jimmy Atherton is still reading with tears in his eyes. His fingers touch the page, almost feeling the words that Mary wrote. There is still garden dirt under his fingernails.

He looks up and shakes his head. "The way we laughed at her. Scary Mary, Mad Mary, even grownups like my dad. This is – is just tormented. I knew she were crazy from things I found out later." He pauses. Again, there's that moment, his eyes turn secretive and he shifts on his chair. There's something he doesn't want to give away.

"She must have been so lonely. Even when her dad were alive he were a nouty beggar, all the kids were scared of him. We wouldn't have dared to play up there while he were alive.

"No one ever found out who the father were. The papers had a field-day with their imaginings. You know there were people round here as thought her dad were the father of the child, but when you looked at it the dates just didn't add up. I heard my dad tell my mum it must have been Ted Bracewell as he were the only one who ever went up there. This fills in some of the gaps. Wonder where this Michael went. He sounds like a heartless bastard. If only we'd realised what were happening to her, had a bit of compassion."

"You were only a kid."

"Yeah but I still feel guilty. And what about the adults? They just left her to get on with it. Poor Mary."

"It doesn't excuse what she did. Poor Vicky."

He looks confused. "I never really thought much about her. She's never really seemed human to me. Mary couldn't help what she did."

We look at each other across the expanse of the nicely polished table, the diary and scrapbook spread out between us. I drop my gaze back to the newspaper cuttings. There are articles from newspapers and magazines scattered over the years from 1988 to 1995 but they're just rehashes of the original news items and it's hard to tell if any of the information is accurate. Just as Jimmy Atherton's account differs from the early reports, so the later articles show discrepancies and there are no concrete clues as to where Vicky ended up. The last cutting is fairly recent, the paper still freshly off white. It's from the *Ormskirk Advertiser* dated Thursday 20th January 2006.

There's a jolly picture of uniformed nurses and doctors. Sister Owens is cutting a cake. She looks smart and self-assured. This is only a few months ago. It's the only clue I've found in the whole scrapbook. Why has he kept this? Does he know her?

"Margaret Owens?"

He's finished reading the diary and he's been watching me read.

"She were the ward sister, where they took the child."

"Do you know her? Do you know where she lives?"

"No. I only clipped it because it mentions the Appleton case." It's as if he can't bring himself to name Vicky, to invest her with a human personality. "Nothing there of much use to you?" He folds his arms across his chest and doesn't meet my eyes.

"Nothing that will help me to find her but, Christ, I'm beginning to understand what happened to her. Why she doesn't talk. It's unbelievable."

"I'm surprised she were let out. Is it safe to let someone like that out on the street?"

"I don't know if she was let out. But anyway, thirty years have gone by. She's not that creature you saw."

"You mean she might have escaped?" He looks alarmed as if he thinks she too might turn up on his doorstep. I can't help smiling.

"I don't know, but she managed to survive on the streets before I met her. People take care of her. There's something about her." I think of the way she touched my leg, how she knew about it, how she knew about Peter, even though she couldn't have.

"She's special." It sounds ludicrous, but I don't owe him any explanation. "Anyway the police picked her up. That's why I'm trying to find her. She needs help."

He looks sceptical. "What's it to you anyway? She got some kind of hold on you?"

"In a way." This makes me smile again. "It's getting dark. I'd better be going."

"Got somewhere to stay tonight? I suppose I could put you up if you like?"

"There's a place for me in the hostel in Skem." It's a lie but I don't want to stay here. He's starting to ask too many questions. Besides I've got other plans.

His hand hovers over the diary. "I'd really like to keep this."

"Sorry." I palm it quickly. "It's not mine to give. It belongs to Vicky."

Now there is guilt on his face when he looks at me.

"Just a minute." He goes out again and comes back carrying a couple of books. "You can have this. I can get another copy."

It's one of those popular books of regional folklore and stranger than fiction accounts with a rather predictable title, *Strange But True Tales Of Lancashire*. The third chapter is titled, "The Curious Tale of the Chicken Shed Girl".

"Thanks." I shoulder my pack. The dog runs up and shoves its muzzle in my hand as I open the back door.

"Hold on." He pushes something into my hand. "You'd better take this. I found it up there a couple of years after it were all over. It were hidden in the lav outside. I never showed it to no one. It belongs with the other one. Come away Jimbo." He drags the dog off into the other room.

I look down. It's a cheap exercise book with a red cover, like the ones I used to have as a child. My heart jumps as I open it and see the familiar pothook script.

"Let me know if you find her." I turn to see his burly shape silhouetted against the open door. I want to stop and thank him properly. I know it's cost him a lot to part with it. I want to stay and read it right away, but the door closes before I can say anything.

It's almost dark as I climb the slope back up to Ashurst Beacon with my fingers clutched round the book in my pocket as if it might burn a hole through the cloth. I want to stop and read it, but I won't let myself, not until I get to where I'm going.

At the head of the lane, I look down into the tunnel of trees. Maybe this isn't such a good idea but it's something I've set myself to do.

Along the top road, although there were no streetlights, the distant lights of Skelmersdale and Wigan diffused the alien dark of the countryside, but in the lane the black is whole, pierced only by the squeaks and scurryings of unseen creatures.

I don't use my torch. My eyes have adjusted during my journey and I need to conserve the batteries for reading later. Still, I stumble up the path once I've got through the gate and just like Jimmy Atherton playing space wars I keep thinking I can see shapes moving in the bushes. Poor Jimmy, he found out too young there are plenty of real monsters out there. They get inside you and then you can never get them out.

There's no moon but it's a dry night, no dew and not too cold. There's a bit of a breeze but not enough to chill. It would make sense to camp in the shelter of the ruined farmhouse but I can't face the singing of the wind through the holes in the brickwork or the rustlings in the ivy that's transforming the structure. It sounds like so many voices telling their stories: Mary's, Vicky's, Mary's father's and more, many more, older, going back, repeating, re-inventing.

It would make more sense not to be here at all, to trek back down the hill to Skelmersdale and throw myself on the mercy of Elaine or Greg but I feel that by staying here maybe I can feel Vicky, sense something about where she is, reach out for her somehow.

On the edge of the field overlooking the motorway, I spread my groundsheet in front of a hedge of brambles. It's a while since I slept out in the open and the air feels fresh and clean after weeks of urban grime.

I make tea on the primus stove and stare into the blue flames, with the age-old attraction of fire heightened by the enveloping darkness. Once it kept away wolves, their greedy eyes gleaming in the dense night, but here there are only the squeaks of unseen rabbits and the occasional bat flying overhead.

Only when I'm comfortably wrapped in my sleeping bag do I allow myself to open the red notebook. The torch glimmers eerily on the paper. The writing starts mid-sentence and, checking the other one, I see it's a direct continuation.

round the new estates, they are crying out for eggs and vegetables, especially spuds. Ted said it's not too late to plant, Mary and I seen him eyeing up the fields. I held my peace. I'm busy enough as it is, but more eggs will be easy enough, providing this new rooster does his job.

Tuesday 16th July 1968
All is fruitful. I am overrun with produce, even selling some to Ted, peas and beans, even raspberries. There are many new chicks too, there will be plenty of eggs next year. Ted rubs his hands. I see the money twinkle in his eye for he is the slave of Mammon but I am hopeful that this prosperity is a sign. In my heart I think God sees my repentance and my humble acceptance of my lot and thinks of forgiveness. Is it possible that my punishment may come to an end?

Wednesday 24th July 1968
Ted brung papers today. All days are the same here except Wednesdays. Ted spies and watches but I can't live without the things he brings for the eggs. I could spend Dad's money instead but then people would know and come here to spy and steal like Michael.

Sunday 8th September 1968
Today I am twenty two. Twelve months already since that day in Wigan with its sinful people. Even here now they drive up the top road in cars and come in the fields, fornicating under the hedges and leaving beer bottles everywhere. If only Barney were still here.

I must watch constantly but I am of good cheer. All is well and my garden is still full of vegetables. God begins to turn his face towards me. An angel come to me in a dream and telled me I am to keep guard. Watch, guard, record, so my sin may be wiped out. Oh, to be free of sin, like the white pages of this book, yet this book come from a sinful place. To be clean seems an impossible thing.

October
It is sick. Should I rejoice? I prayed but the angel would not come. It lies on the floor and leaves food untouched. This morning it would not move no matter how much I shouted or poked it with the brush. In the

end I had to touch it though it always makes my flesh crawl to do so. It were alive still, but hot and sweaty. I filled the water hopper and thought whether I should succour it.

I sat in the lav and prayed and at last the angel come and told me what to do. I went back to the shed and wiped it with a wet cloth. This seemed a bad thing for it opened its eyes and looked at me and I saw Hell in there. I were frickened and ran away and it were nearly dark before I could go back with the blanket like the angel told me to. I were still scared but the Lord's will must be done. I moved the water nearer for it to drink and I come back in to the light and the warmth of the fire.

That were all the angel told me to do. I sat by the fire and thought on why these instructions were given, but it is not for sinful humans to know the Lord's intentions. It is in His hands now.

Wednesday

It has eaten nothing for five days but it drinks the water. Ted were early today and I were still cleaning the shed when he come in the yard but it made no noise so I got out without Ted noticing anything. He frickened me, coming sudden like that. You don't look well, Mary, he says and he looked at me in that spying way of his. Why don't you come down to the village, have a cup of tea with Elsie, see the shop, get Dr Andrews to have a look at you.

I could see the serpent in him and I wanted to drive him away but I can't afford to do that. Don't need no one, I telled him. Just take the eggs and mind your own business. I will have to do something about Ted but first I must wait to see if it will live.

Thursday

It is better. The bread and water I left it were all gone when I went in this morning. Now there is rain, rain and more rain, for two days now like God is displeased. Can it be that I got the instructions wrong or that the angel is the Devil in disguise?

I am unsettled tonight, my thoughts running loose so I can't rest, and strange feelings, like something I don't understand or don't want to think about but it keeps forcing its way into my mind.

When I thought it might die I were frickened when I should have rejoiced and now there are doubts and fears because there seems a gladness in me that it will live. How can this be? Evil must still be rooted in me when I thought I had cast it off. Thoughts of where it must go, back to Hell from whence it came sent shivers through me as I waited to see what would become of it. I must watch my step or I will share the same fate.

Were it sadness I felt when I thought it would die? And there were fear, the fear of change, of what would happen to me. There would be no need for me to stay or to go. This is wicked thinking, selfishness. I do not know God's purpose in all this. I must follow his will without thought, without reason. God help me, I feel I am drowning. I must pray.

Dad come to me in a dream, his eyes full of fire. Repent, Mary, repent your sin. His voice were like thunder and I did repent, but he forced my head down on the open Bible and the black letters on the paper burned themselves onto my eyeballs. I saw the sighting of Canaan by the Chosen Ones, the rejoicing of the wandering Children of Israel. You can never leave here, Dad told me, listen Mary, and he dug his fingers into my neck. On the night breeze I heard the sound of it screeching in the shed.

You see, Dad said and I woke up and dawn were breaking but the noise carried on, the sound of the wind howling round the rooftop, only the wind.

Winter

Snow – bitter, bitter snow. Ten days now and the leeks stiff like stone posts in the ground. I live on eggs and potatoes. Ted has not been I think since eight days gone. There is no flour left for bread. I must be careful with wood for the fire. The snow is too deep to gather more. The chickens have mostly kept to their shed, keeping each other warm. In the other shed it seems to take no mind of the cold. The Devil takes no care of fire nor ice.

Dad comes almost every night. I hear his heavy tread on the stair, the whisper of his leather belt, drawn from his waist. In the mornings I am sore from chastisement. In the shed it gloats, gobbling its food, watching, watching while I scrub the filthy mess it makes.

February. Wednesday

I must hide this book. Ted is always spying. I don't know how you stays here Mary, he said today and he's looking all round the yard, peering through the house windows. It's a waste, young woman like you.

I know you, I told him, I know you of old. I could see the Devil in him like Jesus when he cast out Legion. Get thee hence. I went for the yardbrush and Ted took to his heels but he'll be back. Maybe when I'm not looking, maybe when I'm sleeping. What if my sin should be discovered? It's quiet now, it's so quiet, only now and then it makes noises to itself. What them noises mean I cannot tell but mostly it is quiet.

Spring

Thank God winter is over. The hens are laying well now. Dad telled me to beware of Ted Bracewell. I leave the eggs in a basket by the gate with a list of what I want from the shop. I don't want him nosing around.

There will never be an end. The Bible falls open at Ezekiel. All his righteousness shall not be remembered but for his iniquity that he has committed, he shall die for it. I walked around the fields all grown over and ragged. Today this seems a Godforsaken place.

Will Jesus not save me? Truly I have repented and suffered.

I must put my life in the hands of the Lord. Father, forgive me. Consider the lilies, how they grow, they toil not, they spin not.

And the ravens who neither sow nor reap

I turn the page. It's blank. So are all the rest. Inside the sleeping bag, I'm cold as ice. I can feel her madness all around me; the dark horror of what was done here seeping from the tumbled stones. I want to get up and run back to the normal world of streetlights and traffic and cosy homes. Oh, Vicky, Christ, how did you survive here, trapped with this insane woman? Where are you now?

* * *

marjori e e e e e e   sleep sleeeeeeeep eyes
                              stick

                                         thirsty
marjoriemarjorie   noneedle no   marjorie yes yes
marjorie
          medication   yes be good yes   sleep   sle e e e
e eee
no hermitjack   hermitjack nomarjorie   vicky wake up vicky
wake up hermitjack redgreyblack   redroundvicky   run
vicky run run vicky

runvicky no no stopit noneedle stopit stopitstopitstopit   no ma rjo no   o

* * *

There's no way I'm going to sleep. I turn the stove down low. In the dark I can feel Mary Appleton's madness creeping through the bushes as if it's gained its own separate existence. Jimmy was wrong about those triffids, they're real up here.

I snap the torch on again and try to calm myself by pulling out the other book he gave me and reading "The Curious Tale of the Chicken Shed Girl".

It's a short account, highly stylised and geared to titillate. There's much play on Mary's immorality contrasted with her religious fervour and a lot of speculation on the identity of Vicky's father. Mary's father is prime suspect, ignoring the fact that he died two years before Vicky was born. Although they're not named, for obvious reasons, Ted Bracewell and Gordon Stanley, the post-boy, emerge as other possible candidates. It's as if their shades are here watching even though they may still be alive, as I read their story. It's frightening to be on the spot where the events took place, where these people walked and talked, but it brings me down to earth, away from the insane logic of the later diary entries.

The end of the tale brings new information:

> Children like this are always a source of intense interest to scientists who hope to learn more about the links between humans and animals. Vicky spent several years undergoing rehabilitation programmes designed by psychologists, psychiatrists, linguists and various educational theorists. From 1975 until 1980 she lived in a specialist centre for grossly deprived children.
>
> Although at first she made good progress and learned to speak and communicate, she never developed the full use of language. In 1980 she was transferred to a residential care home.

The book was written in 2002. It's a small local press, Red Rose publications, based in Penrith. Maybe I'll be able to trace the author, someone called Eric Fisher. This is good. I've two lines to follow up, Eric Fisher and Margaret Owens.

When I turn off the stove, the night folds round me and again I'm aware of another world of life going on round me, layered over the older sensation of evil I get from the land and the crumbled buildings. The farmhouse stands silent behind me but I don't want to look at or think about it. I watch the moving lights on the motorway, the M6 that connects here to my home town, the place where friends and family live as if on a separate island.

"*A specialist centre for grossly deprived children.*" I rack my brains but nothing comes to mind. Maybe I'll need to get help to find out more, to spin out a bridge across to that island I cut myself off from so long ago. It's not the first time I've thought about it. Many's the time I've gone into a phone box, stood with the receiver in my hand and my fingers poised over the buttons, but I've never done it.

Even though Jed supported me, covered for me when I was drinking, argued with me, told me the truth and wouldn't let go of me, wouldn't give me up for the useless bastard I was ... even though he visited me in hospital, helped Corinne through the funeral, was always there for me and never blamed me once ... even though he was my one true friend since we met as students, I didn't trust him enough, didn't trust his belief in me or his friendship.

I didn't even tell him I was going. I just walked away, out of the hospital, the day before I was due to be discharged. I was sitting outside the ward in the sunshine, thinking about how I was going to stay with Penny, my sister, instead of returning to my own home. Corinne had waited until I was up and walking to tell me she was getting a divorce but it hadn't been a surprise. I couldn't have faced going back to the house anyway.

There were a lot of things I couldn't face. While my injuries were healing, I was pre-occupied with the business of learning to be a patient instead of a doctor; coping with pain and the persistent effort required for recovery and trying to deal with the concept that I was now a different person, bodily and mentally.

But then I began to realise I was expected to pick up the threads of life again, take up my position and carry on. I was terrified. How was I going to go back to the surgery with Jed, face the silences and concerned looks from the staff and patients? It wasn't fair, to me or to them. My world had completely shifted and the courses I followed before now seemed totally irrelevant. There was nothing to go back for. Penny didn't want me. Her cold face told me that she had nothing but contempt for me. She was only offering me a bed out of her sense of duty to the family.

It was easy. I put my stuff in a carrier bag and went. In the taxi, I felt only relief. When the driver asked, "Where to, mate?" it was like a load had lifted off my shoulders.

All those cars going up and down the motorway, even now late at night; people just like I used to be, maybe even people I used to know, friends and colleagues with places to go, people to see. The pinpoints of light swim in the dark.

This time maybe I can face the scorn if it means I can find out what I need to know. I realise now that Jed would never reject me, even if others will. Perhaps, after all this time, I owe him an explanation. But can I make that walk back now?

Corinne is getting ready to go out. The gleam of the stockings on her legs, the arch of her instep in her high-heel sandals make me want her. I can't take my eyes off her movements. The dull dark red of her dress softens her skin, the cut of the fabric slides, skimming the shape of her buttocks. Delicious! I could go up behind her, put my arms round her and feel her breasts, have them heavy in my hands. My fingers tingle. I could touch my lips to that spot between her neck and her collarbone. My mouth waters. I'm going to do it, going to get up and go to her.

She turns, her heavy gold hair glinting in the lamplight. It's sleek, shiny like an oiled snake. I want it between my fingers; want to rub it in my face.

A single diamond drop sparkles at her throat, my Christmas present to her the year we were married. It's perfect. I'm lost, locked in love and desire.

"How many have you had?" This harsh voice knocks at my ears. Her mouth is a bloodless line. Her eyes are ice. Instantly, I feel myself shrivel.

"Why do you do this Jack?" It's like hammers – no, ice picks – driving in my brain. I put my hands over my ears. "You can't possibly go like this. You'll have to stay here. I'll say you had to work late."

"I'm all right." I get to my feet but the ringing in my ears makes the room wobble. The door slams and there's only the trace of her perfume; the perfume and the musk of her body that she can never quite cover up, that she probably isn't even aware of. Oh Corinne! The Glenfiddich has its own musky scent that soon overrides hers.

The doorbell rings. I'm watching Countdown on TV. Angela's friend Lucy is at the door. She's a pert thirteen-year-old, breasts and body rounding out but her skeleton still retaining the coltish long bones of a growing child. She's neat in Nike top and track pants with the latest designer trainers. She's come to visit the stables with Angela. It's their day for grooming the ponies, but Angela's not here. She's already gone.

"I'll take you," I say and she looks at me thankfully.

It's good to be in charge and I love the way the car responds to my commands. My hands are powerful on the wheel. Lucy is small in the passenger seat . . . and then it's dark and I'm in a cold room. It's so cold and the lights are dim. There's something on a table and I don't want to look.

The door opens, the light floods in and I know that shape in the doorway but there's something wrong with it, something terribly wrong. She comes nearer. There's nothing gleaming now. Her hair hangs in rats' tails, the red dress is dull like dried blood, her mouth is a dark slash. The diamond is ice at her throat and her eyes are just holes.

"It's all right Corinne." I want to run to her but my feet are nailed to the floor. "It's all right, it's not her. It's not —"

At last I can move. I spring at her, catch her hand, drag her towards the table. "It's Lucy. Look, it's only Lucy. It's not —" then the body sits up and looks at me with Vicky's eyes.

I'm awake, wet with sweat and shivering, all my senses floundering as the vision splinters in front of me. Then I feel the cold air on my face, the greasy nylon of the sleeping bag grasped in my clutching hands and the teeth of the zip against my throat.

Relief and sorrow rush in at once but at least wash the horror away. The background filters in. There are noises. In a while I perceive they are sounds of joy; birds, seems like thousands of them, welcoming the grey light that begins to leach the blackness.

* * *

The hospital at Ormskirk is a new building, all glass and yellow brick, but the older buildings round it testify to its cottage origins.

I've little money left after paying the bus fare here, but there's enough for tea and toast in the hospital canteen and a wash and brush up in the toilets costs nothing.

I can't stop myself glancing at the doctors as they hurry past me in the corridor although it's hardly likely that I would know any of them. The girl at the information desk is smart yet casual. Her smile is impersonal.

"I'm trying to trace a nurse. A Sister Margaret Owens."

The smile wavers. "Sister Owens? Do you know which ward she works on?"

"I don't think she actually works here any more. She retired not long ago. I need to get in touch with her."

"I don't recall anyone of that name." Her fingers move over her keyboard.

A porter stops at the desk. "Fran, do you want anything from the canteen? I'm going on break."

"Owens, Owens, Owens." She's scanning lists, her mouth shapes the names, the sound comes out in a low whisper.

"She worked on the mental health unit."

"Sister Owens? She retired in January." The porter looks at me.

"I know, but I need to get in touch with her. Doesn't she live in Aughton?" I'm racking my brains for a plausible reason for contacting her if they ask but he cuts me short.

"Not any more. She died. Had a heart attack two months after she left. Enough to give you goose pimples, isn't it? Happened to my mate just the same. Couldn't wait to retire, took up golf. Bang, two weeks later, had a stroke, dropped dead. Take my advice Fran, carry on working as long as you can."

He turns back to me. "Her daughter works in the coffee shop, voluntary like." He nods towards the hospital entrance. There's a tiny coffee bar tucked to one side. I hadn't noticed it when I came in. "That's her. Rosie Slater. She might be able to help you."

Rosie Slater is dark and slightly gipsyish with a nervous glance. An elastic hairband struggles to contain her luxuriant curls. Her eyes are tired under makeup that is too heavy and old-fashioned.

"Poor Mum." She pours me a cup of coffee that I can ill afford. "She didn't get to enjoy her retirement. She had ideas for setting up a self-help group for discharged patients from her ward. Did you know her?"

She obviously thinks I'm an ex-patient and a few years ago I certainly could have been.

"She once nursed a friend of mine. Someone I lost touch with. I was hoping she'd be able to help me find her."

"Oh, she wouldn't have been able to tell you anything. It's a matter of patient confidentiality."

"It was a very long time ago. You might remember her. The girl who was found in a chicken shed at Scarclough."

She looks bemused for a second, then she recoils slightly and her face wrinkles with disgust. "Oh that. That was years and years ago. I was only a little tot. Of course I heard tell about it over the years but it's not something you want to think about, is it?

"Horrible. You say you used to know her, the girl. What was her name?"

"Vicky. Not then, no. I got to know her recently. We were friends, then we lost touch."

"Oh." Her face is closing. She looks suspiciously at my clothes, my pack, my face. "She's still alive then? I never thought – well, I supposed she'd be in a home somewhere."

"I think she is. I need to find out where."

"Well my mum wouldn't have known. That was over twenty years ago. How would that help you?"

"I don't know. I don't know where to start. I'm just trying anything, anyone who might know anything about her. Maybe she's been taken back to a place she was at years before."

"Isn't that the best thing for her?" She wipes the counter. Her eyes are hard when she looks at me. "I'm sorry I can't help you. All I remember is some talk about her being moved somewhere down south. It was a few years ago, at least I think it was her."

The sun is out when I come through the glass doors and it's unusually hot for late September. I'm starting to sweat under the weight of my pack and my hip begins to grumble as I make my way towards the shops. It's getting near to my lunch-time dose of co-codamol.

Ormskirk's one of those little towns with the standard old church and pedestrianised market area that still pays homage to the original crossroads marketplace. Now it's a mixture of chain-store outlets, charity shops and touristy gift-shops and cafes. The kind of place coach tours stop off to while away a couple of hours.

There's an employment agency but I know it's hopeless, when I go in, by the way the smart lad at the desk watches me as I limp towards him.

"We've only got skilled jobs on offer." He puts on a friendly face, vaguely regretful. "Office work, data input, qualified IT engineers, that kind of thing. We used to have a lot of farm work, and quite a bit of catering, but it's all contracted out to gangs of Polish workers now. If you'll excuse me for saying so, you don't look fit enough to do any physical work. Shouldn't you be on sick benefit at your age?"

Sick benefit? Do I look that bad? I bet I could beat him any day at anything physical, false leg or no. He's soft as a slug from sitting at that desk all day, but then he's always going to be right. He's got his accepted place in society and I haven't.

I sit on a bench under the town clock eating a pasty and watching a busker outside W. H. Smiths. He's not having much luck either. In the end I stop worrying about money and make my way to the library where I ask the attendant how to find out about the Red Rose Press.

She directs me to the *Writers' Handbook* in the reference section and my heart leaps when I see it's listed there. There's a web address and an email address that I copy down, but how am I going to communicate with them when I'm never in one place long enough to receive any messages?

There's another bench outside the library and I sit in the sun and ponder. Even though it's hot and my body's sweating, my inner core feels frozen. All these enquiries seem to come to nothing. I'm no nearer to finding Vicky and now I'm stuck here with no money and no prospects of getting any.

There's an old red phone box near the bench and I keep looking at it, thinking of the lifeline it represents. A lifeline to Jed, not to Matt or Penny, certainly not to Corinne. I think Jed will help me without too many recriminations, but for all I know he might be in a different practice now, even live in a different place.

How long have I been sitting here dithering? The afternoon shadows are lengthening and I've nowhere else to go. My fingers keep rubbing the fifty-pence piece in my pocket. Before I can change my mind I go in the phone box and dial the surgery number. "Please be there, please be there," I'm muttering when the receptionist answers.

"Dr Knox is in surgery at present. He can't take any calls."

"It's urgent, do you hear? Put me through. It's Dr Crabbe." I realise I'm shouting then the phone clicks.

His voice is so familiar but strangely quiet. Is it surprise or suspicion?

"Buster? Buster, is it you?" At the sound of my old nickname tears well up in my eyes.

CHAPTER FOUR

I get to Knutsford services about three o'clock on Thursday afternoon. It's taken a long time. People are more cautious about who they pick up nowadays. Maybe I just look rougher than I think.

I'm on edge. I keep going over what Jed said on the phone for clues as to how he reacted. I spent last night under a hedge near the M58 and, as well as being uncomfortable, I tortured myself with bad memories and fears of what lies ahead.

I'm deadly cold, even though I'm sitting on a bench in the sunshine outside the service station. It's an ordinary scene, with people coming and going in cars and coaches. I don't belong in it and I'm wishing I wasn't here, but I feel the notebooks in my coat pocket and know I have to see this through.

At last Jed comes and I know him at once, but he doesn't recognise me. He hasn't changed, at least not as dramatically as I have. Still got the MG and still wearing the old sweat pants and crumpled tee shirt he keeps in the bottom drawer of his desk so he can rush off to play badminton after work.

He's wandering blindly round the car park looking at people and then he heads off towards the service building. I have to approach him. For a moment I consider just melting back into the bushes, it would be easy to disappear from here, catch a lift to anywhere. I think of Vicky and heave to my feet.

"Jed."

He spins round. "Buster! Jeez! Buster, what happened to you?" He tries to hide his dismay with a smile but it wobbles.

"It's called streetlife." I smile back but my smile falters too. I'm thinking how we were students together at the Infirmary, of all the fun and earnestness we shared. Memories of those days seem to be all highs and lows, everything full of meaning. We were driven by emotion and idealism, then we flattened out into the years of working together, sharing the practice. We both had beautiful wives, lovely children, professional recognition, everything going for us, until I messed it all up.

"Let's get something to eat. I'm starving." What he means is "Let me feed you Jack, you look like you need it." He seems to feel guilty about me. It's written all over his face.

I let him buy me a burger, chips and coffee. At first he doesn't say much, just watches me eat, but soon it begins.

"Where have you been all this time? Why didn't you keep in touch?"

"After what I did? I couldn't face anyone. What use was I to anyone – to myself even? I didn't want to be me any more."

I've managed that pretty well, being somebody else or nobody maybe. Nobody that means anything to anybody. Nobody that's required to do anything.

"Don't talk bollocks, Jack. How could you just walk away like that? How do you think I felt? How do you think Corinne felt?"

Corinne? I stop chewing. Surely she must have been delighted? For a moment I look at him and see the sports-car driver, the respected member of a professional body, the consumer of precious spare-time hobbies, the confident, well published academic. I shouldn't have come. The food tastes like cardboard.

"I'm sorry." I push the food container away.

Suddenly he smiles and he's just my good mate Jed again, as if those bad times didn't lie between us.

"You look different."

"Yeah. I'm someone else. My street name is the Hermit."

He bursts out laughing.

"Okay. It started because of my surname but now it's become me or I've become it. I like it. I like the freedom, the anonymity, the way

I can just move on and leave everything behind when I've had enough."

Is this true? Even now, as I sit here, remnants of those other selves – the husband, the doctor, the drinker, the father – are rising up, resurrected by Jed's presence.

"Why didn't you ring before? Even just to let me know you were okay? And why now? It's been over four years."

"I wasn't okay. I told you. I wanted to be someone else. But now I need your help. I couldn't turn to the family. They wouldn't understand. There'd be too many strings and recriminations. I don't need money or a place to stay. I need you to help me find someone."

He's surprised. He was expecting a request for material help, cash or care.

"What do you mean?"

"I met this woman on the street, in Liverpool. She'd been in care somewhere, I don't know where. The squat we were in was raided and the police took her away. I can't find out where they sent her. I need to find her, Jed." My voice breaks unexpectedly. He's staring at me as if I'm crazy.

"In care? What for?"

"She's got problems, learning disabilities." I don't want to go into the horror of it all now.

"You've been having a hot affair with a woman with learning disabilities?" He pushes his chair back and frowns at me.

"It's not like that."

He doesn't understand. I have to tell him the bare bones of the story and give him Fisher's book to read while I finish my coffee. I don't show him the notebooks; he's not ready for them yet.

He's fascinated, I can tell, quite apart from his desire to help me. As a medical man he's intrigued and perhaps he assigns the same motives to me. Now my search makes sense to him.

He shuts the book, puffs out his cheeks. "Jeez, Buster, is this for real?"

I nod. "No one will tell me anything. You've got contacts. You might be able to find her."

"It means you'll have to come back with me."

"I don't think I can do that, Jed."

"Then how are we going to keep in touch? Come and stay with me for a few days. No strings, you can leave whenever you want. We can work on this together."

It's tempting. Another haven of home comforts and access to information systems, a way of tracing Vicky maybe.

"But what about Becky?" Becky and Corinne were never great friends but we often used to go out as a foursome and after what happened I can't see Becky having any time for me whatsoever.

"Becky and I split up two years ago." He looks away and his face hardens. "She's living in Bournemouth now with an organic farmer. I don't get to see the kids often enough."

"Oh." I forget that other people's lives carry on when you leave them. Inside me Jed has been frozen the way he was when I last saw him. I thought he hadn't changed, but looking closer I can see the lines, a difference in the way he holds the muscles of his jaw. I wonder if the break-up was something to do with me, an outward ripple from the trauma I caused to everyone around me.

"It was nothing to do with you, with what happened. We just grew away from each other."

I hope desperately that he's not lying. I've got enough to feel guilty about already.

"What about Corinne? My family? I wouldn't want them to find out I was around."

There's a silence. His mouth works at the corner. He's dredging something up from inside.

"Jack, Corinne got married again. Eighteen months ago. She's pregnant."

The words hit me like stones. "Pregnant? But she's —"

"Yep, over forty. Forty-four to be exact. Not impossible."

No, not impossible. I hadn't argued when she told me she would divorce me. Nothing could put our marriage together again after Angela's death. At least she'd waited until I was recovering from the amputation. And, yes, sometimes I'd thought about her meeting a new man, but never, ever did I think she might have another child. How could she? As if anything could replace Angela. Now I want to put my head on the table and cry.

"She had a hard time, Jack. Now she's happy. He's a nice guy. She just wants to forget. Make a new life." He's trying to be gentle, not to blame me. "Come on back with me. No one will know. Corinne lives in Gloucester now. You won't need to see anyone if you don't want to. We'll see if we can find this Vicky. You can rest up, make plans. No strings, I promise."

I should be happy for Corinne but I feel betrayed. I'm gutted. I feel so empty I can't think straight and the next thing I know, I'm squashed in the passenger seat of the MG, speeding down the M6 as the darkness closes in.

* * *

The first night he leaves me alone but he's only biding his time. I know the probing will soon begin. Straight-talking he'll call it and I won't like it. I've been free these five years, free to be whoever I want and I haven't had to justify or explain myself to anyone.

It's late when we get back to Worcester and although something's tugging inside me as we travel along the twisting rural lanes that are so different from the flat Lancashire landscape, from industrial Manchester or the decayed elegance of Liverpool, there's little to see in the dark and we soon hit the outskirts of Ronkswood. Jed still lives in the 1930s villa he bought when we set up the practice.

"This place is a bit big for you to rattle round in on your own." The space and silence of the house threaten me.

"I keep thinking the kids will come to stay." In the hall light, his face is woebegone then he wipes it with a cheery smile. "You know me. I'm one of those stay-put people."

Not like me. For a moment all the places I've been in the last few years, all the people I've known briefly, melt together. Was there any meaning in it all? I don't know.

"Want a drink?" He stops, hesitates.

"No, I don't think so. I'm tired." I'm so weary my brain is rambling.

"Me too and I've got surgery first thing in the morning. It's half day tomorrow though. When I get back we can start trying to find your friend."

I lie awake in the cold bed that no one's slept in for ages. I should be comfortable but I feel shut in, frightened of what's coming next. Even Jed, my oldest and best friend, frightens me with his ordered life, his clocks and duties, his possessions and this house that holds him in one spot. I'd forgotten this kind of life and now it seems alien to me. Maybe it's just his hopes that tie him, hopes of resurrecting the past, bringing back Becky or at least the kids. I suppose it's easy to find meaning while you still have hopes.

I thought I'd left all that behind, those excuses that keep hope alive, help you to carry on, but now, after years of wandering, I realise there is some sense of purpose coming back to me, seeds of hope sprouting, planted there by Vicky's vision of Angela, of the car. I want there to be an explanation, whether it condemns me or not. I need a resolution.

I know they said I wasn't drunk when the accident happened. I had to believe them, they'd tested my blood, but I knew it was my fault. There was no one else involved. I hit a tree on a straight road. Corinne knew it too and she made it plain the only time she visited me in hospital, to tell me about the divorce.

"You shouldn't have driven. You had the shakes didn't you? Tell me, Jack."

I close my eyes, grope in my brain. I can't remember. I still can't remember.

Corinne pops up stroking her huge belly. She's looking with love at someone I can't see, a blank space in the distance. It's not that I can't see, rather I don't want to look, don't want to see my replacement, don't want to identify the roundness in her body that will replace Angela, put Angela firmly in her grave.

Spectres plague me all night and when I finally fall asleep I don't wake until the sun is way up in the sky and Jed is long gone.

There's a note in the kitchen telling me to help myself and he's left a set of clean clothes that makes me laugh. He's living in the time when we were both much of a size. He's retained his well-nourished, toned and muscular body while I'm much thinner, my flesh loose and stringy from poor food and the wrong kind of exercise.

I put on my own clean clothes and stuff the dirty gear in Jed's washing machine. The kitchen is spotlessly clean. There are no feminine touches but a multitude of cooking utensils, jars of herbs and spices. Someone here likes to cook. It must be Jed but I'm surprised. He never used to be able to boil an egg.

Over cornflakes and toast I get out Fisher's book and the information from *The Writers and Artists Yearbook*. I decide to make the phone-call.

The phone rings for a long time, so long that I'm surprised when someone finally answers.

"Red Rose Press." The northern accent is muted but unmistakeable.

"My name's Crabbe. Dr Jack Crabbe. I have a copy of a book you published. *Strange But True Tales of Lancashire*. I'd like to contact the author, Eric Fisher. It's in connection with some research I'm doing."

"Eric Fisher? Just a minute." I can hear his fingers clicking on his keyboard. "He hasn't written anything for us lately but we do have contact details for him, if they're still up to date, that is."

"I'd be very grateful if you could put me in touch with him."

"Dr Crabbe, you'll appreciate I can't just give out confidential information. If you'd like to leave your number, I'll see if I can contact Eric and make him aware of your interest."

It's fair enough. I give him Jed's number. "Tell him it's about Vicky, the chicken shed girl."

I make more coffee. This is luxury, to be able to boil a kettle whenever you want, but then there's a price.

There's a bottle of whisky in the cupboard where Jed keeps the coffee. My hand falters but settles on the coffee jar. Poor Jed in this empty house full of shades and memories. I hope he's not going the same way I did.

Don't watch the phone, I keep telling myself. I flick through the *Strange But True Tales* again but nothing goes in. I will Fisher to ring but the only noise is the gurgling of the washing machine.

There doesn't seem to be a washing line outside so I stick everything in the tumble-dryer. The garden looks neat, with tidy lawns, shrubs and a few flowers. My guess is he pays a gardener to take care of it. It lacks the visible passion of an enthusiast. There's still a kids' slide at the bottom end, looking a bit worse for wear now. The phone starts to ring as I come back in.

"It's only me. Are you okay?"

"Checking up on me? Bet you thought I'd run away."

"Why would I think that? I just wanted to let you know I'll be finishing up here about twelve-thirty so I'll be back around one. I'll pick something up for lunch."

I'm on pins all the time he's on the phone. I can picture Fisher dialling, shrugging his shoulders, ripping up the phone number and chucking it in the bin before getting back to his latest manuscript.

I wouldn't admit it to Jed but I am tempted to disappear, dissolve back into no man's land. I can feel this easy living seeping into my bones already. I only have to stretch out my hand for hot water, shelter, good food, a comfortable bed. It's Maslow's hierarchy of needs but even this basic level is something I've learned to live without and it makes me feel unsettled.

The phone rings again. It's a female voice, someone called Sarah, asking for Jed. She's curious, wondering who I am. I feel awkward as I tell her Jed's at work. It feels like a mistake, coming here. Everything's different, Jed's life has changed and learning about Corinne with her new husband and her baby has thrown me. It's more pain, after I'd got used to dealing with the old stuff, or at least burying it, bandaging it. Now it's like a fresh wound or rather an old one ripped open. If it wasn't for Vicky I'd be out the door and headed anywhere a long way away.

And there's more to come. The price to pay for Jed's hospitality will be having to explain the past, justify my behaviour towards him, Corinne, the world. I suppose he'll want to help me return, come back into this two-edged world of comfort and stress. Some people can juggle it and some can't. How far am I prepared to go for Vicky's sake? I don't know.

Jed comes in promptly with a couple of bulging carrier bags and a pizza in a box.

"I'll cook something decent tonight." He's storing the things he's bought in the fridge and the cupboards with an efficiency that strikes a chord in me from the old days. "I taught myself to cook after Becky left. I really enjoy it now. Not like student days is it? Beans and chips and no one ever washed up. Wonder we didn't get salmonella."

He slices the pizza neatly, reaches into the fridge for a bottle of beer then stops.

"It's okay, go ahead. I'll have a cup of tea."

"You've really stayed off the juice?"

"Yeah. It's like hypnotherapy. Every time I'm tempted there's a stock of horror pictures ready to flash up. Shame isn't it, it took killing my daughter to stop me? Now I've no inclination to drink."

"Or to live?"

Only he could get away with saying that to me. I look down. The pizza on my plate looks wooden.

"Don't try your amateur psychology on me." I laugh, but he's right. I've been running away for the last five years.

He lets it go after that and tells me about his morning, the procession of warts, bad backs, crying babies, pregnant mums. It gives me a twinge of nostalgia.

"Coughs and colds are starting already and it's only September. Look at the glorious weather and I've got a queue of sniffling, sneezing patients."

"So much for the wonders of medicine we thought we were going in to when we were green young docs." I can almost kid myself into his world, my old world.

He's finished his pizza, I've barely touched mine. I tell him about Eric Fisher but the phone still hasn't rung.

"By the way, someone called Sarah rang. I forgot all about it." I let a query hang in my voice.

He grins. "She works at the hospital. Medical Records. We met at a PCT training day. We see each other on and off, nothing serious. Let's have a look on the Internet."

His study is neat and modern, all blond wood and stainless steel. We type in keywords, chicken shed girl, Scarclough, Vicky Appleton, Mary Appleton, deprived child, anything we can think of, and we get millions of hits.

It's amazing the stuff that comes up, everything that I painfully dug out of the library archives and much more but nothing that tells us what happened to Vicky after she was found.

It surprises me how many similar cases there have been in England alone, never mind world-wide. And now there are stories of kids abandoned in inner-city centres, running wild with dogs, living in drains, God knows what else.

There's been a lot of scientific interest and debate on Vicky and we end up with a list of articles from social science and medical journals. Most of them only deal with the general facts of a number of cases including Vicky's.

We're only part way through them when the phone rings. Jed comes back with a quizzical smile. "It's for Dr Crabbe."

"Dr Crabbe, this is Eric Fisher."

My heart jumps. "Thank you for calling back. It's very important to me. I'm doing some research on the psychological effects of severe language deprivation on young children and I came across your account of Vicky the chicken shed girl."

"I don't know if I can help you. I wrote that piece quite some time ago and you know it's only a general account, not based on academic or medical research."

"That's okay. I'm particularly interested in cases in England, because of specific cultural values. I've got plenty of stuff on how she was discovered but what I'm trying to find out is where she went when she left Ormskirk Hospital. I need to contact the relevant institution so that I can research her treatment regime."

"I don't know if I've got anything like that. Can't you find out from hospital records?"

"It was such a long time ago. The relevant notes seem to be missing. I've tried the FHSA archive but no luck so far. Part of the problem is that initially at least she had no official identity, no medical records, GP or anything."

"Let me see." I can hear papers rustling. "I've still got my original notes, I never throw anything away, but they're a bit rough and ready. Tell you what, leave it with me and I'll get back to you."

"That's very kind of you. I'm sorry for taking up your time."

"No problem Doctor, I'll be glad to help."

Jed's standing in the doorway, grinning. "That was very convincing."

"Yeah." I almost convinced myself. Now I've put the phone down, I've got a strange dispossessed feeling, as if I've slipped from one person to another and back again, and now I'm not sure which one I am.

"I've found something too. There's a piece of published research. Someone worked with her, made a longitudinal study. It's published as a chapter in a psychology book. I've got the details here."

We can't access the chapter online but we get the publishing details. The book is called *Studies in Language Deprivation*. The chapter itself is by someone called Dr Alexander Soames and it's dated 1980: 'Educating Vicky – The Language and Development of a Severely Deprived Child.'

It's got to be her. I'm elated. "How are we going to get it?" We look on Amazon but there's no mention of it. Jed can order it from the hospital library but it might take some time. I can't wait.

"It mightn't be her anyway."

"Oh come on. Who else could it be?"

"But there are lots of them, loads of stuff here." He's scrolling through websites, links to chat rooms. "It's like a freakshow. Some of it's real sicko stuff."

This sobers me. I think of how Jimmy Atherton still sees Vicky as a monster, of the thrill-seeking public, gobbling up lurid press stories, but if these accounts help me to find Vicky, I'm glad they exist.

I peer over his shoulder. "A lot of it seems academic. Aren't you a bit curious? You've got to admit, it's intriguing."

"I suppose so, there are moral and philosophical issues. Is that why you're so interested in her? Why you've come out of hiding?"

"I told you there's something about her, something special, uncanny even, but she isn't a freak. She's real. Anyway, who says I've come out of anything? I'm only here for a few days – remember?"

After Jed goes back to the practice, I spend another hour trawling through the mass of links on wild and confined children that go back several hundred years. These accounts with their woodcut illustrations seem to bear no relation to the living woman I know. I'm disturbed at the same time as I'm fascinated. In the end it gets too much. Information overload sets in and I switch off and think about going out to the town centre, to the library. Maybe there'd be a copy of the Soames book.

I'm not sure if I can face the town. I might bump into someone I know and then the questions will start. Chances are no one would recognise me anyway but I can't be sure. And I'm not ready for it, not ready for the associations familiar places will set off. In the end I sit in front of the TV staring at the afternoon quiz shows and adverts for stairlifts.

Eric Fisher rings back in the evening, while Jed is cooking chilli con carne.

"I've got some information for you."

"Great. That's fantastic. Thanks so much for ringing back."

"No problem. She went to the Leadbetter Institute. It's a residential place or a rehab facility for damaged kids. It's in Cambridgeshire, or it was. We're talking nearly thirty years ago."

"You don't have an address or a phone number?"

"Sorry. It's just a mention in some notes I took when interviewing some of the staff who looked after her at the hospital. I couldn't use it for confidentiality reasons. Shouldn't be telling you really, but after all these years—"

"My research will respect that confidentiality. It's very kind of you to help me. This may be very useful."

"Might just be a dead end, Doctor. Who knows if the place is still there? Best of luck anyway. Like to see a copy of your research when it's published."

I want to discuss it with Jed right away but he's putting our plates on the table. I try to rein in my excitement. Jed's made an effort to cook and I am starving. He drinks red wine and I have water. Every time he lifts his glass he looks at me. The food is wonderful.

"It's a long time since I ate anything this good."

"You look like you could do with a bit of feeding up."

"Ever heard of the Leadbetter Institute?"

"Can't say I have."

"Fisher phoned back. It's where Vicky went. Some kind of rehab or children's home."

"Will they have taken her there then?"

"Shouldn't think so. It's a long time ago and if it's a rehab, she'll have been sent on somewhere else afterwards."

"I ordered the book but it'll take a few days so it looks like you're stuck here for a bit longer."

"This Leadbetter place is, or was, in Cambridgeshire."

"We can look on the Net."

"You're staying in then? I thought you might be going out with Sarah." The thought of an evening of chummy intimacy summons up unnamed dreads.

"Not tonight." He stacks everything in the dishwasher. In a few minutes the kitchen looks unused again, almost clinically clean. Only the lingering smell of the food records the sensual delights it produced, and, with a spray of air freshener, he even gets rid of that.

He finishes the bottle of wine and opens another in the course of our internet search and now I look at him each time he lifts his glass. There's not a great deal of stuff on the Leadbetter Institute but it's there and it still exists.

Most references are to a Dr U. Singh who seems to be a prolific publisher of articles. We waste a lot of time going through these but none of them refer to Vicky and most seem to have been written fairly recently.

"We'll send them an email, saying we're doing some research and see if we can set up a meeting."

"We?"

"It'll look better if there are two of us and if they check up at least one of us is legit." His fingers are already flying over the keys. "There." He presses the Send button before I can open my mouth.

"You are curious then? Or are there other reasons why you're helping me like this? You might be putting your professional reputation at risk." I don't want it just to be for old times' sake.

"I'm curious, I suppose. But if it was anybody else I wouldn't do it. You're my friend, Buster. What happened doesn't change that. I'm just sorry you didn't see it like that at the time. I can understand how you felt but you could have kept in touch. The fact that you didn't, not a word all these years, that fucking hurt. It still does." He flashes me a look of suppressed rage as he pours another glass of wine. His hand is unsteady as he puts the bottle down.

How can I say that he's part of another time, another me, a whole bad scene I just had to shut away and ignore? I don't want to make things worse.

"You don't know how many times I've stood in a phone box, picked up the phone and put it down again."

"Then why?"

"Have you ever done something so bad you couldn't look at it, couldn't have anything to do with it? Well, multiply that by a thousand. I couldn't face myself, I still can't. Do you think I could face Corinne, colleagues, even you? Look at the mess I left you in with the practice."

"Oh fuck the practice, Jack. We're talking about you and me. You needed help and I thought you would have known that you could count on me."

This is the drink talking. I know the practice means a lot to him.

"I'm here now."

"Okay, but you haven't dealt with anything, have you? Corinne's moved on, let go, but you Jack, you're like Sleeping Beauty. You've fenced it all off, but you've fenced yourself in too." He stares moodily into his glass.

"I can't forget Angela."

"No one's asking you to forget her. Do you think Corinne has forgotten her? There are always fresh flowers on her grave."

I've not only killed her, I've neglected her grave.

"It's time you stopped feeling bloody sorry for yourself."

Sorry for myself! How can he say this? Doesn't he realise how much I hate myself?

"At least looking for this Vicky shows you're thinking about someone else for a change. Do you really think you can help her? In cases I've read about, rehabilitation is really difficult, at best only partial. Do you really think you can succeed when everyone else has failed, after all these years? And what about you, isn't it time you rejoined the real world?"

Rehabilitate her? I don't want to do that. I want her just the way she is. I've got the feeling whatever she's got that ties me to her, her way of seeing things, is something she has because she isn't like the rest of us. Jed's wrong. My interest in Vicky is selfish; I want her to help me.

"The real world?" I watch as he slugs the glass of wine down. "You mean *your* world? Leave me alone, Jed, I'm not one of your patients."

"It just seems such a waste."

There's nothing more to say. We sit for a few minutes in silence, then he turns the computer off and swings round in his chair.

"And if we find Vicky – what then?"

"I don't know."

* * *

supper   fish   marjorie like

    bath   yes good marjorie   medication pinkcup cocoa

darkwarm   marjorie roomquiet   itch   ticklemarjorie

    yes good nice dark yes
                        light   nolight stoplight   martin
nomartin
nostopit nostopit martin   nodirtybitch   no   marjorie be
good   yes
        nomoredirtybitch   martin notellmrsmitchell   no marjorie
good goodgirl
martin noshout no   marjorie scared   martin red   redmartinshout
marjorieblack   red come off martin onto marjorie black hide
wardrobe hidemarjorie hide cupboard vickyhide cupboard novicky
vickymarjorie hide   marjorie dark

* * *

I can't sleep. Jed's words keep going through my head. Rehabilitating Vicky is something that never even occurred to me. She needs protection but I don't see any value in trying to change her. As for rehabilitating myself, I don't see any value in that either. Why should I want to be back where I was before when I made such a mess of it the first time?

Jed seems to veer between pitying me and being angry at me. Why does he want me to be like him when I'm content as I am? Except that I'm not really content. He's right about me fencing things off. I see Corinne putting flowers on the grave I can never let myself think about. The 'if only' game starts again. If only I had put Angie in a cab instead of driving. If only I'd got help before the drinking got out of control. If only I knew for sure what had happened.

The space where my leg used to be aches intolerably. I put my hand out of the bed to feel the unresponsive surface of the prosthesis. It brings the past and present together.

I'm always looking for reasons. Why drink is a demon for me and not for others. Was it all down to circumstances or was it something in my nature, my family, my genes?

In the end I get up and spend the rest of the night on the computer going through the journal articles we looked up. It's a depressing parade of half-human creatures that never quite seem to get the hang of social living. Jed's right about that. Yet Vicky seemed happy enough, going around with Rita and Kindi, trotting along with me, eating ice cream. But she had a dark side too; the times she spent in the cupboard; her fear of the police and the place called Medoban. Even when she was on her own, it seemed she didn't have much control over what happened to her. And yet she could make people do things. I remember the woman in the gardens, handing over her baby's fluffy toy. These thoughts set up a bundle of questions in my mind, questions I really want to find the answers to.

Friday evening, Jed goes out for a meal with Sarah. I can tell he doesn't like leaving me, but I'm glad to be alone. I don't want another evening like last night.

I spend some of the time looking through his photo albums but this is a bad mistake, because it's all there. Me as the green student, all big ears and silly grin, both of us at graduation, as interns, how happy we look, how – clean.

Then the foursomes, girls I barely remember and before long Becky and Corinne with padded shoulders and big hairdos. It's all soft skins, innocent eyes and open faces. I'm depressed even before I come to the one of Angela's christening and then I start thinking about the whisky bottle in the kitchen cupboard.

I put the albums away and sit down in front of the TV with a cup of tea, idly switching channels. Something's trying to form in my mind but I keep pushing it away. I tune into a quiz show but I can't concentrate on the questions. Pictures from the photo albums keep intervening.

In the end I pick a CD from Jed's blues collection and settle down to Sonny Terry and Brownie McGhee. If I'm going to be miserable I might as well enjoy it. I let myself lull into the repetitive riffs.

The music drops back somewhere and the picture comes, the one that's been trying to push its way through the thicket of my thoughts.

It's Corinne putting flowers on Angela's grave. It's more like a sepulchre, a huge rococo affair in white marble with a sad angel on the top. I don't like it and change it for a pink granite square as Terry and McGhee go into, 'Sun's Gonna Shine'.

Corinne can't bend down properly because of her belly. She's talking to the stone, to Angela. Someone else is with her, a man, but I can't see him, only his hands as he takes the flowers from her, puts them in a vase, places it in front of the stone. His hands are soft, manicured with black hairs on the knuckles. A dandelion is daring to grow on top of Angela and his hand plucks it out, tosses it aside. I expect Angela's hand to shoot up out of the soil, like the final scene in *Carrie*. It shouldn't be him.

Nothing happens. Corinne straightens up, puts a hand to the small of her back. She looks old, careworn, till she smiles at him and there's radiance there. I open my eyes. The music's stopped. It should be me.

* * *

       yesmrsmitchell   take medication   yes good-
girlmarjorie
toast pinkcup tea be good yes redwhitepill pinkpill   hot tea
hermitjack make tea   make tea vicky novicky marjorie good-
girlmarjorie   yes sit chair
tv yes peggy   maureen   sit chair   niceandquiet
goodgoodgirl

* * *

Saturday morning Jed plays badminton. I walk in the nearby wood, trying not to think about Corinne or Angela. My leg is comfortable now it's getting regularly cleaned and a fresh sock every day. Even my hip's quiet now that I can pace my walking.

In my memory it is always spring in this wood, with the overpowering scent and colour of a myriad bluebells, but now the trees are brilliant with red and orange.

The turning leaves remind me of Brow Lane Farm. The atmosphere is different here but I can't say why. There's that same sense of presence but it's not as brooding. Here I get a sense of being engulfed in living things. I can't say I believe in a spirit of the wood or any such thing but it's as if something's watching me. It's a benign feeling though; there's none of the horror I felt at Brow Lane. No triffids here.

Only a week has passed since I met Vicky. Such a lot seems to have happened in that space of time. Maybe it's that I seem to have changed so much in just those few days; as if she's a catalyst. Back on the road to the house I think again about going into town but instead I turn into the drive and let the safety of the house swallow me.

Sunday afternoon, Jed takes me out for a drive in the country, which is full of other people driving about. What I really want to do is go to the cemetery and look at Angela's grave but at the same time I'm scared stiff of doing so. I thought about it all last night. Now I've let the image out I'm haunted by it, it's pushing everything out, even Vicky, but it's terrifying. It's as if I were going to meet Angela herself, alive and ready to accuse me.

Monday lunchtime, Jed brings home a list of institutions and homes he's managed to obtain from a social worker he knows. There are hundreds of names but Medoban's not there. After lunch he goes out on house calls. I take the spare key and a deep breath and set out for town.

It's a long walk. There are forgotten memories at almost every step, and though some of them are painful there's a sense of coming home, even though I've chosen to dissociate myself from the place.

When I come to the tall terraced house near the canal, where I lived as a child, I could cry, thinking of my mother cleaning the windows and my father tinkering with his old Ford Pop in the rented garages that used to be next door. In their place stands a modern apartment block. The house itself looks shabby with grimy windows. It looks like a bedsit dwelling with its mismatched curtains on each of the three storeys. Mum would have been horrified to see it like this. I'm glad she can't, just as I'm glad she and Dad can't see me now. They were so proud of me when I became a doctor.

I turn down by the cathedral and take the path along the river, dawdling and stopping to watch the swans. The river is high but in a good mood today, slipping along as if it would never dream of raging over its banks and flooding the streets. Memories jostle my mind at every step. I remember walks taken with Corinne and Angela when she was tiny, and later, those special Saturday afternoons Angela and I had together while Corinne was off spending time with her friends.

There are lots of people out and about, enjoying the late sunshine but I don't see anyone I recognise and this gives me the courage to turn up Bridge Street to the town centre and venture into the library where I ask for the Soames book.

They haven't got it and I decline the assistant's offer to order it. I've no library card and I don't plan on staying long enough to use one.

I can't put it off any longer but my feet drag as I approach the tall gates of the cemetery. Looking at the neat rows of graves, I realise I haven't a clue where Angela is buried.

At the time I'd been glad they wouldn't let me out of hospital for the funeral. That way I could almost pretend nothing had happened. Penny came to see me afterwards and told me how distraught Corinne had been, how she'd had to lean on her father as the coffin went into the grave. My sister's lips twisted as she told me this and she delivered the story to the air above my head without looking at me. Matt couldn't bring himself to come at all. Jed came nearly every day and he never reproached me, but his miserable silences said so much it would have been better if he'd stayed away.

"Okay mate?" It's a gardener with a lawnmower and I'm in his way. I've been so lost in the past I didn't even hear the noise of the engine.

"I need to find a grave. I'm visiting a distant relative."

"Go to the lodge." He points to a stone building across the cemetery at a second pair of gates. "They'll be able to tell you."

When I find it, it's so ordinary; third from the end on one of many interminable rows, not, as I'd imagined, in a sweet shady corner under a tree. The stone is small and plain, white marble, no angels, no sentimental verses, just her name and the dates of her short life.

My stomach is a cold lump as I look at the brilliant chrysanths flaunting their life on the plinth. They're still quite fresh, so Corinne has been here recently, maybe over the weekend, and there's not much chance of bumping into her here. I still look round guiltily for a moment until the grave claims my whole being.

There's not even a curve in the ground to suggest that the con-toured body of a person lies beneath. I think of Angela in there, what she will now look like, the natural process of decay finishing the job that I started.

Up here, everything is neat and tidy. I put my hand out to the stone. It's cold despite the sun and it's hard. "Angela-a-a," Vicky's voice whispers in my head and I remember the way she looked at me as she said it. It's linked to the way she touched my leg that first night.

The sun beats down on the stones, on the rows of rectangular graves. If anything remains of Angela, it isn't here and I'm no longer afraid of being here. I can see the first signs of fading on the petals of the chrysanthemums.

It isn't difficult for me to walk away but as I make my way back along the river there seems to be desolation in the way the branches hang down over the murky water and questions in the way the water shifts from brown to green and back.

I feel as if I've achieved something but my whole body feels weighed down nevertheless.

* * *

"Here." Jed rushes in at four o'clock and slaps a book down on the kitchen table. "Can't stop. Flu vaccinations, then surgery and family planning clinic. Tuesdays are a nightmare."

I'm glad to be left alone with the book. The chapter on Vicky is about thirty pages long and I can't wait to get into it.

"Educating Vicky – The Language and Development of a Severely Deprived Child"
A. V. Soames

In 1975 a female child was discovered in a chicken shed on a Lancashire farm. The child, subsequently named Vicky, could not walk properly or speak when found and appeared to have been severely neglected for a long period.

We will never know the true story of Vicky's early childhood for her mother was found dead on the farm, no one else knew of her existence and Vicky herself was, and remains, unable to tell us about her early years. Who knows what her experiences and feelings were? Physical evidence suggested that she had been almost totally isolated from a very early age.

Some months after she came to us, a small notebook diary kept by Vicky's mother was forwarded to us by the police. This had been removed from the farm when Vicky was rescued and had been overlooked in the property office. The entries in this diary, which covered the period around Vicky's birth, corroborated the evidence of almost total isolation and make painful reading. It was plain that Vicky's mother had suffered some kind of psychiatric breakdown and had been unable to cope with Vicky's birth. Police had been unable to identify or trace her father.

When Vicky was found, she weighed twenty-one kilograms and appeared to be about five years old. However, when she was admitted to hospital, doctors estimated her real age at eight-and-a-half to nine. She had been naked except for an old shirt when found and she appeared to be impervious to heat or cold.

After a three-month period of physical rehabilitation, during which Vicky's weight rose to thirty kilograms, she was transferred to my care at the Leadbetter Institute for educational training and psychiatric treatment.

By this time, she had learned to walk almost normally and was accustomed to wearing clothes. She had begun to respond to those around her and had a small stock of words. "Stop it", "No" and "Shut up" were the only words she had been able to say when first found, but during her three months at the hospital she had learned to name some items, notably things of which she was fond, such as, "redcup", "chips", "coke", and "marsbar".

Apart from these words she did not speak. Whether this was because she had not learned any other words, or whether she did not feel the need to use them, we could not tell. Her speech was only used to express desire or refusal.

By the time she came to the Institute, she was toilet-trained, although occasional bouts of incontinence still occurred. A major problem was her habit of playing with her genitals as a very young child might, regardless of where she was or who might be present. No amount of disapproval would persuade her to desist and the only method that sometimes worked was bribery with sweets or some other desired treat.

Staff at the hospital had described Vicky as exhibiting little emotion except fear. When something frightened her she would hide under her bed or in any confined space, the toilet cubicle being a particular favourite.

After the first few weeks with us, she became more confident in her environment and less afraid of those around her. Occasional bouts of angry behaviour emerged when some desire was frustrated. Her anger took the form of wordless screaming and jumping up and down, rather than violence against things or other persons and soon ended when she had exhausted herself.

Vicky quickly settled down and made good relationships with the nurses and doctors. At this time she had no contact with other patients as we felt it best to concentrate on developing her social skills within a small group of reliable and sympathetic people.

She soon identified favourites, Nurse K, myself, and Dr P. She had learned to smile and laugh but she used these expressions sparingly and usually inappropriately or manipulatively to get something she wanted. It was so rare to see her express any feeling however, that when a smile or a giggle did occur, it seemed intensely meaningful.

This was a concentrated learning period for Vicky but was equally valuable to us. By observing her behaviour over time, we were able to assess her abilities more effectively and plan a treatment regime which we hoped would give her a reasonable chance of survival in the social world and enable her to deal with the mental trauma she must have suffered.

We remained conservative in our hopes for complete rehabilitation however, in the light of previous case studies (Gordon and Philips 1968; Peters and Zimmerman 1971), which tended to endorse the Critical Period Hypothesis, i.e. that there is a crucial period in childhood after which language cannot be acquired. If we accepted Dennis's belief that the critical period is over by the age of two, there was little hope for Vicky. However, Lenneberg's more generous estimation of one to ten years meant that Vicky might still acquire good language skills and Vygotsky's argument that development takes place through social contact and not through fixed developmental stages also held some promise.

Case histories of other isolated children are few and ambivalent. Historical evidence is often anecdotal, or reflects the scientific views of the time which differ greatly from our contemporary knowledge. Overwhelmingly, though, the records show that these children failed to develop full language skills. Those cases that did acquire complex spoken and written language, such as the eighteenth-century Caspar Hauser and Memmie LeBlanc, may well have had the rudiments of such skills before their periods of isolation.

Between January and July 1976, Dr P or I visited Vicky daily and made extensive notes on her behaviour and on any progress we could discern. Video-recordings were also made.

At this time, although her word stock grew rapidly, it consisted only of names of things. She had a few adjectives but these were invariably attached to the thing she named "redcup", "blueball" with no concept of the adjective as a separate linguistic unit. Towards the end of the observation period she acquired a few simple verbs, "give, go, want", but she had no sense of sentence construction, no understanding of intonation.

Language was at this stage an effort for her. She rarely responded when spoken to and did not appear to understand, for example, the particular intonation and syntactical structure that makes an utterance into a question. The elicitation of a response often seemed to have more to do with our body language, signs and gestures than with the content of our speech. She was also remarkably responsive to our moods, even when we projected what we felt was a professional image.

For example, Nurse K's mother died a few months after Vicky's arrival. Nurse K continued to work her shifts as normal, but when she came on the ward Vicky immediately noticed her, watched her carefully for some minutes, then went up to her and touched her eyelids. This was done with such a physical expression of abjection, that we were all led to the belief that somehow she could intuit Nurse K's sense of loss.

At the end of six months Vicky registered a mental age of eighteen months on the Simon-Binet scale. She had a growing vocabulary and most encouragingly she had begun to imitate and repeat words spoken to her, indicating that she had the ability to recognise sounds and split them into words.

Psychological investigations indicated a wide variation of functioning in different areas so that while she had a mental age of eighteen months in areas requiring abstract thought, she was much nearer her physical age in concrete operations such as dressing and caring for herself.

Some nine months after she was discovered, we began intensive training with Vicky. She was introduced to a small class of other children and showed great interest in puzzles, colours, painting and particularly music. Her vocabulary expanded rapidly and she began to respond to others more readily, although her speech still remained mostly monosyllabic.

There seemed to be a widening gap between what Vicky understood of what she heard and what she could verbally express herself. Within a further six months she demonstrated understanding of most conversation going on round her, but although she began to string words together, ostensibly in a sentence, the word string had no structure or meaning, being simply composed of unrelated units.

She could not produce a question and was unaware of past or future tenses. She was unable to use subjective or objective pronouns and referred to everybody, including herself, by name.

By January 1977 she had achieved a great deal in comprehending the world around her. She enjoyed the company of other children and seemed happiest when in the classroom using coloured blocks, letters and art materials. She would sit for hours listening to records or the radio, totally enraptured.

She loved to go shopping and was attracted by clothes and jewellery in bright colours. Unfortunately she had no concept of paying for things and was an inveterate shoplifter, which, added to her propensity for scratching her private parts in public, meant that shopping trips were usually fraught with difficulties. Her carers also noted that complete strangers sometimes came up and gave her presents; items they were wearing, pretty scarves, or costume jewellery. This only happened occasionally but often enough to be noticed. There seemed to be no explanation, Vicky gave no discernible sign to these strangers although she readily accepted their gifts.

For the most part Vicky appeared happy but she was still very quiet and serious for a young child. She could not understand jokes or any of the automatic forms of speech that most of us use in everyday communication such as greetings, swearing, pleasantries. Although she seemed extremely sensitive to the moods of others, we felt that this was due to her heightened ability to interpret body language and gestures rather than any response to intonation. Physically, although she had gained weight and could now walk quite normally, activities such as sports and running remained difficult for her. Physiotherapy sessions were continued to develop her muscular and motor skills.

Her speech remained at the most basic level of communication. Her words were reduced to the bare minimum required to achieve fulfilment of her wants, and her demeanour was that of a silent child whose experiences were still locked inside her.

There is an unspoken sadness in this narrative that fills me with a sense of loss, the loss of the lively childhood Vicky should have had and was still deprived of even after her rescue.

As I read I keep finding little things I recognise in the Vicky I know that relate her to this poor child on the paper. There are pages of tables and test results following this section, which although medically fascinating distance me from Vicky as a person. I have to keep reminding myself that this is Vicky and not just a case history.

What do I mean, 'just a case history'? All case histories are people. I am ashamed that this appears as something of a revelation to me.

I skip through the tests, which mostly show how Vicky's language-use developed from one word names to simple sentences. As the test data unfolds however, it becomes clear that her progress peaked, then slowed gradually to the point where she did not seem to learn further grammatical structures or social constructions. It was as if she had come to the end of the line as far as linguistic ability was concerned. Soames's text, too, becomes disillusioned:

> By the end of 1978, almost three years after Vicky first came to us, we realised she was no longer responding to our efforts to improve her language skills. She was able to communicate her wants and needs in basic word strings but could not be easily understood because of the incompleteness of the sentences she used, let alone initiate or engage in the easy conversation that most people take for granted. We did not think she would be able to function normally in a family fostering situation.
>
> Vicky was now twelve years old and standing on the threshold of puberty. The rubbing at her genitals, which we had been unable to prevent, now developed into full-blown masturbation and she began to show signs of physical attraction to the opposite sex, developing intense crushes on older boys among her classmates and younger male members of the Institute staff.
>
> In January 1979, the decision was taken to transfer Vicky to a small residential unit, where the emphasis would be on attempting to prepare her for a place in a foster family, rather than on intensive educational training.
>
> In summary, our work with Vicky had a positive outcome. She came to us a speechless little girl with no social skills whatever and an extreme fear of other people.

By the time she left, she was able to enjoy the company of others, make her wants known and communicate in a basic way. She had learned a great many social skills. However, her language development was limited. She did not learn to read or write and she preferred to draw answers to questions rather than give spoken answers.

We conclude that her inability to acquire full language skills is due to her early social deprivation and its psychological consequences. Other studies tend to confirm this conclusion (Samson 1972; Whittaker and White 1970a).

While grammatical ability has been shown to be variable depending on individual circumstances, regardless of tested intelligence (Peters 1968), social competence appears to be a crucial factor in developing effective communication. The inability to develop this competence is not primarily a problem of linguistic inability, but one developing from social and psychological deprivation, from lack of stimulation from the outside world, lack of examples to compare oneself with, and lack of others to teach one how humans behave and interact.

Vicky has never been socialised. If the Critical Period Hypothesis upholds, it may now be too late for her ever to become integrated into society. Our research seems to support this hypothesis. Despite her initial progress which gave us high hopes, she remains unsocialised and appears unable to develop further.

While it is our sincere hope that she will continue to improve we feel it is unlikely that she will ever develop sufficient literacy or social skills to enable her to function unaided in the outside world.

So that is the end of Dr Soames's involvement – just like that. There is not much in this chapter about Vicky's emotional life. How did she feel, living in an institution like that? Was she aware of being alone or different? She had been alone all her life before that, but if you don't know you are alone, can you feel lonely?

How would she have experienced the company of others? Maybe at first an overwhelming rush of sensations, fears, delights, an overload of sounds, colours, tastes, touches – but alone in a world of adults. The chapter resounds with the careful creation of an environment, no doubt out of protective motives but also to protect and control the research project of which Vicky had no knowledge. It's so impersonal. Even I can see the thing lacking here, the thing that everybody needs. The love she should have had from her own mother was still withheld, following her rescue, by the failure to introduce her into a family.

This Dr Soames makes me angry. I go out and walk into town again. I want to sit by the river, to be soothed by the serene, unstoppable movement of the water. Outside everything seems better. The sun is still warm but evening approaches, reminding me that winter will soon close in and for a moment I wonder where I will be and how I will fare.

I feel out of sorts, upset by Soames's study of Vicky and the way she was reduced to an experiment. When I pass the place where our family's allotment used to be, I think of how the three of us children used to help my father pick damsons. This plot now has become a mock-Tudor housing estate.

The river is too big a tourist attraction to be meddled with and anyway no one in their right mind would buy a house there because the Severn is so fond of rising up and drowning everything in its path.

I cross the bridge to the quieter side and find a secluded spot. My hip creaks as I get down but it's good to rest in the cool dampness where I don't need to worry about meeting anyone I know, or being disturbed by anybody, except the ghosts of course; myself young and happy, courting Corinne on the path on the other side, taking the pleasure-boat down the river and, later, there I am with the darkness and the drink already settling on me, lifting Angela high on the parapet to throw bread to the swans. Her little legs kick with glee. She wears neat cotton socks and blue glitter sandals. They were all the rage that year, every kid wanted them. I remember thinking how healthy she was and then it strikes.

Dr Soames, Jed, myself – all looking at people as cases; dividing all humanity into a dichotomy of healthy/unhealthy. Instead of people we saw conditions – a healthy baby, an interesting cancer, a problematic kidney, a challenging skin disease – never noticing the power, the control we had or how we were using it.

All of us in our circle, our medical world, reinforcing our way of thinking, joined together in our rightness. What did we see when we looked at our patients, at our families, at ourselves?

Is this why I drank? Did I sense something lacking, something alienating? Yet Corinne – the delight, the first sensations of our love – I can always recall. Surely then I was different? And when I first qualified, I chose general practice from a desire to help people, not study conditions.

I'm groping for those feelings, those sensations but they're like ancient history, dry papers, dusty stones. Corinne grew cold and bitter and blamed me. I always thought it was she who became hard and empty but now I'm seeing myself in another light and I like myself even less than the pathetic weakling I eventually saw whenever I looked in Corinne's eyes.

Across the water, the last day-trippers in shirt sleeves and cotton frocks are ambling back to their cars and coaches, eating ice cream as if it were still summer, but the fading light gives everything a melancholy aspect. The river slinks between us. It does speak, though, as it rolls by. It murmurs "Here I am and here you are". I think of Dr Soames recording Vicky's inability to deal with the past tense. The value of the moment rises up and swallows me so that everything drops away, and when I come back time has moved on and I don't know where I've been. There is a tinge of darkness in the sky. The air is cooler and the pleasure-boat is tying up for the day.

There is a peaceful feeling in me as I walk back, which I identify as a lack of anxiety about finding Vicky. When I first met her I wanted to help her, then to protect her, but now I realise that, even in her absence, she is teaching me, not the other way around. There is a newness in me that is disturbing but exciting, something tender that needs protection, nurture and I know without reasoning that I am going to find Vicky. Our business together is not finished.

When I get back I find an email from the Leadbetter Institute inviting us to visit on Wednesday the thirteenth.

* * *

Dr Singh is darkly beautiful and slender. I put my hands at my back and walk slightly behind her as she gives us a conducted tour of the Institute.

It's quite a small enterprise, houses no more than thirty children at any given time and the classrooms are bright and colourful. The children have their own rooms and the décor here is muted and restful. There's a cheerful atmosphere about the place but it's still got the institutional taint, a sort of ambivalent style somewhere between a hospital and a school. It's certainly not a home.

"Of course, things are much changed since the period of time you are wishing to research." Dr Singh flashes me a brilliant smile. "I think then these areas were still dormitory wards. Some were converted to shared rooms perhaps, but certainly not the en-suite singles we have today."

When we've seen everything, including the gardens and the sports facilities, she brings us into the dining room and to a small alcove at one side where a tray of coffee and biscuits is waiting for us.

"If you would excuse me gentlemen, I have some work to attend to while you have your coffee. The files you want are laid out in the office next to mine and there is a computer set up for you to use with access to relevant sections of the electronic archive.

"When you have finished your coffee we can have a chat about our work here and then I will leave you to your research, although of course I will be around to answer any questions." Another bewitching smile and she's gone.

"What a beauty!" I flop into a chair and blow out my cheeks.

"Been a long time, has it?" Jed grins.

"What?" I act daft but can feel the flush on my face rising up into my hair. I'm not admitting to him that I haven't been with a woman since Corinne. I couldn't bear to see that hard coldness grow in someone else's eyes. A woman would want things from me, expect things I can't give and anyway who'd want to have sex with a one legged tramp?

"It's not that," I mumble. "I thought she'd be a man." Jed says nothing, just raises his eyebrows at me so I shut up and pour the coffee.

On the way back to Dr Singh's office, I catch sight of myself in a mirror and I look fairly presentable. Two weeks of comfortable living have almost got rid of the roughness and the little that remains is quite fashionable. Interesting, I'd call the look.

I've put on a bit of weight and now fit into Jed's clothes reasonably well. I'm surprised to see how quickly I can look like the doctor I once was.

"Come on Romeo." Jed pulls me away. "We're here to work, remember?"

* * *

"Dr Singh, how long have you been at the Institute?" A faint perfume drifts across the desk from her to me.

"Usha, please call me Usha." Her eyes flash when she smiles. I'm captivated. "I came here in 1996. There have been many changes since I arrived. Of course I was not then Director here. I was in charge of Language Development, but I had been publishing research for several years in my previous post and I became Assistant Director here in 1998 and then Director when Mr Rose retired in 2002."

"So you weren't here when Vicky was here?"

"Of course not. That was long before my time." She giggles.

I could kick myself. She can't be more than forty.

"But, you know, this is a famous case. Everybody knows something about it. Since you contacted me, I've read up the old notes myself, so feel free to ask me anything you don't understand. They make very interesting reading."

"Terribly sad."

"Of course." Her dark eyes hold mine for a moment, each of us trying to read the other. "But a unique opportunity for study. Such cases do not occur very often."

"We've read the chapter Dr Soames wrote giving an account of his work with her." Jed's voice is clipped, matter of fact. "He seems to have given up on her relatively quickly. I'd have expected him to continue working with her for a longer period. These cases must take time, surely?" He seems unaware of Dr Singh's charms and pins her with a questioning stare.

The way she shrugs her shoulders is delicious.

"Work with Vicky was intensive for a long period, over three years. The Institute received funding for a precisely specified study and rehabilitation programme. A point was reached when the team agreed that little further progress could be expected."

"So they just offloaded her?"

Dr Singh recoils slightly. Jed gives me a look. Then she gives that expressive shrug and my indignation is defused.

"What could they do? The Institute does not provide the right environment for a permanent home. It was felt that Vicky would be happier in a residential setting. There are always new cases requiring the specialist intervention of the team. This is our function, not providing permanent care."

Jed is nodding. My foot taps involuntarily and I have to make a conscious effort to stop it.

"You will see from the notes that Vicky stopped responding to training. I'm afraid you will find the notation rather difficult to read. Most of it is handwritten and perhaps not as politically correct and precise as today's standards demand. There were not as many central guidelines as we have today." She looks ruefully up at a shelf full of policy folders on the wall behind her.

It's a sign for us to get on with our reading. In the small office she leads us to, stacks of well-worn files and folders are waiting on the single desk. Jed and I take them one at a time and swap when we've finished each one. They've been laid out in chronological order and nothing seems to be missing.

It's a fascinating record of daily life as well as of scientific data but I soon get a cold feeling. In amongst all this observation is a little lost girl who has no idea why she's there or what is happening and she's voiceless among these professional records.

The notes record her eagerness to learn, her early attempts to make herself understood and the terrible tantrums that expressed her frustration at her inability to do so. She's keen to play with toys, educational games, anything colourful but she doesn't get the point of them. And then, at other times, she just switches off like a tap and ignores everything round her. In this painstaking litany of Vicky's days certain themes stand out.

Classroom notes, 19.3.76

10.00 am. Vicky refused to play the picture matching game. When I fetched the game she said "No," and then ignored me while I laid out the cards. She didn't speak or move for fifteen minutes while I played the game myself, talking to her all the time as if she were taking part.

Classroom notes, 19.7.76

2.00 pm. I asked Vicky to fetch the blue box of counters. Vicky gave no sign of having heard and carried on modelling a piece of Plasticene. I repeated the request three times but she gave no response. I fetched the box of counters myself and took the Plasticene away from Vicky. She remained silent and motionless for the rest of the session (about 45 minutes).

The style of the notes is detached and attempts to keep value-judgements out, but there seems to be an undue emphasis on Vicky's lack of social skills and 'moral' development which increasingly seem to be cast in the light of 'bad habits'.

Nursing notes, 4.4.76

11.30 am. Vicky took Amelia's new red scarf from her locker without asking. Vicky had admired the scarf several times this week. I returned the scarf to Amelia and Vicky did not protest.

12.30 pm. Vicky appeared at the lunch table wearing Amelia's red scarf which she had taken from Amelia's locker. I took the scarf from her and explained that it belonged to Amelia.

2.00 pm. Vicky came in the TV room wearing Amelia's scarf again. I took the scarf away and explained again that the scarf belonged to Amelia. Vicky did not say anything and went to lie on her bed.

2.30 pm. Vicky came back in the TV room wearing Amelia's scarf. I told Vicky she must give the scarf back to Amelia and that her sweet ration for the day would be stopped.

2.40 pm. I went to Vicky's dormitory in response to someone having rung the alarm bell and found Vicky tying the scarf so tightly round Amelia's neck that Amelia was choking.

Consultant review, 23.9.76

Vicky's stealing continues to give concern. She has no concept of items belonging to others. Her locker has to be examined daily to return articles stolen from other children and from staff. Vicky makes no protest when the items are taken from her, but she does take pains to keep both these and her own items secreted in her locker. She is reluctant to share her own items with others. She does protest volubly if she is punished for stealing. Neither punishment nor removing the stolen articles prevents her from doing the same thing again the next day.

Classroom notes, 22.5.77

11.30 am. Vicky kept playing with her genitals in class. After three requests for her to stop had no effect, I removed her hand and said "No". I did this several times but she continued as if I wasn't there. Eventually I had to remove her from the class as she was distracting the other children.

Nursing notes, 16.2.78

7.15 pm. Vicky was playing with her genitals while watching TV. Mandy and Paula were present. Mandy began laughing but Paula went up to Vicky and said, "Stop it, you filthy bitch". Vicky did not respond or give any indication of having heard this. I went to intervene but before I could stop her, Paula slapped Vicky and called her a disgusting cow. I placed both girls in separate quiet rooms until suppertime.

As the notes progress Vicky begins to improve, much as Dr Soames reported. She develops the ability to converse in a limited way and her social skills expand.

A review in early 1978 records, "Vicky's incontinence has now disappeared completely. Masturbation or playing with her genitals occurs less often than formerly, so we are hopeful that it will die out eventually. Stealing continues and we have so far been unable to instil any sense of right and wrong with respect to other people's property."

At this point the outlook seems positive but from then on Jed and I agree that the notes take on an increasing tone of failure and disillusionment. There are many more negative statements such as, "Vicky did not respond", "Vicky ignored my request", "We could not persuade Vicky to desist from—".

When we come back to the files after breaking for lunch, it soon becomes evident that Vicky's training and education are on a downward slide. Worse still, the entries seem less concerned with her language development than with her failure to acquire the expected social skills, particularly with regard to socially unacceptable behaviour.

Nursing notes, 9.9.78

6.00 pm. Vicky went on a shopping trip with Nurse K and, despite being constantly watched, was found to have several cosmetic articles and chocolate bars in her pockets when they returned to the car. Nurse K returned the items to the supermarket and explained to the manager who agreed to take no further action.

Classroom notes, 15.10.78

1.30 pm. Vicky was seen masturbating in the playground in front of a group of older boys. This is a worrying development. I have made arrangements for a nurse to be with Vicky during class breaks.

Nursing notes, 18.11.78

4.30 pm. Vicky disappeared from the lounge during afternoon free time. She was eventually discovered in the boys' bathroom with Billy T and it was obvious that some form of sexual experimentation had been taking place. The incident was reported to Sister G and action to be taken will be discussed with Dr S.

Medical review, 20.1.79

Vicky is now twelve and a half and physical developmental signs indicate that she is approaching puberty. The onset of menstruation will pose a particular problem in view of her increasingly sexually provocative behaviour.

We need to consider the way forward immediately rather than wait for events to take their course. Accordingly, a conference has been called with Social Services and Vicky's legal representative in order to determine the best steps to be taken to safeguard Vicky's future welfare.

I scrabble through the next file to the conference and reports section with a sinking feeling in my gut and there is the decision.

We are all agreed that it is in Vicky's best interests for urgent action to prevent the possibility of her becoming pregnant. We have discussed various methods of contraception but these are unlikely to be feasible as Vicky is unable to understand the purposes of contraception and medical opinion is that she will be unlikely ever to be able to use self-managed forms of prevention. The insertion of an IUD device is not considered to be suitable.

In view of the fact that Vicky already shows signs of being sexually active and our considered opinion that she is unlikely to develop the skills necessary to make informed decisions about choosing sexual partners or becoming a parent, and as she has no family to make choices on her behalf, we are unanimous in our decision to make application to the courts for an order for compulsory sterilisation, for her own protection, on the grounds that there are clear and beneficial therapeutic reasons for doing so.

"Look! Look at this!" I shove the file under Jed's nose. My chair overturns as I blunder to the window. "I can't believe it!" My fist bangs the window and the glass rattles.

"Steady on, Buster."

"How could they? What a bunch of bastards."

"Calm down." I can feel him looking at my back. "What did you expect them to do?"

How can he say this? I twist round to make sure it really is Jed speaking.

"Look, it says here, she was already sexually active. What do you think would have happened if they hadn't acted? Add two and two, Jack."

The futility of everything disarms me. The flat fen landscape beyond the grounds, with its drab, harvested fields, is equally meaningless. He's right.

It's a physical pain, this rift between what I want, what I think should be, and what is "right", expedient, the best option, whatever. All I can think is if such a thing happened to my daughter, I would do anything to try to protect her. All I can see is Vicky trotting along, innocent at thirty-five, never mind when she was twelve and still without a champion.

Whatever holds me up feels like it's running down, out of me into the floor.

"I know – but . . . " I sit down and cover my face. I smell Usha Singh's perfume before I'm aware she's in the room.

"Everything okay?" She looks at me, then at Jed.

"They sterilised her." It comes out flat as the landscape.

"Yes. It was thought to be for the best." She sounds like she's talking about the choice of a good school, not a life-changing decision.

"How would you like it to happen to you – or your daughter?" I can't help glaring at her. How would she feel, she who is so pretty, so womanly that every cell in her body advertises a sure sensuality?

"I am not Vicky," she says quietly. "What else could they do?" She's looking strangely at me. This is not the reaction expected from a medical researcher. I need to pull myself together.

"It would not be the same for me." She moves lightly round the desk, looks over my shoulder at the file. I'm distracted by her closeness. It separates me from Vicky, lets me get my composure back. "I would know. Vicky did not. She wouldn't have known what was happening, or what it meant."

"Does that make it better – or worse?" The words still come out bitter. I can't believe that as a woman she agrees with this.

"There are always moral dilemmas in these situations, Jack. You know that as well as anyone." Jed's sending me eye signals to keep quiet. "At the end of the day they had to try and work out what was for the best. Even her solicitor agreed to it."

I'm subsiding, giving way under the weight of their argument. I finger the file. It's the last one. I turn up a note about the decision to transfer Vicky elsewhere and a list of possible new places for her.

"Where did they send her?" I feel exhausted, too tired to search through any more notes.

"She went to The Larches." Dr Singh seems just as fresh as she was this morning. "It was a small fifteen-bed rehab unit near Wisbech. They used it for a sort of halfway house to prepare people for moving into sheltered accommodation or residential homes."

"Was?"

"It closed down a long time ago. I don't know exactly when. It was long before I came here."

"Do you know where she went after that?"

She shakes her head. "There's nothing in the notes."

"You mean there's no record of what happened to her? What happened to the records from The Larches?"

She looks perplexed. "Our records end here. Vicky's case attracted much media interest. Even after she left here, reporters, writers would turn up every so often. When she moved to The Larches, she was given a new identity, a new name. They expected her to have more contact with the outside world."

"A new name?"

"It was deemed expedient for her own protection."

"A new name? But when I . . ." I stop myself from giving the game away just in time. "What was it?"

"I don't know." Her shrug is now intensely irritating.

*　*　*

"How can she have a different name when I know her as Vicky? That's what she was called when I met her last week." I can't get my head round it.

The flat fields fly past the car window. Jed's got the top down and the wind blows my words away so I have to shout.

"Did she actually say her name was Vicky?"

"Yes – well – I'm not sure." I can't remember her using her own name. "But the others called her Vicky. She must have told them it was her name."

"Maybe they knew who she was. Maybe she told them."

"No, I don't think so." I remember the conversation I had with Rita. "No, they didn't know anything about her past. They just thought – well, it was obvious something was wrong. They thought she'd been in care. And she wouldn't have been able to tell them."

148

"Doesn't she know who she is?"

The landscape reminds me of Lancashire, of the bus journey up to Skelmersdale from Liverpool. There are the same sprouts and cabbages, the same greying stalks of harvested wheat, the same wide fields and open sky. I think of Brow Lane Farm.

"She doesn't know her history; either doesn't know or can't tell." It sounds weird but I'm sure of it, thinking about her behaviour. "Oh, she remembers things, but they're isolated happenings, good things or bad things; the taste of ice cream or being locked up by the police. I don't know. Dr Soames noted that she had no sense of the past in her language."

Jed stares at the road ahead. This is beyond his remit. He deals with cause and effect, treatment and cure. I've got no real evidence but just from being with Vicky I know she's got little idea of who she is or where she's come from. I can't explain it but I know it's so. Her memories are like the collection of possessions she kept in her cupboard. I wonder if she remembers me, if I'm tucked away in there to be fetched out at random.

Does it matter, this lack of history? I've got my neatly arranged past, but these last few days have shown me how inaccurate and selective it is; how I've let fictions drive my present, and as far as the future goes, I've no more idea than Vicky.

"Let's stop for a drink." The light's failing and I'm flagging.

"Thought you'd gone to sleep. Thought you were dreaming of the lovely Usha."

I'd forgotten all about her. "I was just thinking."

"Didn't you ask for her phone number?"

"What do you think?" I give him a look, but I can't help smiling.

We stop at a pub on the outskirts of Northampton and it's almost dark by the time we swing onto the M1 and join the rushing horde of drivers who all know where they're going.

* * *

sleep   goodgirlmarjorie   sle e e e e p

tv   s l e e p

supper   redwhite   pink   s l eee

* * *

Two days after our visit to the Leadbetter Institute I'm still sunk in despair. After all my high hopes I've come to another dead end. I don't know where Vicky went or even what her official name is, so how can I begin to trace her?

I'm restless in the house. After Jed's gone to work I walk in the woods and think about Vicky's life. After years of total isolation in that shed, she was shut up in that institution and then what? Abandoned and forgotten in some residential home? But Dr Singh said The Larches was a rehab unit. Maybe they found her a foster home or even a permanent family. Then how did she end up on the street?

It's begun to rain. I can hear it pattering on the leaf canopy but it's dry enough in here. From the edge of the trees I can see the rain falling in slanting lines on the field between the wood and the housing estate.

Someone is running across the field; a girl with a golden Labrador. The dog crashes in through the trees a few yards from where I'm standing. The girl follows. She's about eighteen, long blonde hair swinging round her head as she bends down to restrain the dog.

"Good boy, Rinsky, good boy." She looks up and sees me, hesitates then smiles. "Oh, hello. Unexpected this rain, isn't it?" She waits for me to answer. She's uneasy because I'm a stranger.

"Let's hope it's only a shower. Nice dog." I make the appropriate response. She relaxes, looking at me casually, then her expression changes, her eyes narrow.

"Aren't you – aren't you Dr Crabbe?"

The blood seems to drop down my body and I lean my hand against the nearest tree. It had to happen sometime, I suppose, but who the hell is she?

"Are you okay?"

I must look as shaky as I feel. She takes a step towards me. The Labrador is off nosing in the bushes.

"I'm Lucy, Lucy Mainwaring. Don't you remember me?" She pauses. "Angela's friend."

"Lucy?" I recognise the caramel eyes but that's all. I can see the two of them poring over magazines on Angela's bed, their heads together, one dark, one fair. At the same time I remember the dream where Lucy was on the mortuary slab instead of Angela and my face must register my horror.

Her eyes widen, then she looks away towards the bushes.

"I'm sorry." I struggle for words. "I didn't recognise you. It's been a long time. Your hair's different." Everything about her is different. Five years difference. She's a woman now – just as Angela would have been. "It used to be dark."

She grins. "Blondes have more fun."

"I suppose so." I can't relate that trusting little girl to this confident, beautiful woman in front of me. She's left Angela behind.

"I've been away a long time. I've just come to visit an old friend for a few days."

"Oh." She smiles vaguely. Does she know about Corinne, about me? Does she know the whole sordid story?

There's a silence. We both watch the rain. She must know some of it because she doesn't say anything, doesn't mention that time and neither do I, but I can feel Angela as an awkward presence between us. The dog comes back and noses at her pockets.

"What do you want, Rinsky?" She finds a dog biscuit and gives it to him.

"You must have left school by now?" It's a safe thing to say. Angela shrinks.

"Yes – I've just started a nursing degree. I've got my first placement, start the week after next."

"That must be exciting. I hope you'll enjoy it. Which hospital?" I wish the rain would stop so I can escape but it's getting even heavier. This girl is like an open channel through which painful pasts and pictures of futures never to be come flooding.

"It's not a hospital, it's a community placement, a residential home called Meadowbank. Do you know it?"

I shake my head. I've no breath to speak.

"It's out near Pershore, a bit of a way to travel but I've passed my test and Dad gave me a car for my eighteenth. Not new, but it gets me around."

Her voice falls away. I stopped listening after the word "Meadowbank." All I can think is, it could be, it must be.

"What kind of residential home?" My voice croaks.

"Usual kind of place. For the elderly." My heart sinks. "There are some younger people there too, people with learning disabilities I think. I went to have a look round the day before yesterday. It's a nice place, lovely gardens and the staff seem okay."

I'm itching to ask more but she'll think it's odd. Anyway, Vicky isn't called Vicky and Lucy won't know any of the residents yet.

151

"The rain's going off. I'd better be getting back." She pulls the hood of her jacket over her head. I want to detain her, ask her to meet me again, but I can't. I know as soon as she gets home she'll tell her mother and it'll be all over town that I'm back.

She snaps a lead on the dog and flashes me a perfect smile. "Nice to see you again, Dr Crabbe."

"Sure." I wave as she sets off and wait till she's a small figure in the distance before I go off in the opposite direction.

Back at the house I force myself to sit down with a coffee when all I want to do is to rush off to Pershore. My mind is a jumble; Lucy's blonde hair that was dark, the contrast with her brown eyes, the dream, the mortuary, Angela's eyes devoid of life, Corinne – chips of ice, black holes, Angela looking at me out of Vicky's face, stuck forever at fourteen years old.

I've got to go there now. I can't wait for Jed to come back. Meadowbank. Medoban. Perhaps it's not the right place. I search the study for the list Jed brought home but Meadowbank's not on it. Adrenalin runs through my body, making me want to run, to be on my way, but I don't even know where the place is.

I check the phone book. There are three Meadowbanks listed and the realisation that it's a common name pulls me up, but one of them is a residential home at Drake's Broughton. It's near enough to Pershore to be the one.

Something's scoffing in my head. What are the chances of her being there? Convenient, isn't it? She's been just around the corner all the time you've been here. But someone told me she went to the Midlands or was it down South? And Wisbech isn't so very far away. It's possible she's there and if it's possible I have to go and look.

I've got a feeling about it. What drew me to come here? What caused my path to cross with Lucy's today? It's as if I'm meant to find her and if I don't find her at this Meadowbank, I'll keep on looking till I do.

I've got the phone in my hand, meaning to ring Meadowbank when I realise I've got nothing prepared to say. I'm in no state to sit down and think of something plausible. I just want to go. I'll think of something on the way there. I rifle the tin of loose change that Jed keeps in the kitchen with a pang of conscience. He won't mind and I promise myself I'll find a way to pay him back.

The bus from Ronkswood takes me into town and there I catch another to Pershore which dawdles all over the place before getting on the A44 and putting on some speed. The scenery's lost on me because I'm picturing what I'm going to do when I get there. I could pretend to be looking for a place for a relative but that won't guarantee I can find out if Vicky is, or was, there.

I'm no nearer to a plan when the bus pulls up in Drakes Broughton. When I ask for Meadowbank, an elderly lady tells me it's not actually in the village but is on the main road back the way I've come. The bus must have passed it without me noticing.

It's a beautiful sunny day, more like August than October. It would be a pleasant walk in other circumstances. Now I'm almost there I feel sick, and although I'm walking as fast as my hip will let me, each step seems to be in slow motion.

Meadowbank is set back from the road so I come upon it without warning. There's no sign of a building from the gate and if it wasn't for the signboard attached to the fence I would have gone straight past. Even this gives nothing away, just the name, 'Meadowbank', no phone number, no explanation as to what it is, and this gives me an uncanny feeling, as if there's something here to be hidden away.

The drive curves off between twin lines of beeches and horse chestnut trees. My feet crunch on beechmast and conkers. When the house comes into view I realise I'm in plain sight of anyone looking out of the front windows.

It's a dilemma whether to march confidently up the drive or to creep round the bushes that border the wide lawns. It's a big house, not mansion or stately home proportions, but the sort of place that once belonged to a well-off merchant or small manufacturer.

I decide to brazen it out. I don't want to be caught skulking in the bushes, a sure fast-track to the police station and an end to my search. There are people dotted about on benches, mostly old ladies I see when I get closer. My heart gives a thump of alarm when I spot a few uniformed nurses, but no one gives me a second glance. They probably think I'm here to visit a relative.

I can't get close enough to see properly without attracting attention, but I look at each group, hoping to see a familiar shape, a certain turn of the head, a remembered tone of voice.

The front door is closed and there's a security keypad so there's no chance of just wandering in, but a gravel path leads round the side of the house to more grounds at the back. There's a small kitchen garden, three-quarters cleared and the rest filled with sprouts and leeks. I turn the corner and see a view of the Malvern Hills in the distance behind the house and in between the shiny ribbon of the M5 crammed with cars.

Instantly I'm back at Brow Lane Farm looking down from the hill to the M6. It stops me in my tracks, and when I turn round Vicky is sitting on a bench by the back door of the house.

It must be a mirage. I'm stuck in the past on the farm and I've materialised Vicky from my imagination, projecting her on this poor woman with the slumped posture and vacant eyes. I take a step closer and it *is* Vicky, even though she has freshly curled hair and an empty face. I can scarcely breathe.

"Vicky." It comes out in a whisper. She doesn't move a muscle.

"Can I help you?" The back door bangs and makes me jump. A middle-aged woman in a green overall and gardening gloves looks at me with a pleasant smile that doesn't mask the suspicion in her eyes. Vicky doesn't react. She might be carved in stone.

The woman shifts the empty basket on her arm, waiting for me to speak. I ransack my mind and suddenly a picture comes, something I saw on the bus.

"Is this the kennels? Marchbank? I'm looking for a place for my dog."

"Kennels? Does it look like kennels?" She jiggles her basket impatiently. "Why didn't you ring the doorbell?"

"I – well – I could see this part wasn't the kennels. I thought it might be round the back. You know, like a separate enterprise. My friend recommended it. It's for Goldie, my Labrador. I have to go away at short notice and my usual place is full up. My friend couldn't remember the name properly. He thought it was Marchbank."

"Hmph! Well, there's no kennels here. This is Meadowbank. There's a kennels up the road but it's not called Marchbank, it's something daft like Daisy's Dog Hotel."

"That must be it!" I flash my version of a winning smile. "Maybe the people who own it are called Marchbank."

"I wouldn't know." She picks a pair of secateurs out of her basket and looks at a bed of chrysanthemums in the border.

I want so badly to speak to Vicky but I daren't even look at her. She still hasn't moved, doesn't even seem to be aware of our presence, let alone recognise me, which is perhaps just as well or she'd give the game away.

"I'll try there then. Thanks for your help."

She gives me a curt nod and stands watching until I turn the corner back to the front of the house. There's nothing I can do except leave. I walk along the road towards the kennels because I can't think of anything else to do. I can't think of anything. Any efforts to make sense of what's happened and arrive at some organised strategy are completely overwhelmed by the enormity of finding her.

The kennels is called "Delightful Days for Dogs". I can hear a faint sound of barking.

There's a bus stop just across the road. It's time I went back to Jed's. There's nothing I can do here now and Vicky doesn't look like she's going anywhere.

* * *

Sun

                                              birdsing

              thirsty   flowers

                                                      tired

          man newdoctorman   tirednotalk

                                                valerie

                            greengloves

                    hotsun
                  thirstytired

                                    flowers
                                    cut
                                    cry

              want
              go sleep   marjorie
                      go sleep

CHAPTER FIVE

By the time I get back my mind has cleared. I know exactly what I'm going to do. The plan arrived in my head as if someone else had thought it out and delivered it to me. Will it work? It's got to work.

I have to wait till around four thirty so I make myself an omelette and devour it, suddenly realising how hungry I am. Now I'm on course I'm utterly calm.

At 4.28 I key the number.

"Meadowbank." The voice is professional but friendly.

"Hello. My name's Jim Wallace, from the School of Health Studies. Could I speak to whoever's in charge there, please?"

"Mrs Mitchell? I think she's still here. I'll put you through."

"Claire Mitchell." This is the voice of a busy person.

"Mrs Mitchell, I don't think we've met. My name's Jim Wallace, from the School of Health Studies at the university. I'm Lucy Mainwaring's supervisor. I wondered if I could pop in and have a chat about her placement?"

"Well, Mr Wallace —" She sounds puzzled.

"Doctor."

"Sorry, Dr Wallace. Janet Russell usually comes to discuss student placements. In fact, let me just check, yes she has an appointment here next Wednesday. We've another student coming as well as Lucy, and Janet is coming to discuss them both."

"Yes I know, but unfortunately Janet's been called away due to family illness. I'm covering her appointments until she comes back. I'm afraid I can't make Wednesday, I've an important meeting all day."

"Oh! Well, I suppose we can make it another day. Let me see. What about two o'clock on Tuesday."

"Erm . . ." I flick the pages of the phone book. "No, I'm sorry I'm booked up on Tuesday. I could manage first thing Monday morning."

"Mornings are very busy for us. It's not really convenient."

"I do appreciate that Mrs Mitchell but it's the only time I can get there. I'm afraid it's a bit of an emergency situation with Janet going off so suddenly. My diary's full all week and Lucy's due to start with you the following week." I let my voice tail away.

"Yes," she says irresolutely. "Oh, I suppose I can fit it in. It'll have to be nine o'clock sharp."

"That's fine. Thank you so much for making the time. I'll see you then." I ring off before she can change her mind. There's no way she'll be able to check up on me at this time on a Friday afternoon and if my plan works, by the time she finds out the truth, Vicky and I will be long gone.

Next, I search Jed's garage for the things I will need – a decent torch, wire and bolt cutters and gardening gloves. Among some abandoned bike gear I find a black silk balaclava that might come in useful. I can't wait to get back there, but then it occurs to me that tonight is too soon. My preparations might be discovered before Monday. Much better to wait till tomorrow. I put the packed bag away and wait for Jed to return. It's difficult not to fill the time with thinking of all the things that could go wrong. If only I could fast-forward to Monday. I can't concentrate on TV or music. I wish Jed would come back. I want to share my news. When he hasn't arrived by seven thirty I start to fret. Just before eight he rings.

"Won't be back till late Buster. Got a last minute call out and I'm taking Sarah to the pictures. Get yourself something out of the freezer will you? We're eating —"

I cut him short. "Jed, I found her."

"Vicky?" His voice drops in surprise. I can barely hear him above the clatter and chatter of the place he's ringing from.

"She's in a home near Pershore. I've been there today. I saw her, Jed."

"That's great." He sounds uneasy.

"I can't believe it. All this time she's been so close."

"It's great news. Look, I have to go."

"I'm going back for her Jed, I'm going to get her out."

"Buster don't. Look, don't do anything. We'll talk about it when I get back."

I heat a frozen lasagne, make coffee, watch TV, but all the time I'm planning how I'm going to kidnap Vicky. Can I really impersonate my former self convincingly enough to carry it off? I get so involved in creating and replaying scenarios in which I charm Claire Mitchell into letting me take Vicky away, that I don't notice the time passing until I hear Jed's key in the door. It's after midnight. One look at his face tells me he's not happy about my news.

"Thought you'd be staying out all night." I give him a tomcat smile, trying to dispel the tension I can already sense between us.

"Fat chance after what you told me. I've been worrying about it all evening." He takes off his jacket and reaches in the kitchen cupboard for the bottle of Glenmorangie.

"Sorry to ruin your date. I suppose you talked it all over with Sarah."

"That's unfair, Jack. You should know I would never discuss your affairs with anybody else." He puts two glasses on the table, but I push mine away and get up to put the kettle on.

"So, you found Vicky." He puts his feet up. "What happened?"

"It was weird. I was out walking this morning, in the woods and I met Lucy – do you remember, Marianne and Tom's daughter?" I tell him the story except for the bit about ringing up Claire Mitchell.

"That's amazing. From Liverpool she ends up here and so do you. Are you sure it's her?"

"I saw her." I remember my momentary doubt. "I didn't get to talk to her. She didn't know me, or she didn't appear to. She didn't move. She just sat there."

"Probably medicated to the eyeballs." He gives me a wry smile and pours half a tumbler of whisky. "How did she get to Liverpool? Did you find out any more about her?"

"I didn't talk to anyone, except the woman working in the garden and she wasn't going to tell me anything. I couldn't just up and say,

"I'm Dr Crabbe and I want to know about Vicky Appleton, could I? And, anyway, I don't know what they're calling her now, do I?"

"Okay, now you know she's safe you don't need to worry about her any more do you? Maybe you can get on with your own life now, take some steps back to the life you ought to be living. Maybe this whole thing has been a good experience for you."

What is he talking about? I put my coffee down on the table. "You don't think I want to go back to – that?"

He shrinks back from the horror that I know is in my voice and on my face.

"Look, I know you put yourself out to help me. I know I've been taking advantage of your kindness and your lifestyle for the last week or so and, believe me, I'm grateful, but the past is over and done with, Jed. I can't go back to what I was. I just want to get her out of there and be on my way."

He looks completely bewildered, and hurt. "But when you came here, I thought what you really wanted was to come back. I thought you'd realised —"

"What I was missing? No, Jed. I've been telling you all along I didn't want that. You haven't been listening."

"But it's such a waste, of your life, your talents." He knocks the whisky back in one gulp and pours another.

"It's up to you what you think. All I know is I'm not leaving Vicky to rot in that place."

"You're talking crazy! Think straight man. You can't get her out and even if you could, what then?"

"I'm going to get her out, Jed."

"How? Going to walk up and knock on the door, 'Excuse me, I've come to take Vicky away'?"

"I've got it planned."

"Well you can count me out. Helping you find out about her is one thing. Kidnapping her out of state care is a different kettle of fish. I've told enough lies already for you."

"I wouldn't dream of —"

"Jesus Jack, I don't want to know." He gets up and slams out. The door to his room bangs shut and after a few seconds The Who burst out shouting, "My Generation". He's taken the whisky bottle with him.

I lie down on the bed in his spare room and nothing seems right. I think of all the cold, damp doorways I've slept in with my hip groaning and complaining, all the grotty hostel rooms I've shared with the most unpredictable social outcasts. It's taken meeting Vicky to make me realise that instead of dropping out of an environment I wasn't good enough to be in, I've dropped into another world that operates in different, but equally valuable ways. I don't know which is right or wrong, I only know what I can and can't do, and I can't go back to the comfortable world of Dr Jack Crabbe.

* * *

wakeup marjorie

sun yes day look garden
                               wakeup goodgirlmarjorie

openwindow
openwindow
openwindow
openwindow window shut no

thirsty   thirsty   thirsty tea and toast
yes

medication   water thirsty water
                          want coke   want

valerie garden   marjorie sit   goodgirl yes   tired

* * *

Saturday morning I'm back at Meadowbank but this time I take the risk of creeping through the bushes. It's as I'd hoped. Vicky's sitting in the same place by the back door. She's got the same vacant look on her face, staring ahead but not looking at anything. Her hands are limp in her lap.

The security is not as bad as I'd expected. There are cameras of course, but there is only simple link-wire fencing down both sides of the back garden and a thick hedge at the bottom end. Beyond the fence on the side of the garden where Vicky's sitting is a small copse of Scotch pines.

No point in hanging around for long, it's too risky in the daylight, and if that dragon in the gardening gloves comes out and sees me, my plans will be shot to pieces. I want to call out to Vicky but I mustn't and she looks so absent it would probably be pointless anyway. She doesn't even look unhappy or despairing, just not there. I can no longer see Angela looking out from her eyes.

When I get back, Jed has gone out and that's how it goes for the rest of the weekend as we carefully avoid each other. I suppose that now he realises we're on separate paths he doesn't know what to do about me. I'm pretty sure he won't tell anyone about my plans, but he'll probably want me to move on. That suits me anyway. I don't want to put him in a compromising situation.

On Sunday morning I visit Angela's grave for the last time. I'm able to do this without fear this time. Angela is not there and this is a symbolic farewell. I even feel peaceful but how or why this is I don't know. Nothing has really changed, yet everything is different. There is a fresh bunch of carnations on the grave and last week's chrysanths have disappeared.

"It's okay sweetheart." I am not talking to the grave but to Angela inside my head. Now I'm looking at things from my new perspective, perhaps I can open up the good memories, the good things in my life that she represents, rather than pushing her image away with horror.

In the late afternoon, I travel to Pershore again. I want to check that Vicky's still around, maybe sitting on her bench, but I'm frightened of being seen and remembered so I get a sandwich and a Coke at a pub in the village and settle down to wait. I try to plan where I will take Vicky when I get her out. I can't take her back to Jed's but at the moment I can't think of anything except tomorrow morning. Something will turn up. What did Mary Appleton say? "Consider the lilies."

At last it starts to get dark and I can make my way back to Meadowbank. The sun is almost set by the time I get there and the trees along the drive are black and stark against the last bright stripes as the sun slides down through bands of cloud.

Lights are on in the windows but the curtains are all drawn. Where is she? Maybe she can sense me the way she sensed what was happening to Peter. If only I could clear my thoughts, maybe I could reach her, but my mind is cluttered with plans and all the things that could go wrong. What if it rains? What if she's not there? What if someone else is there with her?

When it's so dark I won't be seen, I cut the wire fence, just enough to slip through, making sure I pick a spot close enough for a quick escape but out of sight behind a bush and away from the security lights and cameras. Vicky's bench is empty and the peace of the garden is broken only by the last chirpings of birds settling down for the night. I stop to hide my bag under a heap of pine needles in the copse on the adjoining farmland before making my way to catch the last bus back to Worcester.

When I let myself into the house, Jed is in the lounge, watching a re-run of *Spinal Tap*. He's got a fresh bottle of Glenmorangie and he sees me looking at it, but neither of us can say what we're thinking.

"There's some curry in the fridge. It's home-made," he shouts over the soundtrack. I'm too keyed up to eat but it's a peace offering. I can't afford not to accept so I warm it up and take it in on a tray. Music fills the space between us and he watches me while I eat, then he swings his feet off the couch and fills his glass.

"This plan of yours. When is it going to happen?"

"Tomorrow." My look dares him to try to change my mind.

"And then?"

I shrug. "I'm not asking you to help me. You've done enough already. I won't be coming back here."

"Where will you go?"

"It's best if you don't know."

"Jesus Christ! I can't believe you're really contemplating doing this. What if it all goes wrong? You'll go to gaol. You'll be struck off!"

"So? I've not kept my registration up anyway."

He stares at me like I just landed from Mars.

"I thought I knew you, Jack, better than I know anybody, but I don't. I don't know you at all."

"I've changed. After Angela died I didn't want to be myself. I hated myself. Yes, maybe you're right, maybe I could have learned to love myself again, forgive myself, come back. But now, because of Vicky, I see all this differently. The way I used to live with Corinne, with you, okay, it's what most people want, but it's not the only way. It boxes you in, shuts you off from yourself. I don't know what it's all about, Jed."

I can see he doesn't know what I'm talking about and I can't explain. Words aren't enough.

"All those years on the streets, I've been learning other ways of living. But it wasn't till I met Vicky and saw for myself how she thinks, how she is, that I realised the value of it. I thought she could help me to go back to the past, to those things that were so painful I couldn't face remembering them, but now I'm not so sure I need to do that."

Jed's face is white. He reaches for the Glenmorangie. I suddenly think of Mabel with her bottle of wine.

"Whatever happens, I shan't come back here. I wouldn't want to involve you."

"You'll need money."

I shake my head. "I might need to borrow some clothes."

He puts his hands over his face and when he takes them away again I see how tired he looks. "Call it off Jack, it's a crazy scheme."

"I can't. Not even for you."

"You're fucking nuts. I'm going to bed." He stands up and rubs the back of his neck. "Maybe you'll see sense in the morning."

When he's gone to his room, I wash the dishes and his empty glass. This time he's left the whisky bottle behind.

In the morning, when I come out of the shower he's gone, even though it's barely seven o'clock. Maybe this is the best way. I choose a dark suit from his wardrobe and put on a silk tie that feels so alien after all these years that I have to crush the desire to rip it off again.

On the kitchen table there's an envelope with £100 inside and Jed's mobile number scrawled on the outside. After a moment's hesitation I put it in my pocket. Maybe someday I'll be able to repay his kindness. I leave his front-door key on the table with a sense of desolation. It's unlikely that we will meet again.

I arrive at Meadowbank at ten to nine. All the way I've been watching the gathering clouds and praying that it won't rain. What will I do if Vicky is nowhere around when I get there?

Think positive. It's going to work, as long as that woman in the green overall doesn't answer the door. Catching sight of myself in the hall mirror as a nurse lets me in, I have to admit that I look the business. I just hope it's enough. If anyone asks to see my ID my goose will be cooked.

I'm left sitting in the hall watching nurses and patients coming up and down the stairs. Food smells and the clatter of dishes identify the dining room across from my seat. I desperately want to go and see if Vicky is in there, but I daren't move and after a minute or two Claire Mitchell appears and invites me to her office.

"Good of you to be so prompt. I've got a meeting at ten so we'll have to be brief."

"That suits me too."

"This is the student pack that we use here." She gives me a sheaf of forms.

"I'm sure you'll find Lucy a very able student. She's only just begun her studies but she has excellent A level results and a good report from her sixth-form college."

"Well, she'll only be here for observation at first. We don't want to frighten her off." She laughs, a tinkly little sound for such a business-like woman. "The other student, Paul Wright, he's a second year?"

"Oh yes. He's had a year's experience on the wards so I'm sure you'll find him very useful. He's a pleasant lad. Of course we'll be setting his objectives with you once he commences the placement."

"I've not met Paul yet, but Lucy seems a very competent girl."

I waffle about the respective merits of Lucy and Paul without letting her get a word in. I just hope they live up to the praise I'm giving them. When I see her beginning to look at her watch, I wind down. "Well, we're both busy people, and everything seems quite satisfactory – if you're happy?"

"Fine with me. We like having students here."

"I would like to know a little more about the home. Maybe you could spare a few minutes to show me round?"

"I don't really have time right now, Dr Wallace, but you're welcome to have a look round. I'll ask Nurse Johnson to go with you. She's been here a long time. She knows everything there is to know about Meadowbank."

Nurse Johnson looks like she should be retired, but I can tell as soon as she looks at me that she's made of steel. She leads me up the stairs and shows me the neat bedrooms decorated in restful colours, the ensuite shower rooms, even the linen cupboards. Downstairs there's a typical TV lounge with Parker Knoll armchairs and artificial flowers. A few residents wander in from the dining room.

"This is the activity room." Nurse Johnson throws the door open and startles a middle-aged man with Down's Syndrome who is working on a watercolour painting.

"This is Robin. Robin likes painting, don't you Robin?" He looks at me and grunts.

"And this is the kitchen." She shepherds me along the corridor and I almost stop dead as I see Vicky getting a bottle of Coke out of a fridge.

"Some of these people seem rather young to be in a rest home for the elderly." I pray Vicky won't give me away but she shows no sign of recognition.

"It's not a rest home as such. It is mostly for elderly people but specialises in care for those with what we call learning disabilities. We only take people on recommendation from Social Services, so we do get some younger cases. It all depends on where there are beds these days, doesn't it?"

The moment is coming but Vicky is inside, not out. I keep willing her to go to the back door but she's intent on her drink.

"Take poor Marjorie here. She's been with us for donkey's years. She was here even before me and I've been here twenty years."

"What's the matter with her?" I lower my voice.

"No one really knows. She's been here so long she's like part of the furniture. There's no need to whisper, Doctor, she doesn't understand much of what you say. Although, having said that, she disappeared a couple of months ago while we were on a day out to Weston-super-Mare and we only got her back last week. The police found her in some kind of squat – in Liverpool of all places. How she got there and what she'd been doing nobody knows. Doesn't bear thinking about, does it? And she can't tell us poor thing. Put that in a glass, Marjorie, there's a good girl."

Vicky turns towards the back door and looks at it like someone in a dream.

"In the glass, dear." The nurse takes the bottle from her and pours out the drink. Vicky accepts it without any change of expression. "She's being kept under sedation for the moment until she's settled down again but she's never very responsive at the best of times."

There's a sudden altercation in the hall and she breaks off. "Oh excuse me a moment, it's those two again, honestly they're always squabbling." She shouts from the door, "Rebecca! Rebecca? Come and get Millie and Jane."

She turns back to me. "That new girl. She's never around when she's supposed to be on duty." The noise escalates. "I'm sorry. I'll have to see to them."

"It's okay. I have to go anyway. I'll see myself out." I step towards the back door and she nods with relief before disappearing into the hall.

"Vicky! Vicky! It's Jack. Come on." She's still staring at the door with the glass of Coke in her hand. "Come on." I tug at her arm and try to take the Coke from her. She doesn't pull away but she hangs on to the glass with a stronger grip than she looks capable of. How am I going to get her out?

She turns to look at me as if I've dragged her away from somewhere else. Yes, now she will recognise me, she'll respond and come with me.

"Doctor," she says, and there's no intonation in her voice, no recognition in her eyes.

I put on my most professional air and seize her by the arm. "Marjorie. Outside. Now," I say loudly and firmly.

It works. She turns like a lamb and lets me push her towards the door, but just as she goes outside, a woman in a green overall comes into the room pushing a trolley full of dirty dishes.

For a second, my heart stops but it's not the same woman I saw on Friday and this one gives me a quick but incurious smile before starting to unload the plates into a dishwasher.

I puff myself up and consult my wrist even though I've no watch. "Would you thank Nurse Johnson for showing me round. I really can't wait for her to come back."

She nods as I leave. Vicky is standing outside the back door, just out of sight from the window.

"Come on." I pull her and, thank God, she follows me without protest. It's like clockwork. Within seconds I've got her through the fence and then it's only a few moments while I pick up my bag, before we're on our way.

I try to hurry Vicky along. My hip's screaming and I'm too breathless to talk as we dodge through the pine trees. I just pray I've timed the bus right and no one notices Vicky's missing till we have time to get clear.

doorgardenbushesfence

coldtrees   shadow

doctorman run marjorie run vicky run   novicky good-girlmarjorie

run yes run goodgirl run

coke

thirsty

tired   no more doctorman no more run   stopit

* * *

166

Once we're on the bus I still can't relax. I pull Vicky to the back seat and I keep peering out of the rear window, expecting to see the police in hot pursuit. There aren't many other passengers and no one takes any notice of us even though we're both breathless.

After a bit I try to settle down, brush the pine needles off Jed's suit and pick them out of Vicky's hair. She's still barely reacting, despite being dragged through the bushes and practically thrown on the bus. This isn't the Vicky I know.

She just stares at the back of the seat in front of her. but when I touch her hair she turns towards me and something changes in her eyes. Now she knows me.

"Thirsty," she says. "Coke." That's all. She still hasn't recognised me. I hadn't planned for this. What if something's happened to permanently change her? This is silly. I know it's the medication. Once it wears off she'll be okay.

We need to get as far away as possible quickly. When we arrive safely in Worcester, I propel Vicky to Foregate Street Station and buy two tickets to Birmingham. It's an extravagance but we could be hours trying to hitch a lift and getting ourselves noticed into the bargain. Bless you Jed, for leaving the money.

"Want Coke," is the only thing Vicky says and I buy two bottles to keep her quiet during the journey. I wonder if she's ever been on a train before. Perhaps it's a good thing that she's so sedated, otherwise she might have caused a scene.

Thankfully, she falls asleep as soon as the train gets going. The last thing I need is her attracting attention from the other passengers. I'm uncomfortable in Jed's suit, it's rumpled and sticky with all the panic I've sweated into it. I take the pink tie off and drape it round Vicky's neck without waking her, then I sneak off to the toilet to change into my own clothes. They'll be looking for someone in a suit, not an old tramp in sweat pants.

All the time I'm in the toilet, I worry about her, but she's still there, fast asleep when I get back. After a few moments of sitting, staring out of the train window, panic starts to set in. What am I doing? I'm throwing away any chance I ever had of going back to 'normal' life. The train goes faster and faster and my racing thoughts match its speed. What I'm doing is criminal, irrational, illogical. The words beat time with the wheels. I think of Jed's horrified face, then I look at Vicky. She's serene in the middle of all this.

As if she senses my thoughts, she awakes and looks round. She's unperturbed by this awful step I've taken. I can't go back. I've burnt my bridges. But when I look at her, I know I'm doing the right thing for us both.

At Birmingham, I stop short at the station exit. A row of police cars are parked on the station approach. Are they waiting for us? There's no sign of any policemen.

My heart thumps as I drag Vicky back into the station and up the escalator to the Pallasades shopping centre. There is anonymity here, in the crowds, and I start to relax. For a while, we wander aimlessly, while I try to think what to do, then I see two policemen walking purposefully towards us. I steer Vicky quickly to the nearest staircase and out into the street. I daren't look over my shoulder until we get outside, but no one seems to be following us.

In the street, it's begun to drizzle. I buy Vicky a change of clothes and a rainproof jacket in a charity shop. We eat lunch in McDonalds. She smiles when I give her the carton containing her burger and fries. It's the first sign of life she's shown and I'm encouraged. I watch her eat and remember the last time we were in McDonalds, in Liverpool, less than three weeks ago.

mcdonalds   cheeseburgerfriescoke

fizztickle   hotfries

                                mcdonalds
                    police   medoban marjorie

no
ray rita kindi peter black
nomore
            nomorepeter
                greybeard yes oldgreybeard

"Hermitjack," she says, and delight spreads through me like warm honey.

"Vicky. You're back." I want to touch her, take her hand, but I don't. She reaches out and strokes Jed's pink tie. "Doctor," she says and her smile falters. "No go Medoban." She looks anxiously at me.

"No, no more Medoban." I try to sound confident. "Not if I can help it."

To escape the rain, I take Vicky into the Bullring but I'm constantly looking for patrolling police.

Vicky turns and turns, staring in delight at the mirrored lights in the glass walls and ceilings. Although she still seems sleepy, she's definitely coming back to her old self. Her wonder makes me smile, despite my anxiety. Suddenly, I see the mall with her eyes, a flying mixture of colours, smells, textures. I see a muddled vision of dresses, shoes, bags, toys, cosmetics, exotic foods, electrical items, all heaped in an Aladdin's cave full of jewelled lights and shiny surfaces, all totally without pattern or meaning.

She starts to pull me to different shop windows, making little squeaks of delight. She's making me nervous, people are turning to look at us. It's time to move on, but where?

Maybe we can stay in Birmingham for a while until I can work out what to do next. It's big and anonymous enough but my gut feeling is to get away. They will know by now that's she's missing and that I'm not who I said I was. They'll be looking for Marjorie and Dr Wallace. They're bound to ask Lucy but there's no reason why she should connect Dr Wallace with me. I hope not, for Jed's sake.

It's not safe to stay here and when I think about it it's obvious where we have to go.

Outside on the street, the rain has stopped, and the sun is shining on the lunchtime crowds. It's so like the day we walked through Liverpool, I can imagine us back there as if the events of the past few weeks never happened. But then I was a different person, trying to lose my past, whereas now I can live in the present.

I check the money Jed gave me. I think there'll be enough. On the way back to the railway station I buy a couple more Cokes for Vicky. In the shop she looks at me with Angela's eyes. She doesn't ask where we're going, barely says anything, but I can see a difference in her. She's becoming more alert, watching people go by.

At the station, I steer Vicky through another entrance, where there are no police cars. I'm hoping their presence is a normal thing, that they're not specifically looking for us, but I'm on pins while I buy the tickets, and during the time we have to wait for the next train.

In the carriage she doesn't speak except to ask for chocolate when the trolley comes by and after a while she falls asleep again. I could sleep too, I'm dropping with nervous exhaustion and I feel safer with every mile we travel away from the Midlands but I can't doze off. My mind keeps running on the possibilities. Maybe the rail staff have been alerted to watch for us. Maybe the railway police will get on at the next station.

Each time the train stops, Vicky wakes up and looks around. Each time she does this, I hold my breath. Don't talk, Vicky, please don't talk. People will notice, remember us. I ply her with Coke and chocolate and as soon as the train starts its rhythmic beat, she dozes off again.

It's after four when we get to Wigan but we pick up a bus to Upholland right away. Vicky plays with the pink tie, sniffing it as if there are traces of me or Jed on it. She doesn't seem concerned about where we're going as long as it's not to Meadowbank.

They might look for us in Liverpool but they certainly won't be looking for us here. The little village seems almost friendly and we go across to the chip shop on the crossroads and get chips and I pick up a couple of sandwiches and yet more Coke for later. There's not much left of Jed's money but tomorrow's another day.

We walk past the housing estate where Vicky's mother once walked and suddenly horror strikes through me as I realise what I'm doing. Why am I bringing Vicky back here to the scene of her early torment? Is it some prurient desire to see if she will remember? Am I no better that the scientists with their funded research?

I can't explain it but it's something I have to do. Somehow I know it's necessary to us both.

Vicky seems happy walking with me. She looks at everything, the houses, the fields, the dry stone walls but she shows no recognition at all. When we come to the turn into Brow Lane, darkness is beginning to gather under the tunnel of trees. Vicky turns to me and her face now is uneasy, almost questioning.

This is your history, Vicky. I wonder what you'll make of it. Will you remember? Maybe it's something she needs to know as much as I do.

trees	"Down here Vicky. Don't be scared. It's okay."	What is this feeling? Is it the end of the day, the end of the journey, or something
hermitjack sad birdsing sad		ney, or something peculiar to this place?
no sun cold	"Come on, it's not far."	
yes cold trees talk vickynotmarjorie		Shadows finger the long hours before

smell earth leaves
flowers

rabbits on grass one
rabbit   two rabbits
squeak squeak hello
vicky notmarjorie

trees   leaves listen

hermitjack tired
no breath

black here black
house no top no
light sad sadhouse

"Give me your hand
– Vicky – your hand.
Over the gate. Come
on, I'll help you."

"Up here now. Be
careful,   there   are
holes, and rocks."
"Come on Vicky,
nearly there now."

"I'll be glad to have a
rest. I don't know
about you."

"hermitjack   give
vicky coke."

night while life winds
down, creatures get-
ting ready to sleep.

The gate bars the
way blackly and up
there, up the path,
the grass, the bushes
seem taller, a last
burst   of   growth
before winter death.
Is it me, or every-
thing   round   me,
holding its breath?
Not   a   rustle   of
leaves, no breeze but
the sounds of our
passage crack and
crush   the   silence.
When we stop at the
top I can just hear
the brook at the bot-
tom trickling over
the stones.
I stop to catch my
breath. To my right
the   remembered
shape, the dark hulk
of the house.

She's stopping too
but she's just staring
at the house – as if
she's seen it before?
Does she remember
it?
Thirsty again. When
will she stop being
thirsty?

house fall down

stones

tired listen

stopit stopit shutup
stopit

nomore

listen house
holes
sing
hungry
thirsty
hungry
thirsty
hungry
thirsty

"Here, it's the last one.
Don't drink it all
now."

"Don't go in the
house, Vicky, it's
dangerous. Come
away."

"no more sad-
woman."

"What?"
"What did you say?"
"Vicky – tell me."

She must feel some-
thing here. Even I can
feel the sombreness
here. It's death and
life and the rotting
house slowly slipping,
while unseen crea-
tures scuttle about
and the moon sailing
up as if to say every-
thing just goes on
regardless and we're
just two more crea-
tures scurrying down
here.

That spot she's
standing on, maybe
that's the place, yes,
there's a heap of
rotten wood. That's
why she's staring,
staring at nothing,
but would she know?
Would she ever have
known, back then? If
you never knew the
company of others,
the warmth of love, a
comfortable home. If
you knew nothing
but the scraps you'd
always eaten, the cold
you'd always felt,
would you feel
deprived, unhappy,
angry, sad?

Did I hear right? No
more sad woman? Is
that what she said?
She's looking at the

"sadblackwoman
nomore nomore."

hole where the farm-house door once was, the place where Jimmy Atherton told me Mary's body was found.
She remembers. Or does she just see?
Those rotten planks – once they were strong. Once they framed her world.

wood
nomore
broken
beetles
no
sleep
vicky
tired

"vicky go sleep"
"Soon. What about the sad woman?"
"nomore"
"You mean your mother. Vicky, she was your mother. This is where you were born."
"mother mothercat motherbook"

The books! They're in my bag.

motherbook   come
back
hermitjack
give vicky

"Here. Here they are."
"motherbook"

She can't read. How does she know?
Someone's told her.
Someone's told her what mother means.
Look at the way she touches it, strokes the covers.
Someone's told her but she doesn't

"That's right. Your mother's book. *Your* mother."
"mother book mother baby"
"Your mother, Vicky. You were the baby."

motherbook

sadmotherwoman

blackwoman

sadblack

redbook smell red-
book
mansmell
hermitjacksmell
badbook

blackredbook
sadbadblackwoman
 no
stopit no
hurtvicky
no
no

"Come on Vicky,
over here. Put the
books in my bag."

"Want a sandwich?
Chicken or tuna?"
"We'll be okay if it
doesn't rain. I'll
make some tea."

understand. She's
clutching the book.
Does she know
what's in it? Has
someone read it to
her? Would she
understand? Maybe
someone's read it to
her, watered it
down, changed the
bad bits to make a
pretty fairy story. It
would be cruel to tell
her the truth.

But she's touching
the other book too
and sniffing at it. She
stiffens. It's as if it's
burning her fingers.

She opens it, turn-
ing the pages as if they
were dirty, unpleas-
ant. Everything about
her looks taut, as if
she's getting ready to
run away.

Maybe it was a
mistake, giving her
the books. I'll try to
get her settled down
for the night.

Groundsheet, sleep-
ing bag, plastic
sheet. Should keep
us warm enough.

In the light of the
stove her face holds
deep shadows. She's

staring out across the plain, every muscle taut. She's like a statue, sandwich poised halfway to her mouth. Suddenly I'm cold. I can feel the house looming behind me.

What's she staring at? There's nothing there. The hairs rise on my neck. Then I see it. It's the motor-way.

"What is it Vicky? What's the matter?"

dark
hills
fields

orangelights
orangelights
orangelights
broken beetles wood
angry
woman stopit shutup

yes shutup rain
on hills snow
yellowfields   green-fields
sun
hungry
thirsty
shutup shutup
cupboard

no more

noscared hermitjack
nohurtangela
nohurtvicky

nomore

"orangelights vicky
see sadwoman hungry
thirsty nomore stones
trees
wood
wood"

"eggs"

It's the most I've ever heard her say.

What does it mean? Is it a view she used to see? How much does she remember?

Eggs?

Vicky lies down. Her face is a mask, turned away from me so she can stare out at the plain.

I can see the lights of the cars on the motor-way. They make me think of the Jaguar and the way I was so drawn to Vicky to get the answers to those missing moments. Now it doesn't seem to

175

no want see silvercar

no
hermitjack want see

want see angela

no no red bad red

sunyellowshine
redbadblack
silver
poorbird

poor

noangelahermitjac-
knono
stopitstopit

"silver car."

"What?"

"silvercar hermit-
jack angela"
"hermitjack red
angry corinne angela
want horse ride
horse hermitjackan-
gela ride car nice
horse in field angela
like horse angela say
look dad
big bird come bird
want food food in
field bird see food yes
hungry big tail bird fly
fast car drive fast her-
mitjack see horse bird
see food no stopit sto-
pitstopitstopit"

be so important, I've
already made my
peace with Angela.

Despite everything, I
feel comfortable
lying here with
Vicky next to me. It's
warm and I feel quite
at home here, as if
the farm accepts me,
because I've brought
her home.

She turns to face
me and Angela's eyes
look at me gravely.

And I remember, the late afternoon, the sun dipping and blinding me, how cross I was because Corinne hadn't come back to take Angela for her riding lesson. I wanted a few hours peace before evening surgery but Angela nagged for me to take her.

I remember the ponies in the field as we drove out to the stables. She cried out, "Look Dad." And then there was the glare of the sun as I glanced away from the road and the thump on the windscreen, the smear of blood and feathers, before I realised what was happening. I remember the screaming, Angela screaming, the way it tore into my brain, then nothing.

"It's okay, it's okay." I hold Vicky and rock her till she stops screaming and her body starts to soften. We stay like this for a long time, until she's quiet. There's a complete feeling inside me, as if a final piece of the jigsaw has dropped into place. My face is wet with tears.

When I open my eyes, Vicky's asleep. I lie dreaming about staying here, building a home for Vicky, after all it is her property, but would they let her stay? We'd soon be discovered here, small villages have eyes everywhere, everybody knows everybody else and the Miss Thorntons and Jimmy Athertons don't miss a trick.

Maybe I'm only thinking about what I'd like. How do I know Vicky would want to stay here? I'm making decisions for her just like everybody else does. Maybe she'd want to sell the farm and spend the money on Coke and chocolate. I wonder how she lived those few weeks on her own before I met her. Maybe she's tougher than I think. She must have been tough to survive all that time in that shed.

I don't remember falling asleep or dreaming until Vicky wakes up screaming and struggling sometime in the night. "No no Medoban! No Martin, stop it! Stop it!" I hold her flailing arms, feel the warmth of her body close against mine, till she stops fighting and her breathing tells me she's asleep again. Christ! What did they do to her in that place?

Early morning a soft rain wakes us. I set up the stove to make tea with the last of our water. Vicky goes off in the bushes and I look round for some branches to rig up a shelter with the plastic sheet but when she comes back she points to the path. She's telling me it's time to go and she's right. There's a clean space inside me where the spectres of Angela and Corinne used to torment me and maybe Vicky's ghosts too have been laid to rest.

"Get chocolate and Coke." Vicky says hopefully as I pack every-thing up.

"'Spect so." I look at what's left of Jed's money. Just over a fiver.

I don't know where we're going or what will happen next. I don't know if Vicky will want to stay with me today, for a week or forever. I don't know how long we'll be able to travel together, how long till she gets picked up again and taken back to Meadowbank.

Just before we leave Vicky takes her mother's diaries from her pocket, scrapes a hole under a blackberry bush and covers them up. She smiles as she stands up and takes my arm.

hermitjackvicky go out of dark   go down hill   vicky see shop
        hermitjack buy chocolate and coke
vicky see houses   gardens   people
     blue bus come   hermitjackvicky geton

POSTSCRIPT

I first developed a real interest in feral children after reading Michael Newton's excellent book, *Savage Girls and Wild Boys,* which was published in 2002. Prior to this I thought that feral children originated from Third World countries or were relics from earlier times when attitudes to children were less enlightened than today. I soon discovered that cases of feral children have captivated public imagination throughout history.

Mythological examples abound in classical Greek and Roman literature, the most famous probably being the twins Romulus and Remus, who were raised by a wolf and went on to found the city of Rome. Medieval literature features tales such as *Valentine and Orson,* in which the twin sons of a great king are separated at birth, one to be raised as a nobleman, the other to be brought up by a bear, only to come together as an invincible power when they inherit their kingdom.

In these early tales, fact and fiction mingle in the telling, but in the eighteenth century   accounts of real feral and confined children reveal common themes that stimulated my interest enough to do further research.

In the early eighteenth century a wild boy was discovered in the woods near Hanover in Germany. He was named Peter and paraded through the courts of Europe as a great novelty, arriving in London in 1726. Peter's origins were never discovered and he never learned to speak, but many stories were written about him, presenting him as the embodiment of natural purity and innocence, and contrasting this with the decadence and corruption that passed for normal behaviour in court life. A clear example of the thought of the time is can be found in the anonymous poem, 'The Savage', published in London in 1726, which is appended to this epilogue. As Peter failed to develop further, interest in him gradually waned and he ended his life in poverty.

In 1798, another wild boy was found in the woods near Aveyron, France. At first he was not named and was paraded in the local village as a freak, but soon he was put on show in Paris and then sent to the Deaf Mute Institute where a young doctor, Jean Marc Gaspard Itard, attempted to rehabilitate him. He named the boy Victor and spent many years trying to teach him to speak and read, with very little success. Victor learned only one word, 'lait' meaning 'milk', although he did learn some social skills. Itard's efforts reflect the ideas of his time, shortly after the French Revolution: the vision of enlightenment and dignified humanity that owed much to the philosophy of Jean-Jacques Rousseau. Here again there is an emphasis on the purity of human nature, before it is sullied by unnatural and false manners.

Itard left painstaking accounts of his work with Victor, but as he realised he was not able to fully educate the boy, he became disillusioned and eventually abandoned his subject to the care of his elderly housekeeper who devoted herself to Victor until his death. Although money was made available for Victor's upkeep it was so little that they too lived a penurious existence.

Perhaps the most famous feral child is Kaspar Hauser, discovered wandering the streets of Nuremburg, Germany, in 1828. Kaspar was in fact a confined child, and eventually was able to give an account of how he had been kept in a dark cellar for many years, by a captor who he never actually saw. This captor suddenly forced the boy, then aged about sixteen, out of his cellar and frog-marched him to the town, where he left him to be discovered.

Kaspar differed from most feral children in that he did learn to speak, read and write fluently. Like Peter and Victor he quickly came to the attention of learned doctors and fashionable noblemen who vied to be his patrons. Passed from one benefactor to another he eventually fell from favour. Having survived an assassination attempt by an unknown perpetrator in 1829, he died in 1833 following a second attack by an unknown assailant. These attacks led to persistent rumours that Kaspar was in fact a royal prince who had been hidden away at birth, and the true story of his origins remains unknown.

These few examples reveal themes common to most stories of feral children: the freak-show interest, followed by the desire to discover his or her nature, the attempt to rehabilitate the unsocialised child, and the disillusionment and abandonment that follows when the child, now an adult, fails to fulfil the agendas of its protector.

This doesn't explain the reasons why their images have lived on to present times with the re-working of their stories in novels, plays and films. Victor is the subject of François Truffaut's well known film, *L'Enfant Sauvage,* first screened in 1969, and also the novel, *Wild Boy,* by Jill Dawson (2003). Many poems and stories have been written about Kaspar Hauser, notably Peter Handke's play *Kaspar* (1973) and Werner Herzog's film, *The Enigma of Kaspar Hauser* (1974).

These fictional images of feral children explore the ambiguities suggested by their stories, contrasting wildness with civilisation, innocence with corruption, purity with decadence. The feral child exists on the borders of humanity, of civilisation, making us re-think our ideas about what it means to be a human being and maybe ask questions about what we were before we learned to speak, to follow the paths of logic and rationality, and to wonder about the power that language has to distort as well as express, to fill up mental space and block out other ways of experiencing the world.

Perhaps this is why these stories continue to fascinate. However, the image of the feral child is not confined to the dust of history books. Fresh instances of feral children continue to surface with surprising regularity, in our supposedly child-centred Western societies as well as in less fortunate countries.

'Genie', discovered in 1972 at the age of thirteen, had been confined in a basement in suburban Los Angeles for most of her life, without anyone in the local community suspecting that anything was wrong. Six-year-old Ivan Mishukov had lived on the streets of Moscow with a pack of stray dogs for two years before being discovered in 1998, and only recently the world's newspapers broke the story of how Josef Fritzl confined his daughter and her children in the cellar of the family home in Amstetten, Austria, reporting that although the children had some speech, they growled and grunted when communicating with each other (*Daily Mirror,* 1 May 2008).

The media interest aroused by such cases indicates the curiosity we still have about who and what we are. It was this curiosity that prompted me to write this book. The wild cards that are feral children serve to remind us that there are other worlds besides our familiar lives. It was not my intention to explain or justify them, but merely to suggest their presence.

Carol Fenlon
May 2008

THE SAVAGE

(Occasioned by the bringing to court a wild youth,
taken in the woods of Germany, in the year 1725)

Ye courtiers, who the blessings know,
From sweet society that flow,
Adorned with each politer grace
Above the rest of human race;
Receive this youth, unformed, untaught,
From solitary deserts brought,
To brutish converse long confined,
Wild, and a stranger to his kind:
Receive him and with tender care,
For reason's use his mind prepare;
Show him in words his thoughts to dress,
To think and what he thinks, express;
His manners form, his conduct plan
And civilize him into Man.
But with false, alluring smile
If you teach him to beguile.
If with language soft and fair
You instruct him to ensnare,
If to foul and brutal vice,
Envy, pride or avarice
Tend the precepts you impart;

If you taint his spotless heart:
Speechless send him back again
To the woods of Hamelin;
Still in deserts let him stray
As his choice directs his way;
Let him still a rover be,
Still be innocent and free.
He, whose lustful, lawless mind
Is to reason's guidance blind,
Ever slavish to obey
Each imperious passion's sway,
Smooth and courtly though he be,
He's the savage, only he.

Anon.
(From *Miscellaneous Poems by Several Hands*,
ed. D. Lewis, London 1726)

References

Anonymous (1726) 'The Savage', in D. Lewis (ed.) *Miscellaneous Poems by Several Hands,* London: John Watts, pp. 305–6.

Dawson, J. (2003) *Wild Boy*, London: Hodder & Stoughton.

Handke, P. (1997) *Plays I,* London: Methuen.

L'Enfant Sauvage (2003) Directed by François Truffaut, MGM Home Entertainment. DVD.

Miller, E. and Mulchrone, P. (2008) 'Child Victims of Cellar Beast Talk in Grunts and Growls', *Daily Mirror,* http://www.mirror.co.uk/news/topstories/2008/05/01 (accessed 9 May 2008).

Newton, M. (2002) *Savage Girls and Wild Boys*, London: Faber & Faber.

The Enigma of Kaspar Hauser (2005) Directed by Werner Herzog, Anchorbay Entertainment UK Ltd. DVD.